Lunch

Lunch

Karen Moline

William Morrow and Company, Inc.
New York

It is the policy of William Morrow and Company, Inc., and its imprints and affiliates, recognizing the importance of preserving what has been written, to print the books we publish on acid-free paper, and we exert our best efforts to that end.

Library of Congress Cataloging-in-Publication Data

Moline, Karen.
    Lunch / Karen Moline.
       p. cm.
    ISBN 0-688-13320-7
    1. Man-woman relationships—England—London—Fiction. 2. Actors—England—London—Fiction. 3. Women artists—England—London—Fiction. 4. London (England)—Fiction. I. Title.
PR6063.O4835L86 1994
823'.914—dc20
                                            94-9496
                                          CIP

Printed in the United States of America

First Edition

1 2 3 4 5 6 7 8 9 10

BOOK DESIGN BY LISA STOKES

To another M

Yet every man has inward longings
and sweeping, skyward aspirations
when up above, forlorn in azure space,
the lark sends out a lusty melody;
when over jagged mountains, soaring over pines,
the outstretched eagle draws his circles,
and high above the plains and oceans
the cranes press onward, homeward bound.

—Goethe, *Faust*

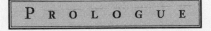

P R O L O G U E

It never would have happened had she not been late for lunch.

Trust me when I say it is so. I've had nothing but time to think about it. An endless, slow looping replay of time, ticking calmly, oblivious.

She was late because the phone rang. A simple thing, choosing that exact moment to call, his voice crackling across miles of fiber optics. She speaks, longer than she means to; she misses him, he is far away. She runs out into a day so gray it is an insult to bring color into it, the sky drooping, about to unleash a storm. There are no taxis on Queens Gate. She paces, waving her hand. Impatient, she ties a scarf, all mauve and green and deeper purples, over her hair and yanks it in a loose knot under her chin. Finally a cab stops. She leans back in the taxi, sighing, and glances at her watch. She hates to be late, she has no patience for people who keep her waiting. They move, they stop, they move again. It is a conspiracy of fate: tempers shortened by sodden skies, the oil-slicked road, the cars' idling puffs of sooty exhaust; an engine stalls, brakes slam, drivers curse. She gets out as soon as she can, into cold sleeting rain. She has forgotten her umbrella. She walks fast, faster, she slips, scraping her palm on a brick wall as she scrambles to right herself. Her scarf slides off her hair, dangling down her back. People pass, heads down, oblivious. She is not the kind of woman who makes heads turn on a damp rainy day. On any day. Not unless they are really looking.

Or rather, that they know what to look for.

She hurries down a long staircase into the restaurant, angry at herself, and the weather, and the disruption of her day. She does not mean to be late when at last she joins her impatient friend at the table next to ours, shaking the rain out of her tangled thicket of hair that glows like molten copper in the flesh-softening lighting of the room, and we saw her for the first time, and it began.

BEFORE

C H A P T E R   I

People call me the Major.

Who I really am is irrelevant. I am known, notorious, in fact, to anyone who deals with Nick Muncie out of the familiarity of the limelight that illuminates him so brilliantly. So many people see Nick, millions *see* him because he is so famous, but they don't *see* him as I do, as all the ingratiating, night-crawling Hollywood hangers-on and professional ass-wipes with wide eyes and wider mouths do, as the producers and publicists and business managers and accountants and lawyers on his payroll do. To them I am the majordomo. A major nuisance, running interference. They must get by me to get to Nick, and that makes them angry, and vicious behind my back.

If any of these people are more frightened of me than usual, which most are due to the imposing size and solidity of my body, large yet not bulky, honed by daily boxing bouts in our home gym, and by the ferocious thick scars crisscrossing my cheeks, the left one a scimitar curving from my half-shuttered eyelid to the outside of my lip to give it an unduly sinister expression, they call me Mr. Major. Nick laughs whenever he hears that. It is our own private joke.

Call him M, he says. M'll do. M is enough.

Think of me as Nick's right arm, his true self, his slave, although we both have acknowledged that he is the slave to my skills of organizational authority, and to the knowledge I keep to myself behind my habitual subdued blank mask. I know more about him than he knows himself. Because Nick lives for the moment, and then chooses to forget. It is easier that way, for him. I choose to remember. It is etched, cunei-form-like, on my face. Besides, what may have temporarily slipped my mind is still all there, stacked in neatly labeled rows of black cassettes, preserved on videotape, just in case.

I am the procurer.

Mr. Fix-it.

M.

I like to watch.

I watch because Nick wants me by him when he's watching, especially during the endless loops of replays. We have done it together for so long in the blue room I'd had soundproofed in the pool house that it is as habitual as the molten Blue Mountain java we gulp in the morning, or the fans who trawl behind Nick like gulls shrieking in wild circles after a garbage barge. People have wondered about us, why we are always together, Nick and his shadow, the weird big man with the appalling scars on his appalling face. We hear their whispers, see the avid curiosity alive in their faces. But we are not lovers, never have been, never will be. We are brothers of the blood, conjoined for life in a symbiosis of necessity and habit.

We never talk about why we are or what happened to make it so. It hovers behind a scrim in the back of our minds, as centuries of soot and grime and waxy varnish will dull the brilliant colors of a wet last-suppered fresco. We wake up to it every morning, for one brief sleepy second it bites us awake, we push it away, we disregard its calling, we play our games. Nick is very famous. Everyone wants to be with him. Everyone wants to be him.

He can afford to play. He can afford to pay, although not even Nick's fervid imagination could have envisioned the incalculable cost of this lunch.

Nick sits, toying with his *puttanesca*, sipping champagne. Jamie is busy talking, James Toledo, the director who has brought Nick to London, confounding Nick's critics who say yes, well, so what if he is the most popular actor in the world, yes he is top of the pops at the box office, can open any picture, any country, can guarantee those grosses, please let him be in my movie we'll give him anything he wants. Confounding those bold enough to state the knowledge that he can't act, what does he have to prove, he just has to open his mouth and bare his pecs and flash the butt shot, there, like that, do it again, thank you very much, with those few seconds you've just packed a few million more of those fat behinds into the theaters, squirming with wet desire.

Jamie keeps babbling, but Nick is not listening. He can give every impression of paying attention while behind that potently familiar facade is a raptor seeking its prey. The room is a delirious morass of pheromones igniting in spontaneous combustion because Nick is there, and Nick means to be noticed, even if he is sitting at a table with Jamie and me, near the back. His seeming oblivion to stares and titters fuels speculation; he feeds off this by-product more nourishing than any stew, as necessary a fix to his daily routine as shaving and jerking off. Every woman's eyes are drawn helplessly to his, their lips are moistened between dainty bites of *carpaccio*, willing him, willing Nick Muncie, superstar, to notice them, look at me, please, look, take me home, take me now, I'll do anything you want, you are the most beautiful man I have ever seen.

These well-bred, well-dressed ladies sit dreaming of Nick's kisses over extra-virgin olive oil. Let them dream. More satisfying these impulses of sweet romance than the debauched reality Nick would impose upon them, even had he found any of them remotely appealing.

Like the rest of London, the lunchtime crowd has only seen Nick's face presenting awards to his colleagues, the packed sardines of the Hollywood elite at popularity contests disguised as official ceremonies, or on the cover of so many magazines, or forty feet high up on a movie screen, the celluloid embodiment of their wildest fantasies. His dark blue eyes seem so familiar to them. Unfathomable, his fans call them. It is also a word that journalists, smitten against their better judgment, are fond of writing, although to me the snickering irony was that the only mystery lurking in their depths was the wonder that no one had yet discovered the utterly banal single-mindedness of Nick's ambition.

What brings Nick Muncie here, a self-launched one-man invasion of the soundstages at Pinewood and the grimy streets of Shoreditch, is Dr. Faustus, of all things, the legend updated, transported to Edwardian England, the tormented soul slinking with his hellish guide into smoky dark corners of East End slums, setting up the number-one box-office draw for mocking scorn and muffled snickers.

"Faust? *Faust?* What are you, crazy?" said McAllister, Nick's agent on one of the infrequent and priceless occasions where I saw him literally blanch, and then try to dissuade Nick from working. "Whose idiotic idea is that? And what the hell reason do you want to play Faust for? He's just some character in a book written by a dead German with a name no one can pronounce." He shook his head in bewilderment, then stopped and paled further when he saw the grim, intractable grin on Nick's face. "Suit yourself," he said, trying for an insouciant shrug, knowing his client well enough to let it drop. He'd be working the phones for the next year, or more, he realized, trying to sort out this nightmare of negotiating anywhere close to Nick's usual megamillion fee as healthy insulation, pay or play, against the inevitable industry disbelief. "It's your funeral," he sighed. "You could've at least done Mephisto."

"Too predictable," Nick said.

"Are you kidding?" McAllister countered. "Like Faust fits in your repertoire of the classics? I can see the poster now: '*FAUST: The Movie!* He Sold His Soul to the Devil! Rated R!' "

"Just set it up," Nick said.

Particularly vehement in her disapproval was Belinda Beverley, the she-devil of Southern California, Nick's infrequent leading lady and caustic companion. She'd protested the risk to his stature with much flouncing until I locked her in Nick's sauna one balmy afternoon, and only let her out when she'd stopped screaming and was more amenable to my politely worded request for peace and quiet.

Such a pair, they are, she so svelte and gilded, all flowing blond mane and liquid legs, he so sleekly dark and chiseled, the epitome of the bad boy, brooding as is his wont, both impossibly beautiful, draped around each other at premieres, at watering holes so exclusively trendy they have neither telephone nor identifiable entrances, at A-list parties, out dancing. Catch them flying around town on his Harley, Belinda trying not to scream at every bump Nick speeds over with deliberate skill. He knows exactly where to place the welts that will hurt the most when Belinda parks her perfectly toned and liposuctioned posterior on the back of his bike, wincing in pleasurable pain because she likes the whip, that is her dirty little secret, their dirty little playtime fun. She eggs him on, so eager, he lets her beg and he lets her have it where it will

never show. Nick knew he'd never find another Hollywood
specimen so pliable, so presentable, the ideal living twin to
the peculiarities of his demands, and she knew she'd always be
able to jump-start her teetering career as long as she remained
available to give Nick whatever he wanted.

Belinda is far away where she belongs, stuck shooting a
remake of *Grand Hotel* in a heat wave in Hollywood, far from
the damp seeping chill of cobblestoned streets slick with ma-
nure from the misbehaving stallions pulling the carriages of
shivering extras, and far from Nick's suite, the Sinatra suite
they gave him, the Thames roiling gray underneath his window, at the Savoy. I expect that at this hour she is not sleeping,
wired awake by a multicolored supplement from her usual
stash to help her through an abominably early call. Instead
she will be lying under the supple ministrations of Ivan, her
masseur. He makes house calls, of course, anything for Belinda. He also keeps his mouth very shut, anything for the
Major. Belinda's welts have healed into snaking thin white
lines she lets Ivan trace gently with neroli oil as she plots
revenge for Nick's professional infidelity, wondering when
he will return to the sprawling ranch house of his fortified
compound high in the Hollywood Hills that she often visits,
only to be chained to the bed, screaming behind her gag because she likes it so, yes, just so, a little lower, please please,
do it there, you bastard, and then do it again.

A flick of a gold lighter, the quick inhale of a Turkish cigarette. The mindless signals we exchange when all eyes pretend
not to be on us. Jamie is blathering about Faust's quest for
knowledge, the sacrifice he owes to hell, the alluring, potent
force of seduction by the devil himself. Actually, he's done
his research and his comments are interesting, but I will not
give him the pleasure of acknowledgment and my fascination
with the story because he is still afraid of me even after all the
preproduction work we've coordinated together, deferential in

his worry that he'd offend me with an inadvertent implication
that I might not understand the intricacies of Walpurgisnacht.
He should be worrying about Nick, instead. Nick is pretending to listen, being nice since he knows enough not to
antagonize his director before the shooting starts, when he is
really floating off on the billowing waves of adulation coasting
airily by. He smiles dreamily at the impeccably soignée
woman sitting at the next table without even seeing the pleasing evenness of her features, or that her edgy impatience with
the lateness of whomever she's expecting is clearly tempered
by proximity to the world's most famous bachelor, almost
close enough to touch. She smiles back, surprised by his casual
interest, and as a blush spreads over the flawless cream of
her cheeks she pats a nonexistent stray hair from her blond
chignon.

I am just beginning to wonder who she is, comparing her
understated elegance with Belinda's streaked vulgarity, when
her friend arrives suddenly, a whoosh of breathless wet, her
back to me, shaking the drops out of her hair.

"I am so sorry," this woman says. "On days like this I almost
wish I were back in Chicago. This weather is so incredibly
disgusting." Her accent is American. "First no taxis, and then
we got stuck, and I couldn't stand it so I got out and ran." She
looks down at her palm, surprised to see faint traces of blood
where the bricks had scratched it.

"Darling, I *must* apologize for dragging you out of the house
during your witching hour," says the chic blond with great
affection, clearly accustomed to such extravagant outbursts,
"and am therefore prepared to forgive you for being late."

"You can't even let me be a bitch," says the American.

Nick is listening, idly curious, until his eyes alight on the
stigmata scrape, and he sits up at attention. The woman runs
her fingers through the mass of her hair again, so much of it
curling that it is almost a living thing, a twisted ringleted

creature. Her fingers are very long, one sparkling with the light of a diamond ring, the nails cut short and blunt, a kaleidoscope of colored pellets dotting them.

I cannot see her face.

"Olivia," Jamie says.

She turns to him, surprised to hear her name. "Jamie," she says, smiling tightly and leaning over to kiss his cheeks. "Mr. Toledo. How are you. I haven't seen you in ages."

She is not beautiful, this Olivia, her face is too round, her features slightly off-center, but the color of her eyes is irresistibly peculiar, the queerest I've ever seen. Pale gray, like fog, flecks of green dancing inside, a ring of gold around the iris. I suspect they shift in hue to match her moods, and they make me wonder who she is and why she is here.

They make me want to look.

They didn't match her coloring, these eyes, nor her darker eyebrows, nor the pallor of a face that should have been freckled to match the fire of her hair.

"I've been working in L.A., but we're just about to start shooting here now," Jamie says. "Do you know Nick?"

Cut to the chase, I've seen it a thousand times. She will melt, he will shrug, and then pounce, if he so chooses. She is faceless, he is Nick Muncie, superstar.

"No, I'm afraid I don't," she says. She is not pretending. There is no quickening interest in her queer eyes, no curiosity in her voice. These are words Nick has not heard in many years. I see him stiffen imperceptibly with the trained reflex of the vain, intrigued by what he perceives as a slight. The curiosity is fomenting, the plot to seduce a Muncie virgin too compelling. By the time he is finished with her she'll never forget just exactly who he is.

"But how do you do." She extends her hand, forgetting it was scratched. Nick squeezes it, hard. She winces and pulls away. He smiles.

"And this is the Major." I nod at her. She scans my scars, does not shudder, and nods back.

"Major of what?" she asks me.

"Major trouble," Toledo says. Idiot. I stifle the urge to smash his face into the table. Olivia has ignored his comment, her face molding into a polite blank. It is a skill particular to Nick, as well as myself, seen rarely in the women we meet. Nick is definitely piqued, the boredom of this lunch suddenly enlivened by a simple encounter with a recalcitrant woman.

"This is my friend and dealer, Annette Isaak," Olivia says.

"Very pleased to meet you," Annette says, coolly professional, a stain of blush still on her cheeks.

"How do you know James?" Nick asks. He has to say something to Olivia.

"My fiancé played most of the score for one of his movies," she says, "and then Jamie wanted me to paint the star's portrait, and I wouldn't do it."

"Why not?" Nick asks.

"Too boring," she says. "No character in his face."

"What about my face? Would you paint me?"

"No," she says, after looking hard at his features. "No, I don't think so."

Jamie laughs. "Don't mess with her. She's quite picky about whom she paints, and she's one of the most stubborn women I've ever met."

"From you," she says, "that's a compliment." She is rubbing her sore palm gently, an unconscious gesture. The diamond catches the light. "Well, enjoy your lunch." We are dismissed.

Nick's face is a cipher, but I know what he is thinking. A quick diversion with an American, just what he needs in this sprawling city so far from home. And she is such an odd duck, this one, self-possessed. Harder to conquer, but ripe for it. A woman's ripeness. Not lithe and leggy like Nick's favored chassis, the Belinda model, those faceless starlets he plows through with such impunity. Tall and streamlined, they were built for speed. Olivia is built for comfort, round but firm. His eyes are alight, he is a jungle cat breathing deep, a long delicious whiff of her peculiar scent of vetiver, pungent, not sweet, breathing deeper, marking his territory, claiming what he wants to be his.

He smells blood. There is a faint trace, still, on her palm, and he means to lick it.

Olivia scans the menu. They order. She gets up. I watch her walk away. I watch Nick watching her, waiting, then excusing himself, and following, a chorus of sighs in his wake. I watch Annette, watching them both, sighing with just a bit of amiable resignation before pulling out a cigarette. I lean over to light it, startling her just a little, and she thanks me. I glance at her wedding band, and our eyes meet. We know. It's obvious. She smiles, conspiratorially. She must be a good friend, honest and true.

Nick is standing by the telephone when Olivia comes out and nearly walks right into him.

"What can I do to make you change your mind," he says.

Her eyes flicker, frightened, and narrow. "Nothing." She frowns. He has startled her, there in the narrow hallway, and he is standing too close, tall and feral, an unswerving presence.

"I want you to paint me."

"I choose the people I paint. They don't choose me." She shrugs by him back to the table.

I see that the angry fear has darkened her eyes into shiny steel. I was right, about them.

Nick inhales the aphrodisiac of her response and soon returns. A brief glance at me, running his fingers through his hair. A panther, grooming.

Their food arrives. Nick's eyes are on her, burning, heated. Even if she switched places, switched tables, ran out into the rain, she'd feel those ferocious eyes boring into the back of her skull. His plate is empty, he may have eaten, but now he is hungry. She feels his hunger. He wants her. He wants to eat her alive, he will devour her whole.

He is looking at her like she is lunch.

A spasm of lust so pure, so unwelcome in its unexpectedness, floods her with such sudden speed that she involuntarily presses her legs together. I can see her do it. Nick, too, feels that fear, he can sense that tension, smell it rising off her, a smoke signal of desire. He has been waiting for that moment, thrilling to a slight recoil of her shoulders, willing it, more delicious than any dessert spun of golden sugar.

We linger. Oh how Nick can change in the blink of an eye, transforming himself into a gracious novice, grateful for discourse about the German Romantics, avidly hanging on to every word of his devoted director. He flirts with the waitress, he toys once more with Annette when she turns to look at him as she pulls another cigarette from her purse and he leans sideways to light it. She bends forward, her face a delightful flush, to whisper to Olivia, who sits stiff and wary, her back defiant. He signs autographs and kisses cheeks, he orders a special grappa, he throws back his head and laughs.

The room is abuzz with the sweet indefinable pleasure of sharing a secret moment with a living god.

Only Olivia will not acknowledge us. She picks at her food, drinks a glass of red wine. She is wearing a long column of a dress made from some shimmering dark velvet, and thick stockings. I cannot see her legs. She is tapping one foot, un-aware of it, her chunky boot heel Morse-coding a rapid stac-cato, her calf muscles tensing, knotted, belying her nerves as those eyes will her to respond. And she is responding, though she can't articulate why. Desire grabs at her, whispering in her ears, caressing her curls, invading her pores, it tickles, pinpricks of cravings crawling up her spine.

No man has ever looked at her like that before. Not her

lover, not her former husband, not anyone. She has met many men of power and potent persuasion, she has painted them and sometimes bedded them, but this man is different. Never before has she felt such an awful, insidious yearning, a dull merciless ache lingering like a bee sting between her legs, demanding satisfaction, gripping her tight, this uncontrollable, unmistakably female reaction to undeniable lust.

They are nearly finished. We get up to leave. Olivia must look up at us when we say goodbye, and there is an electric flash of recognition between her and Nick, a weighted breathless moment before Olivia blinks her eyes as if she could somehow will her acknowledgment away.

Nick blows Annette a kiss. I beckon to the maître d' and palm him two fifty-pound notes, whispering instructions. We go up the stairs.

Olivia comes up first. The maître d' is detaining Annette, as I had bidden him, with a spurious message.

Nick is standing at the top of the stairs, blocking Olivia's path. She looks up at him, a long moment, and her heart begins thumping a strange wild rhythm.

"Are you always like this?" she asks.

"Worse, usually."

"Lucky me."

"Don't go."

"You must be joking."

"We'll drive you home."

"No."

He steps down toward her. She tries to flatten herself against the wall. This pleases him. He comes nearer, too near. She trembles, she cannot help it, he is hungry, starving, she is there to be eaten, and he means to eat her, because she is lunch.

Nick lifts her hand, he turns it over, he traces a thin line on the pink scratch there, and kisses it.

"I will find you," he says, and is gone.

Procuring is easy. It is especially easy when you live with Nick Muncie, superstar.

The scenario is simple: Look at a woman, a body, admire the color of her hair, perhaps, the curve of her hips, her breasts swelling, her nipples hardening instantly when she sees your face, sees who you are, see her as yours, and then she is yours, because you can take what you want. It had worked so well in the past. Nothing profound. Nothing but the deliberateness of mindless pleasure. The disposable-glove relationship, easily discarded.

Olivia will shatter our simple rules. She has to be taught the games, and is not a willing player. Nick had grown lazy with conquest, and with the security of his armor protecting him from intrusions. Olivia has already startled him from the shameless facility of his habitual patterns, because she doesn't care who he is, or that he wants her, and because she loves another.

I imagine her now, home, sitting on her bed, no, she is sitting in a rocking chair, she is rocking, because to me she is the kind of woman who sits, thinking of faces she will paint, rocking, her eyes closed, images a vivid tarantella in her head. She sits, rocking, the shadows deepening, the twilight comes so early here in winter and is so easily extinguished, she is sitting in the shadows, wondering at herself, wondering why the silly dull ache does not leave her, wondering.

She wishes she could see Nick as no more than a spoiled selfish man used to indulging the obvious inclinations of the conquering hero. Such men, these elegant barbarians, bore her. But such men do not regard her with the kind of animal admiration usually reserved for the leggy beauties she expects Nick squires around Hollywood with bored impunity. Such men do not stand by the door of a ladies' room in a restaurant, leaning insouciantly against the wall by the telephone as if nothing else in the world existed but the need to say what he wants to her, to try to touch her, to gaze, to bore his eyes through her, because for him she has unwillingly become the only meal worth eating, and he is ravenous. No, she must admit, Olivier, her fiancé, her beloved, has never looked at her like that, with quite that unwavering intensity, although he looks at her with quiet passion simmering, yes, he looks at her with love.

Olivia does not know what to do, so she does nothing.

She has no idea.

Nick is sitting too, in our suite in the Savoy, eating chocolates from their curt little square box. He eats them slowly, licking the smooth outer shells till they crack, licking them as he wishes to lick the thin faint smear of pink he kissed on Olivia's palm, his tongue circling.

He is plotting.

I am witness to it, as I am ever. Only very rarely did Nick

venture out to forage on his own, fearful as we were to the possibility of blackmail or a lurking paparazzo. On his solitary excursions, when he needed to be more discreet and well-behaved without me to override any boorishness, his most potent pleasure came later, with the telling of the tale. Only in recollection did Nick truly come alive, playing the scene as the impassioned suitor he'd pretended to be. His eyes alight, he'd kick off his boots and lie back on his custom-made bed with the sculptured bedposts and the lacy yet sturdy ironwork grilles between them on each end, his breath all raggedy, telling me what impossibly ridiculous thing he'd just done. He did not need any response, did not expect one; the more outlandish his descriptions, the various boring sagas of how he'd just used his special toys, the more pleased he was by my customary inscrutability. I never judged him, there was no point. At these moments, he didn't need me for advice or counsel.

He simply needed an audience.

The depths of what made Nick who he is are utterly unfathomable to anyone who first meets him. Blinded by the aura of his fame, they see his beauty, what they perceive as his fresh, unpretentious presence, only because he allows them to.

Distracted, they must have been, by the famous forelock of black hair that kept flopping endearingly over his forehead, pushed back in an impatient gesture copied from Gary Cooper, or perhaps by a whiff of his orris cologne, a peculiarly old-fashioned smell, odd and slightly bitter, the signature scent of Louis XIV, because if it was good enough for the king, he said, then it was good enough for Nick Muncie.

Or distracted by the uniform that subtly limns the long lean lines of his body: a custom-tailored poet's shirt bleached and starched to an impossible crisp white, the sleeves billowing into thick cuffs linked with an odd gold insignia that matched his heavy gold ring, one he mockingly identifies as the family heirloom. A belt of smooth black leather just thick enough to impress a wide welt, a vivid souvenir of Nick at night, clasped with an intricate buckle of hammered silver given to him by a fervent fan who'd had it blessed by an Iroquois shaman after he emerged from a ceremonial sweat lodge, or so she said. Tight black Levi 501s, button fly, please, so they can be hastily unbuttoned off. Black leather Nocona boots, well-worn. Black jacket, either Armani or motorcycle, depending on the weather. A perfect study in black and white and blue, what on any other man could have veered easily into the effeminate but on him embodied a masculinity so iconoclastic it has since become known as Putting On the Nick.

And then they see me behind him, the pale, thick scars on my face slashing a wide swath from ear to nose, and wonder yet again who I am and why we are together.

A century or two ago such a debt of honor, dueling, would have made ladies swoon and men pull me aside for a snifter of cognac and a *mano a mano* blow-by-blow. Now, however, the scars inspired little more than fear and repulsion, although Nick sometimes teased me that there were plenty of groupies out there who got off on the bizarre. I expect many people in Hollywood may have questioned why, with all Nick's money, I never had them fixed. Actually, I had gone for a consultation. The surgeon examined me gravely, shaking his head. "Whoever stitched you was a butcher," he said. "I've never seen such a botched job. The skin wasn't able to heal properly, especially around these burns—acid, right?—and the scar tissue is unusually thick." He sighed, his professional pride affronted. "I'm sorry, but this is the rare exception where trying to fix things might make them worse. I can't recommend it."

It didn't matter. I was relieved. A smoother facade might've altered the subtle balance of our life together. I'm used to them, they are part of my face. I've grown accustomed to the convenience of this mask. It serves our purpose. I don't have to answer any questions, because nobody dares ask them.

No one ever figured out that my scars are the tangible reminder of the fearsome genesis of Nick Muncie, superstar.

He has willed himself to forget who we were, where we came from, and what we learned there, and he cannot admit to himself that even forgetfulness has its price.

It took so little time for Nick to become famous that we were giddy with the shock of it, greedy, buying in to the churning machinery. Nick was so eager to please then, because pleasing meant work, and work meant money, and money meant power, and Nick meant to have as much of it as he could stash in his feverish plots of ascension. Deprivation had made him hard, and determined; excess made him indolent, and mean when there was no need for him to be charming.

The meanness, hidden from all save myself, only melted once, for one infinite second, for one interminable, aching moment, which by sheer coincidence I captured on videotape.

Nick never saw that tape. He never knew what I saw.

I saw everything.

It was mine, but all that remains for me is one frozen moment.

None saw him as I did.

He had only to lower those darkly blue eyes and raise them shyly in a move slyly practiced by Princess Diana, bat those impossibly long black eyelashes, the kind women said were wasted on a man but they weren't wasted on Nick, oh no, one sideways glance sufficed. It was a gesture that made him famous practically overnight and took us out of the dump of an apartment we'd rented off La Cienega, 246¼, Nick liked that. A quarter human, that's us.

He was discovered by a casting agent who saw him at the

Sunoco station in Beverly Hills, filling up her Mercedes with super unleaded right after he'd fixed Cary Grant's flat tire. He must have had a quixotic look on his face, and so she asked him why he was smiling. "Did you see who that was?" he asked her, goofy with the unexpected proximity to a celebrity. "Cary Grant's not supposed to get a flat tire," he said. "That's not supposed to happen to people like him."

"You mean because he's a living legend."

"A legend, yeah, I guess so."

From such eloquence a star was born.

"What do you do besides inflating flats?" she asked, her honed eye zeroing in on the planes of his face under the grime, the body under the uniform, the hunger under the eyelashes, unwilling to drive away from such a physically perfect specimen without some form of teasing flirtation.

He smiled. "Why do you want to know?"

"You have the kind of face I'm looking for," she purred.

"Looking for?" His smile slowly faded. "Looking for, for what exactly?"

She handed him her card. "Call me," she said, "and I'll tell you."

He called her, waiting a few days, already his instincts guiding him, he made certain he was the last appointment of the day, because he was not stupid, he knew what had to be done, came whistling into her office, pulled the chair he was meant to sit on under the doorknob, and fucked her senseless on her desk, though she was large and ungainly, fucked her for hours, piles of head shots and résumés fluttering to the floor as she moaned beneath him.

He fucked her, and as many others as were necessary, and he was careful. Nor did he mind. It was purposeful, and they were so happy afterward, sated, pleased with his discretion and abashed apologies, he fucked them whenever he felt they were pulling away, always in their offices, these sad lonely women, knowing why he was so willing yet forgiving him because he was so naive and so sweet to them, grateful for any work they threw his way. He told me about them, but never mockingly like so many of the others. It was a job, on-the-job training, he called it, it was work, acting so impassioned, and in a very short time he learned to do it extremely well. He found he was gifted with the instinctive intelligence actors must possess, or at least pretend to understand, and a quick wit replete with the requisite repertoire of wry lines and snappy comebacks I'd carefully written for him and that he rehearsed in front of me for hours to hone his delivery.

From there, Nick's career spiraled upward: model, actor, famous face seen at dinners and premieres, unfailingly polite, as generous as a man who divulged nothing could be with journalists, endlessly posing for pictures, uncomplaining. He was never late, sent flowers, praised his colleagues, played the game, showing up at the right parties, flirting, cajoling, slyly insinuating his growing capability as a professional charismatic with a self-deprecating humor so that he soon became indispensable, a requisite presence, because he was so unbelievably handsome, and vulnerable, and seemingly so alone among the sharks that you couldn't not want to throw your arms around him and tell him that you loved him.

In those days he was well-behaved. He knew enough not to blow his chances on indiscretions.

Once Nick became essential, with McAllister signing him with a flourish and the requisite cacophony of shrill and basically useless people surrounding him, clamoring eagerly to do his bidding, he had them arrange all the paperwork. One day he came to me, barely suppressing a smirk, and handed me an envelope: passport, driver's license, bogus birth certificate made out to John Q. Major. He'd already done the same for himself years before, obtaining the necessary documentation through the mail after a large payoff to preserve his anonymity.

Editors had already screamed loudly at their journalists in frustration, trying to find the truth behind his origins, and eventually gave up in despair. The tabloids and even some of the studios had hired private detectives, all in vain. We had covered our tracks deliberately, and so well that we were untraceable, orphans, sprouting like wild things from the sea, nameless, discarded, dredged from hell.

I ran away, was all Nick ever said, I can't tell you what I ran from, I'll let you imagine how hard it was, and how horrible. I never knew my parents, they died in a car wreck when I was a baby, and eventually I came with a friend to Los Angeles.

They learned not to push him: all the better to pin the mythical tale of the woebegone urchin onto the donkeylike fans, inventing a baroque history to exploit the pain of his life. Beset by devils and surrounded by despair, this little boy, nameless and unloved, had become the other, magnified in all his magnificence forty feet wide on a movie screen, the waif sprung phoenixlike from the ashes of an unknowable life, discovered at a gas station wiping windshields of the rich and infamous, transformed into the star triumphant, king of his world, ruler of his universe.

It played much better, this myth of Muncie. So much easier for them to see only the surface, the instant stir, not its aftermath. So much easier for Nick to deny the dangers of the public's mirror, the falsehood and fickleness of its reflection. What remained after the spots had blinked off, the boom mikes were lowered, the cameras were dismantled, and the sets were struck? What was left for Nick Muncie, superstar—his films, finished and, for him, forgotten, unspooling, for others, in the dark? Or the light reflected off his eyes as he sat watching the preferred images of his choosing in his private movie theater, the one in the blue room of the pool house?

Every time Nick closed his eyes he could open them into another realm, recreated as anyone he chose to be, an invention entirely of self. How could he exist as anything other than the player he'd become?

Those who belittled Nick's talent had no idea how skillfully he acted every waking moment.

Any life I had away from him, Nick knew about. It was subsumed into what had become the reality of our days together, and the simple rhythm of their hours. There was the real work, and Nick was unstinting with his energy during filming, no matter how bastardized the scripts became once he'd committed the requisite Muncie persona to these projects; and then there was the unreal: the adulation, the photo sessions, the workouts, the drugs, the dinners, the parties, the pliant bodies, not always in that order. Nothing else existed.

Any woman I had, and I didn't have all that many, Nick wanted. I didn't mind; I chose them for him. I needed them only for sex, for some mindless sort of physical release, and often not even for that.

Love was not something I ever thought about.

I had no wish to make others pay for my past unhappiness unless they tried to provoke me, but few did since my reputation had become more fearsome than my scars, magnified from a whisper to a sharp, keening scream. Don't mess with the Major, they said, if you value your life.

Don't mess with the Major.

But Nick, who could not allow himself to be daunted by the things that to other men were so daunting, loved to extract that payment. It was so easy when they came so willingly, offered themselves as slaves to the sacrifice, head down, arms outstretched, beseeching, but they paid such a terrible price, vexed with the memory of what he did to them, and worst of all they paid with their silence. They paid when they would awaken, still, months later, from the soundest of sleep with the remembrance of having been taken, used, and discarded disturbing their dreams. This forgotten terror plagued their muscles, twitching the very fibers like the legs of a dog lost in slumber, a scary sensation as taut as the silken cords that had bound their limbs to Nick's vast, sculpted bedstead as they'd lain there, begging for mercy.

These lust-numbed ladies I met in my guise as the procurer, befogged with the power that is Nick Muncie, superstar, pretended my face and demeanor did not repel them. They acted as if they truly wanted me, wanted to fuck me, not simply as slender ruse to get close to Nick. There was the buzz, a whiff of possibility, strangely oblique, enticing enough to lure these girls with their firm proud bodies and sleek hair and capped white teeth into the murky shallows of hopefulness.

I knew how to select them, so it was quick, and simple, and I was cautious. I picked them up and drove them in the big black Range Rover with the windows tinted dark so prying eyes could not see in, drove them through the honking slow traffic up to the slow curves at the top of Mulholland where Nick's compound was hidden behind an electric gate and wired hedges. They never saw the entrance anyway; the rule was they had to be blindfolded when they got into the car. Security, I said. No one ever protested, no, they shivered instead in the bliss of anticipation for a chance to be allowed into the proximity of Nick's inner sanctum.

Once inside, I'd already said her name, many times, so that Nick knew what to call her, he knew what to say when he came into the room after he caught a glimpse of her through the hole he'd bored in the wall opposite his bed, hidden artfully just behind the edge of a seventeenth-century Gobelin he'd bought during the bankruptcy auction of McAllister's ex-partner.

He looked at me, ready.

I hit my marks. I never missed.

No matter what I was doing to the woman in his bed, I would shift my position, turn her around, lie on my back, she astride me, facing my feet, facing the tapestry she could not see because the blindfold stayed on. She gladly acquiesced when I took her hands in mine and told her to do as I said. It was better for her not to see me, her revulsion masked behind black silk. It was easier for her to pretend I was Nick, she is in Nick's house, perhaps this is Nick's bed, she is touching his sheets, Nick is coming to her, to be with her, she is the chosen one, he will see her and sweep her breathless into his arms, murmuring words of desire. It is all she wants to hear, his voice, the longing for it pouring off her backside as I rake my nails across it and she barely shudders, oblivious. It is all she is yearning for even as I fuck her, fill her, she does not feel me, I am not real because I am not Nick.

She is moving slowly, I have been gentle, for me, she cannot see. She hears a voice, soft. It cannot be. It is. Nick. Her heart stops. It is Nick. Nick is here. She is trembling with giddy pleasure, she strains away from me, I no longer exist. She feels his hands on her breasts, she knows them, instinctively, those fingers, she is desperate to fling her arms around him but I am still holding them. She hears him murmur her name, murmur that she is so beautiful, she is dripping, disbelieving, she is delirious, she is desperately grateful even when Nick pushes himself rudely into her mouth, how eagerly her lips seek whatever Nick deigns to present to her, never had she welcomed me or any other man with such eagerness, never had she thought she would be blindfolded and gagging, still astride another, Nick Muncie, superstar, pushing himself deeper still as she starts to pull away, pull back, but she cannot, she is impaled on me, and she is starting to panic because she cannot move, she cannot breathe, her hands are jerked high above her head and bound together, she is struggling in earnest now, terrified, this cannot be Nick, not he, not this demon choking her, she cannot move, she cannot breathe, and that is exactly what Nick wants.

Nick pulls away suddenly and caresses her cheeks, wiping away her tears. There are always tears, shock and pain loosened and made liquid. Darling, he says, darling, you are so beautiful, thank you, thank you for doing that to me, so sweet, my darling. He kisses the tears away. She is relaxing again, I can feel the stiffness melting back into the magma of desire. She is turned around, gently, so I won't slip out, I am still hard because Nick wants me to be, and she sits, captive, facing me, and I am rocking her imperceptibly back and forth, back and forth, Nick's lips in her hair, murmuring, always murmuring, the fantasy fulfilled of his voice, her name, it is Nick, really Nick, touching her, sweet, even as her hands are lowered, bound and helpless. Nick's hands cup her breasts, he holds her close, whispering of delights to come in her ear, trailing his famous slim fingers down her back, down where she wants to be touched, she is moaning, his fingers swirling, my movements small, rocking, back and forth, near imperceptible, she is screaming for him to stop, she can't help herself, she is coming in waves, she is engulfed in a rush of pleasure so intense she is sure she will faint, she cannot bear it, please, stop, she says over and over, she is begging for Nick to stop please stop, she is begging for Nick.

She is still begging when he slaps a gag on her pleading. There is nothing he likes more than a muffled moan, there is nothing more deeply satisfying than reaching for the whip stashed under the bed and bringing it down with a thin high whistle before it smacks full on her behind, one straight red welt rising thin on each cheek, nothing better than the surprised confusion he can feel as he pushes her down as I slide backward, still holding her arms, her head on my chest, she could hear my heart beating if the roaring were not so loud in her head.

It happens so quickly it always takes a few seconds for the most primal panic to register in her befuddled senses. She who has been so suffused with pleasure only seconds before cannot voice her fear, she cannot believe the same creature who made her come with such rapture is pounding viciously inside her, oblivious to her distress even as he feeds off it.

Her tears stream out from under the blindfold and fall, rolling sideways off my chest into the sodden sheets.

Nick knows when she's had enough, he always knows, he slows down, he pulls out, he caresses her body with his famous slim fingers, he is whispering again in her ear, kissing her cheeks, the pulse thudding wildly in her neck, thanking her, thanking her for making him happy, she is so beautiful he couldn't help himself, she gives him so much pleasure, he wants her, he wants her to be happy, he wants her very much, his hands caressing, does she want him, will you be mine.

Yes, she is trying to say behind the gag, yes of course I'm yours, she tries to say because she does not know what she is saying, she cannot think anything more real than the fantasy she has nurtured to be lying where she is now, burning yet senseless, deluded yet delirious, violated, take me, she wants to say, take me like that again if it pleases you, take me I'll do anything you want as long as you do it to me.

She is no longer crying.

Nick turns her over gently, and I slip away, unnoticed and no longer needed. Her ass is on fire, stingingly sore, her mouth on fire but she no longer feels it because Nick has yanked off the gag with a sudden loud rip, and he is kissing her, she is a limp rag doll, he does crave her, he wants her, he is kissing her deep, sweet, he says, so sweet, my beautiful darling, she will be his, be helpless once more as waves of pleasure snake through her body, rippling when Nick pulls her close and takes whatever else he desires.

He always makes them come, those silly girls, desperately eager, powerless, exposed, spread-eagled, bound and blind, pleading, dazed, sandwiched between two men who could just as easily break their necks as stroke their thighs, not knowing if each further second will bring pleasure or pain, the kiss or the whip, the caress or the teeth, biting, not caring how they are turned and twisted because it doesn't really matter, Nick has his arms around them.

And so they never breathe a word, these initiates thrust so carelessly into Nick's realm and scarred by his rituals, once he said how magnificent they were after he'd come violently inside them, once, more if they particularly pleased him, their thighs strong and waxed smooth, their ripe asses firm from dreary months on the Stairmaster, ripe for welts crisscrossing the tan lines of the bikinis they flaunted on the beach at Malibu. He left them with a lingering long kiss on their lips, at the nape of their necks, between their legs, deep, sweet, please they said, stop please stop.

They do not dare breathe. Instead, they shiver.

They are stunned into silence, dazed, they think they are dreaming, a bizarre nightmare of cruel sex and whispers of their beauty. When Nick signals to me I dress them, sling them over my shoulder in a fireman's carry, then ease them down, meek and pliant, into the backseat of the black Rover, driving out through the gates that slide back silently, driving them home, or back to their cars in the parking lot where they'd left them, unwinding the blindfold, pulling them up, and out.

The sight of my face brings them back to earth with a harsh jolt. Do you want to see Nick again, I ask, he likes you very much, he thinks you are beautiful and very sweet. Yes, they nod mutely, still in shock, unable to meet my eyes. Don't worry, I say, we know where you live. At the threat implied in my calmly bland voice they pale, all of them, poor trembling birds, even through their numbed, dazed stupor they can recognize the chilling voice of terror.

That's why none dared speak of what I did to them, what Nick did to them. Not one ever saw Nick again, of course, not that way, and even if they did see him out, laughing with Belinda over vodka martinis, or walking out of a screening, or on the TV, beaming, or on the screen, intense, soulful, and magnificent, they never said a word to anyone. They knew I would find them, and then they would never again have anything truly useful to say to the world.

In Hollywood, everyone wants to direct, they say. Not Nick, not on a real movie. He was content with this scenario, surveyed from the hole bored behind the Gobelin, the hole just wide enough for the lens of his state-of-the-art camcorder. He'd written this script, filmed and recorded it, rewound the tapes, then settled in his crimson velvet dressing gown from Sulka, lounging comfortably on his favorite overstuffed sofa in the blue room of the pool house, and dimmed the lights, hitting Play on the remote with a soft sigh of anticipation. The watching was as much a ritual as the act itself, perhaps even more intense because Nick could see himself, admire the relentlessness of his smooth, vicious thrusts, feel once more the supple body straining against him, pleading.

The script and camera angles never changed. Only the duration, the shapes of the bodies, the texture of the hair clenched in his fists, their murmured names. All else was the same, an endless repetition of his variation on a theme, the melody heard only by Nick, the whining fluted whistle of a whip that so swiftly raised the straight narrow pinkness meant to be caressed under his famous slim fingers, the muffled oboe of a woman's voice, the basso profundo of Nick, whispering sweet lies in a sweeping cadenza.

Nick heard this melody.

Whenever he was feeling particularly engaged, he made me watch. Instead, I watched him engrossed in his listening, his breathing slow and even, a toying smile at the corner of his lips.

I never made a sound.

I could have told Olivia. I could have spared her.

The price for that cowardice is incalculable.

CHAPTER 3

At first it was no more than a game, his interest piqued by Olivia's physical peculiarities and obvious disdain, a simple distraction from rehearsals and the tedium of London fans, waiting patiently for him on the Strand, shooed away from the Savoy by impatient doormen, their photographs and felt-tip pens poised for the satisfaction only his scrawled signature on an 8 × 10 glossy could buy.

Anything to get close to Nick.

As days flew by, weary days of costume fittings and dialogue coaching, the unfamiliarity of true hard work with thought behind it, the repeated muttering of lines bored into memory, the delving into a complex character with a depth and passion that Nick worried, secretly, he did not possess, hiding his fears of inadequacy under a nonchalant facade, he chose to fixate on a woman he'd briefly encountered, by sheer coincidence. Some small part of me admired his calm determination to plow forward, his refusal to share the burden of his anxiety with the only person he trusted, smothering his apprehension instead with dreams of a woman who'd scorned him, a woman who loved another, if only to prove that his seductive powers, as natural to him as breathing, had not deserted him.

Nick's charm, when he meant it to be, was as unforced as it was devastating. Such a talent is inexplicable, you think you will be impervious to its creeping insidious power even as it invades your pores, irresistibly magnetic. It worked on Annette, less invulnerable to his charisma than Olivia, he tells himself, or perhaps she was simply a businesswoman astute enough to have arranged this lunch. Or rather, Nick figured out how to arrange it through Annette, plotting, beguiling, and determined.

I try to imagine what Annette said to entice Olivia here today.

But I was wrong. It wasn't Annette's cajoling that would bring her to this lunch, no, it was Olivier, her fiancé. She will be here because Olivier laughed. She heard his laughter over the phone from his hotel room in Hong Kong when she told him that Nick Muncie, superstar, was pestering her for a portrait, heard him laugh at her stiff indignation, heard him laugh at the prospect of how she could paint him, how she could demystify the icon, transfer the image so beloved by millions into the myth of her own design. "Do it," Olivier said, "it will be good for you."

"But I don't like him," she told him. "He's a jerk. I don't like how he looks at me. He's so used to taking anything he lays his eyes on that I don't want to be part of his craziness."

Olivier was still laughing. "Even more reason," he said. "He's already got you *complètement folle*, my darling, so throw that frustrated energy into your painting. I can just see him now, Monsieur Sex Symbol, trying to seduce you with his charm, and you telling him *va t'en faire foûtre*."

She laughed then, relieved. "But I've still got a bad feeling about him."

"Don't be silly. It will give me intense pleasure to imagine his *égoïsme* trying to invade your studio. I shall think of you when I'm rehearsing, you my darling, you and the most famous actor in the world, and you will think of me, when you are looking at his face, knowing that I am laughing at the puncturing of his *esprit*. So do it for me."

"Well, I'll think about it," she said, sighing. "But only because you ask. And if it goes wrong, it will be entirely your fault, and I hold you completely responsible. Then you'll be sorry."

"Say it again."

"What."

"You'll be sorry."

"Why?"

"Because it sounds sexy."

"You're crazy."

"Yes. Crazy without you."

"Does this mean you miss me?"

"Horribly."

"Likewise."

"I must go now."

"You're tired."

"Very."

"Is it going well?"

"Very."

She sighs again, she cannot help it. "Well, sleep tight. *Je t'embrasse.*"

"Darling," he said, and hung up.

We are at our usual table in the back, and Nick is in a state of unsurpassed impatience, the signs of which—a nick shaving, a tap of his boot on the floor, his hands ruffling his hair, making the ladies lunching sigh with frustrated pleasure, imagining how much they'd like to do that very thing with their glossy polished nails—were remarked upon and registered silently only by me.

I have never seen him made anxious like this by a woman before. It alarms me, this obsession, because it is growing, here a tiny weed, needing only the first few rays of slanting winter sunshine to sprout and spread, unchecked, soon covering the plots of our nasty bad habits, and choking the garden of our solitude.

I wonder what it is about Olivia.

His greeting of Annette is genuine pleasure, and she flushes with grateful surprise, knowing all eyes are upon her. She really is pretty, her cheeks blooming as Nick pulls his chair closer to hang on her every word as if the teller is far more intoxicating than the tale. Her hair naturally blond, streaked with subtle highlights, her makeup understated, her figure slender, her wedding band glinting pale fire, she is a seductive woman who adores the slither of silk underclothes hidden under the mannish yet provocative cut of her Yohji suit. She would almost be Nick's type if she weren't so smart and posh, speaking in the clipped proper cadence of the well-bred, running a gallery on Cork Street, married to a suitable investment banker, driving their silver-blue Range Rover to the country house on weekends, flicking off the attention of unsuitable lovers as if they were no more substantial than annoying marsh midges.

That she has a husband is worthy only of a yawn from Nick. She would almost be his type, if she were not Olivia's friend.

"Tell me about your business," he says. "Tell me about how you find your artists."

Not artists. Olivia.

"It depends. For instance, I've known Olivia for ages," she says. "I was acquainted with her ex-husband when I was

working at the Tate, and he went off to teach at the Art
Institute of Chicago, and Olivia was a student there, and they
fell in love and came over here and it was a huge scandal
because he was quite a lot older and married at the time to a
certain very proper lady."

This could be more interesting than I thought.

"Is that why she still lives here?" Nick asks.

"Yes, and why she's got such a marvelously huge studio.
Geoffrey turned into a real bastard, and it's why Olivier is
so—" She flushes a deeper rose. "I don't know why I'm telling
you this. Olivia will murder me. I'm still not even sure she'll
do the portrait. It's never up to me, not really, much as I wish
it were, although I am her dealer."

Nick calmly pours her a glass of champagne.

"Still," he says, "I imagine you're lucky to represent her.
She appears to be very successful." He doesn't mention how
well thumbed the catalogue from Olivia's last show has become, the slim volume I picked up from the concierge at the
Savoy after he called the gallery, pretending to represent a
sheik in town on a shopping spree.

"Yes, quite. She is. Despite her peculiarities, as she calls
them."

Nick suppresses a smile. He likes that.

"Her support was one of the reasons I could open the gallery," Annette is saying. "She's a wonderful painter and a
wonderful friend."

"Tell me about her fiancé."

He has segued so smoothly into the sole topic of interest that
Annette barely notices, seeing no farther than the dark blue
eyes smiling into her own.

"Olivier."

"Olivia and Olivier. How cute. Sounds like destiny to me,"
Nick says with a saucy grin, "or a bad romance novel."

"Why do you want to know?"

"Curiosity. He's not in town, is he?" he asks. She shakes her head, surprised that he would know. "And hope. Hopefulness, I mean, that it will give me some leverage and persuade her to paint me."

His candor is unforced, and since he is telling the truth, she believes him, and finds it easy to talk, hypnotized by charisma.

"He's a pianist, quite famous, I'm sure you've heard of him. He's on tour now, in the Orient. He's booked for years in advance. I don't know how she can stand it."

"The separations, you mean."

She nods.

"But isn't that better for you, that he's away, and so she keeps herself busy with work?"

"I suppose. I know she misses him dreadfully, but they're both quite independent, and Olivia would never stop painting to follow him around on his tours like a puppy dog. They both seem to thrive on isolation and longing, it becomes part of their work. Strange, isn't it." Her eyes are fixed on Nick, who doesn't think it strange at all. "That's why Olivier is so perfect for her."

Nick appears mesmerized, smiling gently, as if he were an unaccustomed audience, thrilling to a slowly rising curtain. He caresses a nonexistent hair off Annette's forehead, watching her melt, liquid putty in his fingers as she unknowingly tears bits of her bread into crusty shreds of nervous tension, silently thanking her husband, who has no interest in her extracurricular activities, for marrying her, so she has a built-in excuse to either end or prolong Nick's flirtatiousness, should he wish it.

"Tell me how they met," he says.

"Olivia had just been in Paris, working, so I suppose she still had a soft spot for Frenchmen when he came into the gallery."

"Why was she in the gallery?"

"Covering for me." She giggles. "It really was quite a nasty trick."

"Go on."

This story does not really interest me, because I know I will hear it again, from Nick, hear it over and over again as he muses upon endless provocative possibilities.

I prefer to imagine Olivia in Paris, a city I know well after spending months there while Nick was shooting that mini-series, an abysmally ridiculous remake of *To Catch a Thief* too low-budget to shoot on the Riviera yet inexplicably earning that year's highest ratings and a Golden Globe for Nick's performance.

It is easier to imagine Olivia in Paris, reading myths, for inspiration, reading of the Five Nations, and the Celts, and the Etruscans, sitting on a green iron bench in the Jardin de Luxembourg, or wandering in a contented daze through the Musée d'Orsay and the Louvre, sketching. I picture her sitting in a teahouse she stumbles upon one cloudless afternoon, tucked in the Cour de Rohan near the house where Voltaire once lived, it is claimed. They begin to know her there after a while, warming to her shy smile and hesitant French, giving her the table where the light is best, near the window in the corner, upstairs under the low-beamed ceiling, close to the fireplace that illuminates her odd beauty, flickering quietly, rendering her alabaster skin translucent, her eyes pale, and throwing the strange planes of her face into sharp relief as if she were a Caravaggio peasant come to life. Soon she comes to sketch the *propriétaire*, the waitress, the pastry chef peeling apples for a *tarte tatin*, she gives them these delicate miniatures, received with grateful delight, and they ask her, beg her, really, to paint a mural on their walls. Persephone, she decides, prancing in the wheat fields of her mother, eating a pomegranate, seeds staining her teeth the same sweet ruby as the tea scented with *eaux de fruits* she likes so much, deep crimson, scented with *cynorrhodon* and *pétales d'hélianthe*.

In the evenings she lies in her small bed in the flat she'd rented in the Fifteenth Arrondissement near the Eiffel Tower, the top floor, deliberately, so she can have the roofs to herself, the city at her feet. She could see the very top of the tower, glowing yellow, a nightly beacon reflected and repeated, golden little flickering dabs like pats of butter on her window-panes. Sometimes as she scribbled in her notebooks, a glass of wine on the floor, a candle scented with rosemary and lavender lit, flickering, the radio playing odd bits of jazz and blues, she heard the clickety patter of her neighbor's cat scrabbling up the slate shingles of the roof, or the high chattering voices of the children of the concierge playing games, echoing in the courtyard, laughing, or the quick clatter of high heels on the cobblestones below, or a phone, ringing, or the sudden clap of shutters pulled close, the world shut out, safe for the night.

Paris is a city of secrets. We secret-sharers recognize that in each other, and belong there. Push open the heavy green door, slightly crooked with age, and a courtyard beckons, thick heavy curtains fluttering in the windows, hiding the life inside.

I see her in the market on Thursdays, under the shade of the elevated Métro, admiring the carefully constructed moun-tains of fruit, piled *cerises provençales*, glowing white pyramids of mushrooms, curling green snakes of *frisé* and *haricots verts*, she gets yelled at when she touches the fat fingers of white asparagus, the jeweled heaps of beets and turnips. She laughs when she sees the table of fish, gleaming, neatly quivering silver, for they remind her of the market she once stumbled upon, years ago in Hong Kong, there where her lover is now, his fingers on keys of ivory, the audience rapt, the sounds silver, silver like the scales of fish there in the night market, an open-air market at a crossroads in Kowloon, the tabletops roiling, a wriggling mass of every imaginable variety of creature that crept and crawled in the sea, gathered up, squirming, by bored impassive cooks, dumped into squat black caldrons of boiling water, scooped out seconds later, and as quickly devoured.

Those tables, writhing, alive with the near-dead of the deep, became the background for the painting that launched her career when she was still in art school, the portrait of Mao and Stalin, cooking together, stirring the boiling morass, the witches' brew of the Orient.

"I was home with the flu," Annette is saying, "and I was in a terrible dither because an important buyer had said he might be coming by, but he was in transit and therefore unreachable, and my secretary was on holiday, and I quite didn't know what to do."

"So you called Olivia," Nick says.

"Yes. It was the last week of her show, actually, and she knew the art, obviously."

"Obviously," Nick agrees, filling her glass.

"So, after I begged and pleaded and promised her the moon she came round for the keys."

Nick is calm, listening, his eyes never leaving her. I stare at the bubbles in my champagne, cream-colored effervescence, until my eyes blur, unfocused, and the room dissolves to nothing save Annette's voice, softly speaking, I can see the gallery she is describing, the calm white interior, I see Olivia behind the desk, reading, the only noise the slap of rain on the window, the smooth moan of the wind. I imagine her lost in a book, her paintings on the walls, the discomforting presence of being surrounded by portraits that had once occupied her so violently yet now have passed on to their owners, and no longer have any hold on her life save a vague disbelief that she created them.

She is sitting there, reading, when she hears the door open and the snap of an umbrella shutting, and she barely looks up when a man says *Bonjour* because she has completely forgotten he might be an important buyer, and so all she says is Let me know if I can help you.

He wanders around, this stranger, his presence negligible until she hears a great jolt of laughter, the kind of infectious laugh that makes you smile through any tears, and she cannot understand what could have amused him so, because they were her paintings, and she did not think they were funny.

She gets up, annoyed, and moves over to join him. He is tall and thin, with wavy dark hair that needs cutting, staring with eyes the color of her Siberian amber beads at her favorite of all in the show, the naughty one, a portrait of the cello player Antonio del Campo, painted in the setting of *Le Déjeuner sur l'herbe*, naked on a blanket in the forest, with a string quartet serenading him in the background, the quartet he often played with. Poor Antonio, she is thinking, such a bastard and yet at this moment so maligned, so naked, hanging on a wall, an object of humorous derision for a man who has walked in out of the rain.

"So this is the famous portrait," he says, his English heavily accented. "Forgive me for laughing, but I know Antonio, and she's captured him perfectly, that arrogant smile. *Quelle gueule!* May I ask, do you know, what did he do when he saw it for the first time?"

"I heard he was stunned into what, I was told, was for him an uncharacteristic silence. The shock of the truth, I guess, when it dents the fragile eggshell of someone's ego, can be a bit frightening. Seeing yourself exposed like that, I mean."

"She's a great talent, don't you think?"

He turns to her, thinking she is the receptionist, and his eyes are shining, like a tortoiseshell comb catching the light even as it lies hidden in the thick bun of a woman's hair, and when she sees him full in the face she decides, a surprising quick decision rare in its clarity and strength, that if she could she'd like to paint him, whoever he is, she will somehow contrive to paint him as a cougar, sleek, rain-wet, prowling, an elegant dark shadow, in the corridors of a palace. Versailles, perhaps, or Vaux-le-Vicomte.

"Do you know," he says, as if reading her thoughts, "but, of course you must know, how does she arrange her commissions? Do you think I might be able to ask her to paint my portrait?" He flushes. "It is not only that I admire her work, but it is a sort of—"

"Sort of what?"

He bites his lip. "Rivalry." He looks at her quickly, then away, embarrassed. "It is quite silly. We often worked together," he explains, his gaze back on the portrait. "The first violin used to be my wife."

"I see," she says, "but that's still not a very good reason to sit for a portrait. Rivalry, I mean. It's an important decision, not to be taken lightly, and Olivia is quite fussy."

"And that was a very stupid thing to say. *Vous avez raison.* But, you know, the truth is . . ." He runs his hands through his hair, as she does to her own. "The truth is I live in terror of losing my hands, although that fear is probably quite ridiculous, and I'd like to be painted while I am at this, how do you say . . . this place." He flushes again. "*Excusez-moi,*" he says. "All I seem to do is apologize for the idiotic things I am saying. *Je m'exprime beaucoup mieux en français.* But these paintings, they are so open, their *caractère*, they make you want to drop your guard and be painted as she sees you, not as you see yourself."

There is a glimmer, only a flick, in his eyes that she suddenly wants desperately to capture, to reanimate in her studio, illuminate on canvas, and in doing so make that illusion be real, immortalized.

He catches her stare. "I'm sorry, but you look familiar," she says, her turn to blush even though she knows perfectly well who he is.

"Olivier de Chabrol. I am very pleased to meet you."

"Of course," she says. "The pianist." Before he can ask her name she tells him the particular demands of the artist, the capricious selection of her subjects, the lunchtime sittings in the pose of her choosing, the numbing curiosity unsatisfied by her curt refusal to show any work in progress, her penchant for settings and highly stylized backgrounds among the oddities of mythology and folktales, complete payment in advance, unrefundable and irredeemable.

"I understand," he says. "I am leaving quite soon for a tour in America for several months. Do you think I might meet her before I go?"

"I can put in a word for you, seeing that you liked poor Antonio so much. She was very pleased with that one. Let me have your number, and if she wants to, she'll call you to arrange a meeting."

"I'm at Brown's, only until Sunday. Will you try?"

"I'll do my best. This is her gallery, after all."

"Could she meet for tea, or a drink?"

"Lunch. She prefers to meet potential clients at lunch. There've been many arguments about this, I must say, but she claims the sittings must take place then because the light is best, even when it's not, and that's when she wants to see people, to talk and make her decision." She smiles, secretly a bit aghast at her audacious description of her own stubborn temperament.

"*La dame des règles*," he says. "I like that. It is much the same for me. I can play even if the light is extinguished, but still there always are rules."

He sighs, and she nearly sees that flickering look again, although she doesn't need to, because she has already decided.

"Please," he says, "I know my asking is very spontaneous, but I would like this very much to be arranged."

"I understand."

She goes back to the desk and hands him one of Annette's cards. He pockets it, still assuming she is the receptionist, or Annette.

"You may ring me at any time," he says, shaking her hand, his fingers fine and strong.

It has stopped raining, and he forgets his umbrella.

That night she conjures his portrait, conceives it as a living vision, he moving through it, prowling down the corridors of a palace already so deep in her head that she dreams it finished, seeing his face smiling at her in her sleep.

She had told Annette everything, and Annette makes her call him the next day to put him out of his misery, he disbelieving and grateful.

"Lunch," she says. "Friday."

"How will I know her?" he wonders.

"Don't worry, she knows what you look like," she says, trying not to laugh. "She is a bit of a fan."

His thanks are effusive, embarrassing, and she feels a naughty pang of conscience, for only a moment.

At lunch he is waiting, sitting stiff and anxious, clearly expecting to be disappointed, the fingers of his right hand trilling a nervous sonata between the fork and the spoon.

When he sees Olivia, carrying his umbrella, his face falls. It is only the woman from the gallery, come to tell him, no doubt, the regretful news that the artist had changed her mind.

"She doesn't want me," he says when she sits down.

"Yes, she does."

"But she has sent you in her place."

"No, she hasn't."

"But—"

Olivia smiles. "Please, forgive me," she says. "I didn't mean to do that to you. It was terribly rude."

He forgives her, of course, he will forgive her anything, and they sit, eating, picking at their food because they are not hungry, they are too busy talking, both sending a silent prayer of thanks to Annette for having the flu, curious, their eyes shining, his a beacon of pleasure when she gives him the number of her studio, the number only a handful have, but he does not yet know that, talking about everything and nothing, wary and delirious, wondering and not caring why, there is always time to wonder why.

They leave, sharing a taxi to drop him at Brown's.

"Call me," she says when they turn near the hotel. "Call me as soon as the tour's over."

"I will call you before then," he says, "and I wish it were already over."

"It's better to wait."

"Not always."

They are staring at each other, flushed, it is time to go, and they don't understand, they want this moment to linger, it is enchanted. He leans over to kiss her cheek, one, then the other, and then his lips slide to her mouth and he kisses her, hard, with all the passion locked in his soul, and they both pull back as if shocked, their hearts not beating, looking at each other in blank astonishment, and then he gets out and stands watching her as she turns around to wave farewell.

She counts the days till he gets back.

"That is a story," Nick says. "Very romantic. Except that they are rarely together. How long has it been this time?"

Annette shrugs. "Nearly two months, I should think. But they manage. Olivia goes to see him whenever she can, but she's quite in demand as well. They've entirely overloaded their schedules so they can take a long honeymoon, whenever that is, and it's making me quite cross, actually, that she's working so hard. Olivia's insisting on a long cruise, no telephones, no fax machines, no people, no distractions, but it will probably be a year before they can take it, knowing them."

Nick smiles. That is all he needs to know. The longer they've been apart, the better. "Thank you for telling me," he says, absolutely sincere, for him an uncommon occurrence. "She is very lucky to have you."

"I'm lucky to be here."

He picks up her hand, and kisses it. "So am I."

Annette would happily do anything he said, if he said it to her then, with the heat of his lips on her flesh, but he has no need to, has never any wish to, because he looks up and Olivia is standing at his shoulder.

There is a sudden rush, an electric jolt, and she is cursing herself, furious at the deep twinge of proprietorial annoyance when she saw Nick leaning so close to Annette. I should never have come, she silently, vehemently berates herself, this is so ridiculous that I am jealous, he makes me cringe, his smug surety and his big blue eyes, he is such a bastard to women, I know he is, I can feel it, he fucks them and then he fucks them over, why couldn't I stay away?

She is as peculiar-looking as I remembered. A casting director would see her face and, at best, say nice hair but nothing memorable, her features small and even, save for her eyes, her mouth not wide and pouting, her cheekbones too round, yet she possessed an extraordinary quality of animation felt only when she fixed her queer eyes upon you, pondering, alight, the color ever shifting, eyes like the sky before a storm, the same frothy hues of the sea when it was whipped into angry waves during the hurricane that trashed our beach house in Malibu.

Her hair does not match her coloring, does not belong to the pale splendor of skin that should have been littered with freckles, does not complement the somber pewter of her eyes, it is too darkly red, gleaming chestnut and mahogany and as much like leaves burning crisp in their last indelible glory, and so much of it, long, halfway down her back, a curling mass

begging to be brushed, brushed as Olivier, who buries his
head in it and begs her not to cut it every time she pushes it
off her shoulders in annoyance, brushes it in the evenings.
Her hair should have been dark blond, like newmown hay, or
dark, blue-black as ink, to set off that peculiar lightness of her
eyes, like ice cubes melting, almost reptilianly opaque when
she is stern or flummoxed, as she is now, becasue she has tried
to tell herself she does not want to be anywhere near Nick,
and yet here she is.

She sits down after kissing Annette hello, somber, and we
order. Nick has gauged her mood instantly, fearing as much as
his ego will let him that any forcefulness might drive her away,
and changes the subject, regaling us with stories I'd overheard
and told him about the wardrobe mistress and the extras in
period costume, wandering ghostlike in the artificial moonlight
down the cobblestoned streets of Shoreditch, where they have
just started to shoot, appearing to float in and out of banks of
fog carefully blown in by grips manning the giant-size fans.

Olivia pushes her food around her plate, listening to them
talk, distracted. I see her perplexity. She cannot help but
wonder why he, who could have anyone he wanted throwing
herself at his feet, has chosen her. It doesn't make sense, and
she wants to understand it, why she has allowed herself to
be so stunned by the relentless strength of Nick's libidinous
charisma.

She underestimates it. Nick is the riptide of sex. You're
sucked under before you've got a chance to think, and when
again you surface you've been pulled far out to sea, bobbing
and adrift.

I can't take my eyes off her, watching her bewilderment as
emotions flit unknowingly across her features, kindling her
eyes, turning down a corner of her mouth, raising an eyebrow,
caressing a lash. I have never seen Nick's precise effect on a
woman's psyche reflected so clearly back, ever before.

But then, Nick has never before been entranced by a woman who is real.

I see Olivia worry that her very presence at this table somehow diminishes her love for Olivier, a love that is calm and steady and does not leave her though they are often apart. I see her curious, challenging herself not to react, to prove herself disinterested even though she is not, to prove that her response to Nick, so sudden and shocking in its uncontrollable fierceness, had been a fluke.

I see her relax, finally, secure in the understanding that, no matter where her thoughts lead her, she knows she is loved.

If I told her that Nick, in his own way, is as perplexed by this attraction as she is, she would not believe me.

She sits there, cool and self-contained. She has been content with the rules and structure she has imposed on her days, so calmly aware of being alive, of having some purpose. She has a life here in London, although she sometimes longs for the familiar comforts of the homes she knew before, she has work filling her days, work that pleases her, work she loves, work that brings her some small acclaim amid the privacy she craves, work that buys her freedom from worries of mortgages and the cost of brand-new sable brushes and commissions from people she does not want to paint.

She has a life where people like Nick Muncie do not enter, or if they do, in the unlikely circumstance of her painting them, they are as easily dismissive of the woman she really is behind her professional facade as they are dismissed by her.

They clamor for her portraits, these millionaires craving the exclusive, not to own in pleasure but to gloat over in front of jealous colleagues, and she paints the odd living legend or industrial mogul not for the money but because she saw and was piqued by a hint of the bizarre in them, or the strange quirk of an eyebrow. They blab happily during these sittings, conversation fascinating only to themselves yet absorbed with skillful necessity by Olivia in her concentration, their desultory dronings stunned into speechlessness when they see what Olivia has done to them, not from malicious intent, though it is well deserved, but simply because that is how she sees them, as they are truly: naked, exposed, and shamelessly vulgar. They have been immortalized by the famous Olivia Morgan, and yet when she is finished and the painting shipped off to the mansion where it will hang illuminated in a niche of honor, impressing the same vulgarians who continue to beg, vainly, for her time, she has already forgotten their names.

"Nick, I have to ask you something," Olivia says after we order espresso. "Why is it so important for you to be painted?"

"Not just painted. Painted by you."

"By me, then."

This is his cue. We have already rehearsed this scene, many times. Nick wanted it perfect: somberly conceived, yet spontaneous. Flawless.

The amount of thoughtfulness he has decided to invest in this preoccupation with Olivia has my senses on alert. Nick is not known for concern, or plans for seduction more premeditated than the few seconds it took a trembling, docile body to acquiesce. There is some strange need surfacing, something I'd seen fleetingly on his face once before when I caught him reading the dog-eared copy of *The Iliad* I'd left by the pool and he grinned up at me with sheepish embarrassment. "It's the quest thing, isn't it?" he said.

It's the quest thing that has drawn him to *Faust*, that has brought him here today, though he would deny it.

It is the magnet turning back on us. I am only surprised it hasn't happened sooner.

I don't like it, but I still can't take my eyes off Olivia. I should mind more, but I don't want to, I can't help myself. I want to trust her as I could never have trusted any Belinda-like creature before.

I slide my glance back over to Nick.

Like every skilled actor he has waited a fraction of a beat before answering. This is the audition of a lifetime, and he's not about to blow it.

"I saw a painting you did in Los Angeles," he says, finally, looking off into the distance as if to conjure it up before him—which would have been a marvelous feat of recollection, since I was the one who'd seen it, and described it to him before this lunch—"the portrait that you called *The Director*. I never forgot how it made me feel, that it was a soul, or in his case more like an absence of soul, made visible, painted and two-dimensional, and yet alive."

"Why did you think that?"

"I don't know. It's like asking yourself why you breathe." He sighs. Pause. Perfect. "I want to see how you see me. I want you to make me live."

She fixes her gaze upon him, trying with all her strength to maintain the cold blank professional curiosity that darkens her eyes into polished pewter, unaware that the expression in them is still many light-years from the typical fawning interest Nick has grown to expect from every female who has ever heard his name.

She wants to know, I feel it. She is the alchemist of looking. Her curiosity is as avid as Nick's determined will to possess. She wants to know his secrets, she will puncture the hollow shell of his evasiveness, and she is not afraid to ask.

Their eyes are locked, hers a baffled mixture of blunt denial and inquisitive, subliminal desire, his a silent imploring, desperate to win her over to needs he never thought he'd be able to acknowledge, desperate because losing is not a possibility he allows into his life, desperate because he cannot articulate why this woman attracts him so.

And in that look it comes to her in a flash, she sees it, she knows what to do, the composition of his portrait, his face, who he would be, the specter of his painting comes alive in her mind's eye, whooshing in on a breathless rush of his pheromones, the scent of seduction, odorless, as invisible as carbon monoxide and just as poisonous, unknowable yet all-pervasive, seeping into the chinks of her subconscious mind, and pushing all other thoughts away.

She opens her eyes and sees him truly, there, only for an instant do they see each other, and she gives in.

The restaurant has emptied, slowly, and we are lingering, reluctant. Annette wipes her lips and excuses herself to the ladies' room and the phone.

"I dreamed of you," Nick says to Olivia when there is only me to hear him. "I dreamed that you were at the beach, the ocean near where we used to live, and you were standing on a cliff, your hair loose in the wind, just standing there, staring out to sea."

She frowns. "And where were you?"

"I don't know. It was just you."

"Just me."

"Just you. You don't mind, do you, that I dream of you, Olivia." He says her name like a kiss. "Little olive."

Her frown deepens, she is still fighting him. "Don't call me that. It makes me sound like a martini."

The next day a motorcycle messenger arrives at her studio with a large beribboned box. Inside the soft layers of silken tissue paper lie two martini glasses with stems so thin she marvels that they don't snap in her fingers. And a jar of olives.

There is no note. There is no need for a note.

There is no need because she is standing on a cliff, staring out at the dark illimitable sea, wavering on the brink, ready to fall.

C H A P T E R   4

Nick is standing, lounging really, against a pillar, posing. That is easy, he knows exactly what to do. He is happy, elated, able to watch Olivia, he is close enough to catch the faintest whiff of vetiver and hyacinth, she is moving, her hands move, sketching, she looks at him but through him, she sees his face but her gaze does not linger, he is free to watch her and think his wicked thoughts. She is there, and he is free to watch her.

I am sitting in the corner, watching him watch her.

Usually, Olivia said, she has very strict rules, not just about whom she paints but how she paints them. The quick lunchtime interrogation when she questions their needs and desires. She hears a tale, she makes them tell it, they think it is innocuous, trivial, nothing of importance. From this secret knowledge the portrait begins its formation, magical, she determines what she will paint, how she will paint them, who they will be, what myth is theirs, the transformation awaiting.

She is painting Nick as the Minotaur, a beast, yet still human. He is standing in a maze.

He stands waiting, a ball of string in his hand.

I know that normally, no one else is allowed in the studio during a session, although it is large enough for dozens to hide in corners, unobtrusive. Olivia's living quarters are downstairs, locked to us, although the kitchen and a small bathroom have been built into one side, their doors usually shut to us as well. The studio is white, all white, the only colors her paints, her paintings, her smock smeared with memories of other faces, the only color her hair, gleaming richly red, and the paint freckling her fingers. This used to be a ballroom built specially and detached from the house next door; that is why the ceiling is so high and the room so full of light, Olivia told us, the floor is sprung, it keeps me up. There are cartons of props stacked in neat piles, *objets* peeping out, gleaming things, white bowls on the floor, brilliant Spanish piano shawls folded to hide the bright richness of their woven threads, pushed back behind the cartons into the shadows. They are meant for draping over the chaise, draped over a woman, her skin like a luscious ripe peach in the light of the studio, a *maja* reclining. There are several chairs of white-painted wood, their cushions a splendid white brocade, pulled near a large round table covered with layers of muslin, falling in soft cream piles on the floor. Centered on it is a scruffy wooden tomato basket, filled with clay pots overflowing with white hyacinths. She has staggered the planting, some stalks only just poking through the earth, other buds swelling, others blooming, I can smell them, delicate, delicious, I can see her deft slender hands spreckled with paint, holding the fat dark bulbs, I can see her fingers rounding a hole in the dirt, I can see her pressing down a bulb, covering it, patting it, sprinkling it, grow, she says silently, bloom for me.

I prefer to sit in the far corner, a book in hand, there only because Olivia asked me to at lunch, her eyes soberly begging. Nick had been waylaid by his fans when Annette was on the phone, leaving us temporarily alone, and me not knowing what to say. She'd smiled at me, then, with no pity, and I felt my heart begin to thump. I could sense her wrestling with the inevitable questions about my face, about Nick and me, wondering how discreetly she could begin to satisfy her curiosity.

"Can I ask you something, M," she said.

"Yes." I steeled myself, involuntarily.

"How do you stay so fit?"

"Fit?" This was not what I'd expected.

"Yes. You're very strong, it's like your strength is there, it's solid, and believable, but not pumped up. Hidden." She was still smiling. "It makes me feel safe."

"I make you feel safe?" I was astonished. I half-turned my head to see if Nick was watching, but he was table-hopping on the other side of the room, autographing napkins, and I sighed in relief that he could not see my face.

"Yes, you," she said. "I don't know why, I just feel it. You must make Nick feel safe, too, or you wouldn't be together, right? And you're observant, as I try to be, but I expect that no one ever notices because of your face."

I inhaled deeply, calming breaths. Maybe it was anxiety about Nick making her talk this way, and I couldn't blame her if that was so, or maybe she just wanted to know. I couldn't yet let myself relax into trusting her.

"Well, I like your face. And the least you can say," she added, sensing my discomfort, "is that it's unique."

No one had ever said that to me before. I didn't believe her, but I tried to smile. I knew she wanted me to, and I wanted, absurdly, to please her.

"I'm sorry," she said, folding her napkin into neat triangles. "Sometimes I talk too much. You can get very self-conscious,

being an American in London, when people are always judging
you by the way you talk, and how fast, and not by what you
say."

"Even you?"

"Even me. Especially me." She sighed. "I'm just hypersensi-
tive. And somehow I get the feeling Nick is going to be a
handful."

I did smile, then, that time for real. "Boxing," I said.

"What?"

"How I stay fit. I never answered your question."

"Oh," she said, biting her lip not to laugh. "Right. I should
have guessed." She looked at me, sideways. "So can I ask you
to do something for me?"

"Yes."

"Will you come keep me company during Nick's sessions?
There's plenty of space in my studio. You won't be in my
way." The words came tumbling out, the only true marker of
fears she'd rather have kept hidden. "I think you'd keep me
calm."

Safe, she meant to say. She is watchful enough to have
imagined what I do, why I am always with Nick, to keep him
in line, to save him from himself. To save her from him. This,
yes, she knows.

How could she imagine anything else?

All she knows is that, instinctively, she needs me. She needs
to be protected. She feels Nick's eyes, she feels his desire rising
even though he hasn't moved. It is perfuming the air, invisibly
potent. She sees his face, but her training is too fine, her
concentration is fierce, she feels it, yes, she knows it is hovering, a mist seeking to invade her pores, but she wants to
paint, and so she ignores its full implications, and instead
plucks it from the air and transmutes it into the face beginning
to take shape before her, grinning softly, wickedly sensual,
and very hungry.

She will make him breathe on canvas, standing in a maze.

I close my eyes. I do not need to see her. I hear the soft rustle of her movement, her busy hands swooping up and down. There is music playing, always. I know it is Olivier, his supple fingers scampering over the keyboard, Chopin, Schubert, a sonata, quartet, ballade, it is flowing over us, tranquil and yearning.

There is a world outside, a horrible, gray, empty world, but we are sealed, three figures in a large white room, the ceiling high above it, the dim noontime sun filtering through the skylight, the floor gleaming, burnished, thick Moroccan rugs the color of pale cream scattered around it, needed, she explained with a laugh, for all her prayers when the painting was going badly. Bolts of Belgian linen and stacks of canvases are turned toward the wall, we see only their stretchers and faint streaks of paint along their sides. Jars of the pigments she grinds herself, oils and bristled brushes, a funny-shaped spray bottle of fixative, and tubes of paints are aligned in perfect rows like little fat soldiers on her work table. It smells of primer, of supplies bought in delirious abandon at Cornellessens, of linseed and turpentine, of the wonder of creation.

The ghosts of portraits painted sit near me in the corner. I can feel them, lingering in the peacefulness of this room. Even they are silent, content. There is no need to talk. Only the soft sound of a piano, and a charcoal stick sketching.

We do not wish to leave.

Be there by noon, don't be late, she told us, if you're late I won't let you in, this is the only time I can have the sitters here, don't ask me to explain it. Four sittings, four sittings only. That is all she requires, for the face, for the body, the rest she can imagine. The rest fills her hours when the sun swings west and fades from the skylight, when the images float through her head and are transferred, miraculously, to the canvas, where they take shape and form, recast, born in layers shimmering, their souls captured, living forever.

We are back, a week later. Olivia is relaxed, happy, it is going well, I can see it on her face. She is humming, idly, along with the glorious shower of Schubert's notes. Different hyacinths are blooming.

Nick stands, lounging comfortably against the pillar, easily sinking into the pose. This time he feels like talking. She feels like talking too, he can sense it.

"Olivia," he says, the very syllables a caress, "can I ask you a question?" He is going to try the pseudo-intellectual approach, proving that he can indeed talk about subjects more pungent than the latest restaurants or box-office grosses.

I'd often thought Nick should divulge more of his buried self, although he wouldn't have believed me had I told him so, but he remained convinced that it was better for me to write the lines, clever but not too brilliant, and for him to say them. In that way, he gave me my voice. I hear it as he speaks now, calm, unthreatening. He'll talk, she'll grow accustomed to his talking, and she'll begin to crave hearing the sound of anything he might have to say.

After that he can pounce, when she is lulled into believing the silken cadence of his words.

"Mmm," she says. She has barely heard him.

"How do you paint?"

She looks at him, bemused.

"No, I mean, where do your ideas come from? What do you think when you're painting? What's in your head when you look at me?"

Her charcoal stick dances across the canvas. "I don't know. The ideas, if that's what you call them, just arrive, I see them. I wake up with them."

She steps back, cocks her head, steps forward, a minuet.

"We meet at lunch, as you know. Even then, no matter how much they want a portrait, I'm still waiting for—I don't know, this sounds a bit crazy—but something unique." She smiles to herself, thinking of Olivier. "A word'll jump out, or a sigh, or the way they cock their heads, and it's as if this meaningless gesture becomes, instead, the actual DNA of the portrait, the key to their essence. That's when I can hope it might work."

"So that's what you were thinking when we met," he teases.

"Well, not all the time."

"Oh, so there is some hope."

" 'Fraid not, dearie."

"I'm crushed."

"Sure." She rolls her eyes. "There's not a whole lot I can do to make a dent in your ego. That's one of the things I admire about you. During a sitting, even with someone as full of himself as you are, it's like automatic writing for me. I mean, even though I paint what I want, deep down I still want to please my sitters. I try not to show that because I really wish I didn't feel that way. Being freed from it might make my work better." She sighs, deeply. "So it's a constant struggle, because I have my own ideas about what I want to do, but I still know that drawing is just finding out what the drawing will do. It's like groping in the dark for something you know is there, hidden in the shadows. The marks come and you have to accept them. Only then does the painting really begin to happen. It's like discovering the heart of a pearl, there, buried beneath the layers of nacre, the pearl's true color. Even though I can't see it yet, it's not tangible, I still know it's buried there under what I haven't yet created. My hand moves, I don't think, I look, I see, but it's already there."

"How can you be such a poet and so mean to me at the same time?"

"I'm not mean," she says in mock protest. "Try to make me believe you don't get off on it."

"Why, Olivia," he says, drawling, "I do believe you're flirting with me."

"Dream on," she says, laughing. "It's just chitchat to keep me going. Maybe I make it sound so easy, but it isn't. I'm just used to it, I guess." She wipes her elbow across her brow. "People are at their most vulnerable during these sessions. Even someone like you, who's used to being looked at. All you've thought about who you are and how you appear to the world becomes terribly exposed."

She glances over at me, and smiles, soft. "Artists know that—or should know that—and feel torn between this incredible responsibility to that vulnerability, and the struggle between their own intellectual ideas and their gut instinct guiding them, or guiding me, I should say, to what I hope is the truth." She frowns, eyeing the canvas. "Anyway, isn't it a bit like acting, when you're so submerged in character that your unconscious takes over?"

"I guess," Nick says, looking thoughtful. "I try not to think about it either. If you think too much it never works. I just do it."

"You empty out your self so something else can flow in. There's an old Chinese proverb: When you're taking a boat through the rapids, you haven't got time to think."

He laughs. "Never anything that profound, especially with all the wonderfully trivial movies I've made."

She smiles. "Yes, but I can't do much with my talent. Actors can reach millions and millions. They see you, they want to touch you, they want to be you. All I can do is react to the moment in my own imagination."

"I don't think you should put yourself down like that."

"I'm not, it's just what painting is. I was born into the wrong century, I suppose. No one appreciates us portrait painters anymore, not truly, not the way they used to be appreciated. Why paint? Take a picture instead, even though a successful portrait can be so much more alive, more truthful, than any photograph will ever be. It's because people's faces change all the time. It's why we look at photographs and say, 'That's not me, I don't look like that, really, do I?' A photo is only a snatching of one teeny part of a second. But a portrait, well, it's a record of changes over time, of how much your face changes even as I'm watching it, of who you are and all the emotions flooding out of you and colliding with mine.

"But now," she adds, "it's 'Here, smile for the camera. Look, it's a Polaroid.' Instant gratification. I get so exasperated. In case you hadn't noticed." She grimaces. "Put it on film. Watch it. Watch it again."

Nick turns his head to look at me.

"Don't move," says Olivia.

"Sorry."

"Actors," she says, gently mocking.

"I thought you didn't know who I was."

"I didn't really, but I do now. Besides, I have painted a few of you before, usually against my better judgment."

"And here I was just beginning to think you liked me." He can risk the glib lines, the pleasure of this easy banter loosening his limbs, tripping his tongue as he would have it trip over Olivia's breasts.

She is smiling. "You, all those actors, all that idiot Holly-wood bullshit, how can you stand it? It's such useless energy, all that gossip and deal-making and my car is bigger and my parking space is closer. What an utter waste of time." She steps back again, coolly regarding. "All I know is that everyone out there drove Olivier nuts, when he was working on Jamie's film. All that energy sucked out of him for no reason except to stroke someone's misguided self-importance." Her eyes nar-row in concentration. "You, all of you precious stars, you're what painters used to be. Important." She sighs. "We mean nothing save to the very few who choose to seek us out."

"I'll tell everybody I know to buy your art."

"Please don't. I can't think of anything more revolting than a bunch of so-called superstars begging me to be immortalized."

"Excuse me, your royal highness," Nick says, mockingly pompous. "I suppose I should kiss your feet in grateful appreciation."

"Well, I am too harsh," she says, shrugging away a smile. "I don't want fame, or adulation, or the public panting to examine my dirty laundry. I'm lucky I'm successful, that I can choose who I paint. That's very rare. Most of my friends, artists I know from school, certainly can't. But choosing my subjects is the only control I have, really. I'm only doing you so you'll get off my case and leave me alone." She stops, steps back, steps forward, concentrating. "And because . . ."

"Because what?" Nick says. He is too eager.

"I don't know," Olivia says. "Never mind."

It is the first time she is really letting herself relax into a true look at him, not as a subject she knows she needs to paint, not as a curiosity, but as a man. He feels the heat of her gaze, he grasps it instantly as if he were starving, the potency of his presence is palpable, inescapable. The air is suddenly thick with the surprising fog of unspoken wishes.

"Painting a portrait is a little bit like working very hard on a courtship," she says, she must speak, she cannot bear the weight of his eyes upon her, she turns back to the solid ground of her work, her eyes hooded. "It's so intimate, and so revealing. When it's finished and they see it, see themselves for the very first time, it's like the moment of your courtship when you declare your love for each other. Either they don't like it, or are bewildered by your vision of them and your hopes are dashed, usually because you can't fulfill their expectations. Often, with my work, they simply don't understand the setting I've put them in. Or, if they do like it, you're swept right into their arms." Her eyes on Nick. "Metaphorically speaking, of course."

"Of course," he says.

"Other painters say that a portrait is no good unless the sitter likes it," she goes on, "although that's not always true for me. What I hope is that, perhaps, someone, someday, will be able to read a deeper meaning into what I do. That they will find a sort of—oh I don't know, this sounds so pompous—a sort of profundity, maybe one that is even unintended, and it will move them. Shake them. And if that happens, I will have given a stranger an unexpected gift of seeing another reality, if only for a second."

"But doesn't that happen every time?"

"Are you kidding? Of course not. I'm always telling myself that each one is the last one."

"But you seem so, I don't know, confident. Capable. Fluid. Sure of yourself." Long pause. Long pregnant pause. "Sure of what you want, and who you want it with." Another pause. "And who you want it for."

She stops. Even from where I sit I can see a flicker of panic light up her eyes and her shoulders tense. "Why do you say that?"

Nick shrugs.

"Well," she says, attacking the canvas once more, "you don't see what I do every day before I start." She smiles ruefully. "I am the world's worst procrastinator."

Nick is surprised. "You? I don't believe it."

"Believe it. Every time I wake up I wonder how much courage I'll find that day. That I will have lost my instincts in the night, that even when I start this will be the last one, the Bobby Fischer of my paintings."

"But even he came out of retirement," Nick says.

"I know," she says with a rueful grin. "Still, I'll look at the

light and say it's no good, it won't do. I'll look at the mail and
say there are too many bills to pay, oh right, I'd better read
this magazine, I might get inspired. I'll look at my hair and
say it needs a wash. I'll look at my shoes and say the heels are
worn down and I must go get them fixed. I'll look at the pile
of nice clean canvases waiting to be painted and say I need to
prime another, it takes six weeks, and I'm not ready. I feel my
little jars of pigments and tubes of paint behind me, I feel
them boring into the back of my head saying take me, touch
me, use me. Usually that's when I can start. I don't know."
She shakes her head. "What am I talking about?"

    She was not talking to Nick, to me, she was talking to
herself, she doesn't even hear it. Her charcoal stick dances
wildly, she is moving, shifting, she looks at Nick, she looks
at the canvas, she looks up at the sky, her eyes narrow in
concentration. She is talking to keep her mind free for what
she is drawing, she is talking because she needs to, because if
she does, Nick cannot talk back. He cannot say what he is
feeling, so surprised is he to be feeling it, he cannot tell Olivia
that she is looking at someone without realizing that what she
sees is a sham shadow of his real self, appearances are so
deceiving. He cannot say that she might think she can figure
out what fearsome insecurities and cravings fuel his life—and
they are there, little butterflies of apprehension hovering over
the opened flowers of his ego: Can he do it, is he slipping, do
they love me, will I always be a star—but she will never truly
know what machinations churn ceaselessly in his mind.

    He cannot say he is transfixed by her odd beauty, mesmer-
ized by her words and her seeming confidence in the telling
of them so openly, aching to tear himself away from the pillar
against which he lounges, appearing so cool and relaxed, and
grab her in his arms, throw her on the work table, on her fat
tubes of paint, crush her down on them, their weight squeezing the tubes till they burst, the colors running together, on

the table, staining their clothes, he taking her, not just her body but everything that makes her, she cannot escape the firmness of his grasp, he will not let her go, her back a riot of colors, flowing together.

It is a painting of their own frenzied creation, born of his insatiable desire.

I am sitting in the corner, watching them, unnoticed.

If she keeps talking she cannot listen to the thoughts running through her mind as wildly as her charcoals and brushes scream across the canvas, she cannot touch what she does not want to be feeling, this inexorable response to the primitive raw hunger that scares her so. She feels him, she sucks it in and transfers it in a wild passion, the fire of him is engulfing her arm and the fingers clamped around her charcoal stick, his potency is driving her brushes, forcing her paint this way, and not that, moving her feet in a fervent blaze across the sprung floor.

She sighs. Her hands drop to her side. "Sorry," she says. "I need to take a break. Do you want some tea or a drink or something?"

I know why she has stopped. She is wavering. It is exhausting, fighting him.

She covers the portrait and moves over to the end of her work table, the dirty end she calls it, where all the mess of painting is contained in grime-encrusted tins and soup cans and bottles and bits and pieces, broken-down brushes, rags for wiping, screws and nails in glass baby-food jars, palette knives and razor blades, little tokens from friends, a shaky snowstorm with the Statue of Liberty in it. She fusses with the kettle, running her fingers through her hair. Nick stretches, a languid feral thing. I join him. He is patient. He is supremely patient. He is lurking in the high grass of the savannah, waiting, awaiting the precisely perfect moment before he will pounce.

We sit at the table of the hyacinths. Olivia brings a plate of cookies and a fat pot of tea, she pours it, we drink, she sits down, rolling her shoulders back and forth to relieve the strain making them taut with tension.

"Sorry," she says again, picking at crumbs. "You're here for such a short amount of time. I don't usually need to stop. I don't want to stop." She yawns.

"Should I be flattered that I'm wearing you out?" Nick asks.

"Go ahead," she says, smiling back. "I'm sure flattery is as necessary to you as eating."

"*Touché*," he says good-naturedly. She is relaxing, slowly, she thinks she can trust him not to be anything other than a sitter for a portrait, she is not pulling away, he is going to bide his time, he is going to wait as long as he has to, he is going to have her, she cannot repel this strength, he is too secure.

"We'll come back," he says.

We came back.

CHAPTER 5

Nick had laughed the first time he saw the motorcycle messengers in London, leather-clad clones, hunched over their bikes in thick black overalls and chunky black gloves, with stiff, scuffed knee-high boots and opaque black helmets hiding any trace of their own identity as they went weaving, fearlessly speeding, in and out of traffic on rain-slicked streets.

Darth Vaders on a Harley, he called them, sending me out to buy twin sets of gear far too heavy for the balmy evenings of riding in the Hollywood Hills but perfect disguise for quick rides during stolen moments on the set in London, Nick zooming off to clear his head, leaving a coughing furor in his wake, makeup and wardrobe and Jamie and the insurers screaming at him to come back, the bastard, and then screaming at me to get on my own bike and find him.

It was on one of the bikes that he sent me out to find the flat.

It would not be easy, because we have very particular requirements. Absolute privacy in an empty building. Up-to-date wiring, for lighting that would be discreet yet high enough to record. Walls thick enough to muffle noise, although not too thick to drill a hole wide enough for the lens of a camera.

It would not be easy because my presence is off-putting, especially to London real estate agents, and so I asked the girls in makeup to smooth some sort of putty on my face to make my scars less noticeable, not only so that I'd appear to be a proper American businessman, complete with bogus letterhead and impeccably bogus credentials thanks to the production assistants, but to protect Nick's identity, as many in town had already seen us together, and he wanted no one to know where this flat, the solemn embodiment of his desire, would be.

None of these elaborate precautions mattered much in the end, really, although they diverted me from the daily chores and pleased Nick and kept him humming, and also pleased the crew, flattered beyond all reckoning to be privy to my secret mission, anything to help their superstar keep his sanity during the grueling months ahead, away from the girls standing shivering outside the Savoy, away from prying eyes, safe and cozy in his little hidey-hole, wherever it might be, the poor chap. None of it mattered, because money makes the most succinct dialogue, and the large quantity of loose pound notes I had packed in my briefcase made all negotiations a mere formality, just in case.

On days when Nick would be working too hard to need me I'd get on the bike in my messenger gear, and cruise slowly, perusing the real estate agents' signs. You'll know it when you find it, Nick said to me, it'll just be there, and you'll know.

I am riding slowly, mindlessly, content, icy wind whistling under the visor of my helmet, lost in curving streets with ever-changing names, past neat squares of prim brick row houses, indistinguishable save for the colors of their doors and the patterns on the shabby lace in the windows, past concrete blocks of council flats and the sordid smallness of High Street shops, bored teenagers lingering outside, smoking idly, or cramming french fries into their fat faces, a film of grease on their lips. Past the red Victorians behind Harrods, the color of dust in the desert at sunset, past solid white Edwardians, imposing order on smooth crescent streets, so unlike the bungalows and their parched cropped lawns in Los Angeles. There are no lawns in London, not where I am riding, only paved concrete terraces and pots of frozen geraniums.

I find the building one dark afternoon, just off Queensway. It was the name that attracted me at first, nearly straight across Kensington Gardens from Olivia's studio in Queens Gate Mews, a silly coincidence that Nick would certainly see as symbolic. I find it around the corner from the Porchester Baths, the large FOR RENT OR SALE sign flapping, forlorn, and I remembered one of the grips talking about the baths, the steam rooms and the sauna, the shivering quick descent into the plunge pool, a massage in the heat of comfortable nakedness, to sit, sated, in the billows of mist, tangled thoughts and stress made liquid, melting into an unstoppable stream of sweat, at least for the moment.

The houses are four-storied and white, all the same, their pillars round and smooth like Olivia's arms, like Olivia's thighs, smooth and gleaming. The rows of these houses hug a curve in the road, all the same, only their numbers are different, Gloucester Terrace on one side, Porchester Square on the other.

Nick will be safe here. No one would ever think to look for him in this neighborhood, polyglot nationalities hurrying to do their shopping, arms laden with paper sacks from the Arab grocers, heads bent against the rain, drooping. It is wet, it is dark, movie stars do not belong here, with bags of shopping, or waiting in interminable lines for the bus to take them to work on the other side of the city. No one will ever notice us, a biker on an errand, a station wagon dropping off a passenger with a hat pulled low, and a woman walking with swift purpose, her hair hidden beneath a vibrantly colored shawl, hands thrust deep into her pockets, lost in thought.

Only the white of the pillars gleams, ghostly white in the dark, beckoning.

The real estate agent shows me the house, repressed eagerness giving a slight twitch to his right eye. His glasses need cleaning. "A diplomat's house," he says, "very well maintained, recently redecorated to a high standard, as you must see, oh yes, all the very best indeed."

"Who lives here?" I ask him.

"No one, as yet," he says, his eyes sliding away, "although we've had quite extraordinary interest. There are only five flats in it, one on each floor save the second, as I'll show you." He points to a large door just off the staircase, and then a more modest one down the hall. "The previous owner wished to have a *pied à terre* here, and so he created this cozy flat. It's only one room, with a very small kitchen area and bath, but quite comfortable."

For his assignations, no doubt. "Does it connect to the other flat?"

"Oh no, sir. Not in the slightest."

He takes me into the larger flat first, opening into a lovely square room, the ceilings high, their moldings elaborately carved, the parquet floor polished amber, a kitchen off a narrow hall with sleek cupboards and a gray-green slate floor, the tub in the bathroom so long and deep even I could stretch out in it without bending my knees. But what cinched it was the small flat next door, compact, just big enough for what I needed to install in it, and myself. As if some unknown soul had designed it strictly for Nick's purpose.

Nick will be very happy.

I rent the entire building, cash up front for six months with an option to renew, although Nick's shoot will not go quite that long. The agent is ecstatically obsequious, especially after I slip him one thousand pounds and tell him we expect no problems and want to be left quite alone, thank you very much.

Nick and I go through the phone book one dreary afternoon, finding names to attach to the other buzzers to trick any visitors into thinking all the flats are occupied. Security, I tell the agent, who quickly attaches the names. Alderson, Andrews, Fairley, and Scott. The space next to Flat 2 says that only, #2. That's how Nick wants it. No name. No indication of what awaits, a gilded wonderland, inside.

When I am through, it is a beautiful room. I have struggled around the clock, freed by Nick from his demands for this more pressing matter, one that must be finished, created and embellished, before his portrait is. I hire only the best, dispensing thousands and thousands for the finest technicians and workmen, none knowing what the other is doing, their silence necessary, bought with large palmed payments, a momentary flash of greed flickering into their eyes and as quickly out, replaced by the terror only my reptilian smile could evoke. Even the maid is scared of me, the slender Dominican who says her name is Dulcie, and little else. She comes early in the morning, twice a week as I have asked, and I am always waiting, because I would never give her a key. I sit in the kitchen, reading, while she cleans the large room and the bathroom in silence, efficient, for there is little to do, and then trade places. Do not ever touch the mirrors, I have told her, I will do them myself, and she is obedient. When she is slipping on her coat I always give her two fifty-pound notes, which is far too much, and she nods her head and scurries off, slipping into the street below.

It is a room of enchantment, all gold and wood and cream, deceptively simple. I am proud of my handiwork, and the lovely things I have found, though not their purpose. It is meant to be a haven, latent with dreams, luxuriously calm, waiting expectant, so Olivia will never find out the worst of the secrets it is hiding.

When she first walks in she will see only the curved vase of Murano glass, wrought of red and golden hues so opalescent, as if the essence of Olivia's hair had been captured between the artist's unknowing lips and blown with serene delicacy into tangible glowing life, filled with peonies that I change as soon as they start drooping, more arriving at extravagant expense to the Savoy every other day from a hothouse in Holland. It sits atop a round mahogany table with lions' heads for feet, and the two Regency chairs, upholstered in brocade, beside it. And then she will see the bed, the immensity of it, the fat creamy-colored comforter atop it scattered with dozens of soft, small down pillows, begging to be sunk into, and not that the bedposts are shaped into such graceful slender columns with the sculptured golden rings at the top and bottom, for she is not Nick, and does not share his impulses, and cannot imagine what might be attached to them in a frenzy of lust.

She will see the neatly folded, crisply ironed Irish linen and plump Turkish towels stacked in the vintage Vuitton trunk at the foot of the bed, and not the assortment of Nick's custom-ordered toys and necessary objects, boxes of nasty surprises, hidden beneath a false bottom. She will toss off her shoes on the deeply piled carpet, remarking on its thick comfort, thumbing through the CDs near the small portable player, the piles of books and scripts strewn on it, not realizing how well this carpet muffles sound that might carry to the neighbors downstairs, although of course there are no neighbors, and no one will hear anything outside this room except me. She will admire the pale shimmering brocade of the heavy draperies, matching the chairs, caught back with several silken cords, cream and gold and silver, looping yards of braided cords backed with velvet, not knowing Nick prefers them above all other cords, because they do not chafe on sensitive wrists. She will hear the calm ticking of the ormolu clock on the pink marble mantel, the framed photograph of a Mapplethorpe lily above it, and regard her pale startled face in one of the two mirrors with their baroque filigree frames, flanking the fireplace, thinking she has stepped into a dream.

She cannot know how discreetly these mirrors hide the elaborate video equipment I have set up, cameras activated by a light switch, hidden in the dimmer, that can record even in candlelight. It is my own private network, just on the other side of their room, in the neighboring apartment, that quite comfortable small room just large enough for me to sit in an overstuffed chair and observe Nick's activities in case he should go out of focus, that quite comfortable small room where I will sit, silently watching. Nick knowing, of course, that I am watching. He is not one to miss a moment.

He always needs an audience.

CHAPTER 6

Nick is in the shower of the small bathroom, washing off the grime from a night shoot gone overlong, cool needles stinging him into wakefulness, his desire for Olivia far more potent than his need for the oblivion of sleep.

I am standing in the hyacinths, wavering with fatigue.

"You read a lot, don't you, Major?" Olivia says, coming to stand by me.

I nod yes.

"What's this one?"

I turn it over to show her.

"*Germinal*," she says. "I didn't think you were one for Zola. Not that . . . I mean—"

I know what she means. It is a constant cause of tittering on the set, the Major's classic taste in reading, as the crew sees me engrossed in Balzac, Trollope, and Dickens and wonders why. I have always been a reader, at first to save myself from all the downtime on sets, but then discovering how losing myself in the comfort of words, savoring them, alone and at peace, helped diminish the endless stretching hours of my solitary nights.

"You should write someday, Major," Olivia says, covering her embarrassment.

I look at her, genuinely surprised. We had only really spoken to each other once before, at lunch. She smiles at my bewilderment.

"I mean it," she says, "because you like to watch."

"How do you know I like to watch?" A nervous tingle of dread starts to climb up my shins even as my face remains a blank.

"Because of how you talk, when you do talk." She is teasing, and I relax imperceptibly. "And you look, yes, I've seen you. I told you this already, didn't I? I'm sure I did. I meant to, anyway."

Of course you did, I want to tell her, you told me in the restaurant when you said you liked my face and I didn't believe you. I hear you speak, I listen, inhaling your words, and I remember everything you say.

"You look at people as I look at them," Olivia is saying, "but you don't imagine them as I like to, a fantasy sketch in my head, a few blobs of color, a myth or a fairy tale and a dream of a painting, of how I might try to capture their character.

"When you *do* talk," she goes on, pausing to find the right words, and I realize that she has responded only to me, my behavior, not Nick's, and I push the fear out of my body, "you have an uncanny knack for getting right to the heart of things. Maybe because you say so little. It's what I want to do when I paint, but it takes so long to come to me. Do you know what I mean?"

"Yes."

"Do the scars make it painful to talk?"

They did, I want to tell her, no one asks me that, no one looks at me with an observant eye and such sweet concern as you do, they'd hurt unbearably, and for such a long time that I became accustomed to the silence of the disregarded.

"They're not as bad as you think, you know," she says.

I shake my head no. Not to me. "Not to Hollywood," is all I can tell her.

"Is that why you're so taciturn, then?"

How can I tell her the truth?

"You said I like to watch," I finally say.

She pushes her hair back in that familiar gesture of impatience. "No, I'm serious," she says. "I'm not asking just because you know more about Nick than anyone, and he's closer to you—but because I'm curious. I can't figure you out."

"I've never much liked to talk about myself," I manage, and then an image flashes into my head, of my mother, no it wasn't my mother, I never knew my mother, it was some other woman, and there was something I wanted to tell her and she was smacking me with the metal beater from the Mixmaster she'd picked up out of the sink where she was washing it, and then the image flashes as quickly away, buried back with others long forgotten.

"I'm sorry, I didn't mean to pry," Olivia says, turning away. "Forgive me for asking. It's none of my business."

"It's okay."

"No, it isn't. It was really thoughtless. If I'm going to ask any questions, I should ask them of Nick. Besides, I usually want people to talk when I work. It relaxes them."

I nod in agreement. I wish she would stop being so nice. So perceptive.

"But I wanted to talk to you, anyway," she says, "to thank you."

"Thank me for what?"

"For being here because I asked you. It must be hard to sit there and have to see all this." She clasps her hands together, the diamond catching the light in a sudden spurt of clarity. "I might not look like it, but I am very aware of your presence, and the weird thing is I like it, you watching us. I was worried at first—not about you, about me, and all the rules I impose upon myself to make me be able to work. But it was really selfish to need you because I was afraid—" She stops, and I see her blush.

"You don't have to tell me this," I say.

"Yes I do. It's the least I owe you, making you sit here."

She can't imagine how easy it is for me to sit and watch, how I do it all the time.

"It's not just Nick," she says, moving over to examine the hyacinths. "It's me, painting, and feeding off that energy, yours and Nick's. I know what can happen during these sessions, how much you want to connect into that unconscious state where you're doing, you're *creating*, but totally unaware of your being. It's like watching two people fall in love. It's happening to them, not you, you can be happy for them, sure, but you feel this energy all around you and you're not ever going to be part of it. It can make you terribly self-conscious and terribly lonely."

I want to sit down, I want to go away, I want her to keep talking to me as if I really mattered.

"It's like that at rehearsals sometimes," I force myself to say, "when the actors use each other to make things happen. Or at least to try and stay in the reality of the moment."

She smiles, relieved. "I knew you'd understand. And I am glad you're here. I hope you believe me."

Nick steps out into the room, his hair damp and curling, and I am spared having to answer.

She is painting now, she is loquacious, animated, teasing Nick, their easy flirtation flying, keeping him awake.

"Okay, let me ask you a question," she says.

"Sure."

"What really happened?"

"What do you mean?"

"I mean, how you two met." She looks over at me. For half a second I panic, again, wondering how she could possibly know, but her face is shining only with simple curiosity. She'd told me she would ask questions of Nick, but I didn't think she would ask this one so soon.

Nick shifts position, turning his head away.

"Don't move," she says.

"I can't tell you that."

"Why not?"

He looks at her, steady. "Because it's done with."

"That bad?"

He shakes his head, drooping. "Don't ask me."

"It's all right if you can't talk about it."

He smiles sadly. "It doesn't matter."

"Well, it does matter." Her embarrassment pleases him. He has played this unexpectedly touching scene perfectly. "Still, I'm glad I asked, because I want you to not move a muscle. You've got just the look on your face I want."

He nods imperceptibly. For Nick, posing is a snap. He can sit, unruffled, sit as I am accustomed to, motionless and inscrutable. He knows Olivia's thoughts are focused on him, his life, what really happened, she is wondering what was so horrible, what secrets is he hiding, and he sits, so still, his expression far away and giving every impression of being tinged with the pain of recollection although his thoughts consist of nothing but tearing off her clothes and tumbling her to the floor, pinning her, plunging into her, making her say his name over and over and over again.

I am the one who remembers.

I will say only this: We were young, too young, way too young to have been on our own as long as we had. I first met Nick in Dallas. He'd hitched there from Pittsburgh, and all I needed was one look at his face to know he'd fled from whatever house was meant to shelter him for the same reason I'd left mine, and we became brothers, closer, even, because we were young and strong and streetwise, and we pumped gas to appear legit and we turned tricks if we had to and we learned quickly where the real money was. I headed the gang and I had all the girls because I wasn't tempted by a quick high, no, I knew what kind of price you'd pay if you let yourself lose control. There were fights, constantly, we lived for the sweet quick thrilling rush, we lived for the cover of darkness because we were young and strong and indomitably good-looking, but this one last fight was different, nothing like a cop show on TV or *West Side Story*, there were too many others, attacking wildly for what they perceived as honor: an adolescent's delusion.

We were outnumbered, and we lost. Nick was like a madman, but we could not beat them back. My face was slashed and then there was some hideous burning pain bringing me to my knees, and all I could see through the blood and my screaming was Nick, down, for an awful instant I thought he was dead, curled next to two other inert dark bodies frozen in the death grip he'd given them. My pain disappeared when the raging surge of adrenaline uncoiled my fists and I stabbed wildly at the others still on their feet with the Swiss Army knife Nick had pinched for me, useful, he'd said sarcastically, to clean my nails. I kept on stabbing, blindly, plunging the small silver blade into the boy who'd slashed me, and because I could not see I stabbed two other dim figures, shocked by the gaping wounds on my face, who tried to intervene. I could not have known they were cops, working undercover, poor lucky fools, their lives saved only by the blood that fogged my eyes.

Nick was not so badly hurt, after all, and he hauled me out

of there, threw me in the basement, and found a Chinese doctor who for the requisite baksheesh glued my face back together. Such perfect blank clarity illuminated his features as he examined me, the depth of the injuries rendering them temporarily numb, that I remembered only the color flooding from the face of one of the boys now dead in a heap, the ruddy flush of superiority dissolving into a pale shadow, a prematurely triumphal sneer locked permanently on his lips, and not the grim determination of the Chinaman who stanched the flow of blood that soaked through the filthy mattress, dripping from the bedsprings onto the cement floor below it.

We hid for weeks in the basement. Nick nursed me as I licked my wounds, incoherent with pain; buying food, forcing me to eat, bringing news, finally loading me into a car in the middle of the night and driving for hours, slowly and carefully because he was too young for a license and too poor to own the car we had stolen and repainted months ago. On and on he drove, stopping only for food and fuel and a few hours' rest in the shadows of the semis in the truck stops, their hulking girth aligned in perfect rows like giant black wombats, fitfully dreaming the dreams of the unloved, driving until he could drive no more because the highway ended at the sea.

After that journey our relationship shifted. Rival brothers, leader and follower, reversing quietly, subtly, to master and his savagely scarred majordomo.

I could not forget that he had saved me, and he knew I would never say what he had done with his knife, like a madman.

It was easier this way. I did not want to need anymore; I sought only the simple demands of being needed, and some tangible purpose. Nick was pleased with my quiet acknowledgment of this new reality. I had healed slowly, and badly. Moving any muscles of my face was excruciating. Nor could I bear to feel the weight of eyes upon me in my mute agony.

Nick made me get up, get out, and face life, because there

were things that wanted doing, mindless at first, and then
increasingly involved. My face had changed, obviously, not
with the scars but with what lay behind it. It was as blank as
I could make it, as impenetrable as the Chinaman's, the same
empty gaze. Rage and fear and nearness to death had molded
it. People shunned it; I smelled of it. It made me very useful
later on, when Nick's fame threatened to become a nuisance.
Only Nick had no fear of my blankness, or my temper. It was
buried, buried deep, buried with the agony I had already
endured.

From then on he always called me the Major. Who I'd been
and what I'd once allowed myself to dream of was slashed
away with the straight, once eye-turning angles of my face,
and was now meaningless, no more substantial than a ghost.
Nick knew I preferred the simplicity of his commands to the
pain of the irredeemable. Don't ask questions. I will do what
you say, I will make myself indispensable. Just don't ask me
to feel.

And so I did whatever he said, annoying sometimes, or
stupid, but never complicated. I did what he wanted and then
he could do what he wanted, it was so easy, and as his fame
swelled like the silk of a hot-air balloon it became too easy to
slip into nastiness, because no one ever said no. Once Nick
felt secure in the patterns that had quickly shifted into habits,
he was clever enough to admit that his increasingly twisted
desires could never be so facilely indulged without my help.
Especially when I watched. He always wanted it more if I
could watch.

For the small satisfaction of knowing that Nick needs me
more than I need him, although he will never admit it, I am
grateful, and silently acquiescent.

There is no question of my leaving, of where I might go and
what I might do. For any other person, mine is not a desirable
presence. Nor have I any real skills except as an organizer or

a bodyguard. What binds us is that vivid knowledge of the other, what we have seen each other do in abject despair, and what we vowed, silently, never to reveal to another living soul. We are so used to existing in this symbiotic stasis that we have grown complacent, denying the rage percolating beneath the surface of our world like the viscous brew in a witch's caldron.

We belong together, brothers in blood, partners in complicity. Family. He who is and he who watches. He who exploits and he who aids and abets, writing the scenes Nick performs in daily life, the procurer, linked together by the curses of fate and the raised pale skin of unhealable scars.

This is why he'll never tell.

"Nick, will you do something for me?" Olivia says, breaking what had been a companionable silence, Nick sitting, slightly hunched, quietly smoking one of the two cigarettes Olivia has grudgingly allowed him, because the smoke makes her sick. It is two weeks later. He is reading his script, memorizing lines, and I am reading Bulfinch's *Mythology*, because she talked of it. Chopin is playing, Olivier's fingers weightless sprites on the keyboard. Outside it is raining, we hear it strumming on the skylight.

He looks at her, his eyes alight.

"Will you take off your shirt?"

Only momentarily stupefied by such a plain request, for no one ever need ask him to strip, Nick rallies, bringing his wrists together in an almost prayerlike gesture, loosening his cufflinks, which fall with a soft clink on the floor, reaching to unbotton his crisp white shirt, slowly, his fingers caressing the buttons as if they were a lover's breasts, then pushing it back off his shoulders to drop in a heap.

His eyes do not leave Olivia's. She is staring back at him, at his muscled splendor.

"Is this okay?" he asks.

"Yes, thank you. I just need to see your shoulders for a minute."

"You're blushing."

"I am not."

"But you are." He smiles. "I like it. It's sweet. Women don't usually blush when they see me."

"What *do* they do?"

"They're so busy being with the legend they don't even bother to look."

Olivia puts down her brush. Her face softens. "I hadn't thought about it that way," she says slowly. "Of course, I haven't much thought of it at all."

"Why should you?"

"Well, because it's you, it's about *you*, who you are, how you feel, what's in your face. That's what I am determined to capture. And it's driving me crazy." She wipes her hand across her forehead.

Her eyes have not strayed from his.

"Crazy," he says.

"Yes, crazy," she mutters. "Absolutely stark raving looney tunes."

"Absolutely."

They are staring at each other. Nick's raw maleness is overpowering, filling this studio, flooding its white walls, puddling between the canvases, pooling at her feet. His gaze will not leave her, leave her be, he is again looking at her like she is lunch, yet he is softer, kinder, because he is here, near her, in her space, and she knows he will stand, posing however she asks, stand motionless, the music in his ears, her eyes flicking over him, looking, searching for the chink she will not find, not here, not yet, because he is too polished at posing.

I cannot read her face, but her cheeks are red, flaming, alizarin crimson.

They cannot take their eyes off each other. This time she is really looking. Something in her is gentling, less wary, and Nick feels it, grabs it though he hasn't moved a muscle, kisses it, sweet, buries his head in it, cradling it close.

There is no way she could ever know that he has never been like this before, with any woman, so pliant, acquiescent, so willing to please, so eager to wait.

He sits, waiting, and watching.

It is an impressive performance.

He is acting like me. Except I will never possess his charm, his beauty, the ease with which he can simply be, his palpable charisma a hot hovering specter floating effortlessly to Olivia, capturing her, snatching away her will to fight him, carrying her away, carrying her up into the flat that awaits them.

We come, a final time, the portrait is finished, it was finished the week before, Annette told us, but Olivia wants us there, in the studio, she wants to be there when Nick sees it, she wants to see his face, she wants to be sure.

"Why did you want me here to see it?" Nick asks her when we are inside, there in the whiteness, light streaming in, clean, welcoming, a safe haven. By habit, we have assumed our places, Nick lounging against the pillar, me near the hyacinths. The ones I last saw have bloomed, and shriveled, and others, lilac and pink, have taken their place.

Olivia finds it hard to meet his eyes.

"You wanted to see me," Nick says. "Tell me it's true, I know it is."

"I wanted to see you when you saw it," she says, finally. "Sometimes it's so hard to let go. Especially this."

He stands there, a looming tangible presence, breathing in, waiting, she knows he is waiting, he will keep waiting, she feels helpless in the wake of it, lost, wandering in the maze she has painted, needing to be found, begging for it, yet dreading the moment when she must confront the man who has chased her into it, locked the door behind them, and thrown away the key.

She is flicking a brush idly, her breasts rising and falling, her nerves straining. I wonder how many bristles there are in a brush. I've never tried counting.

Nick comes over to her, slowly, and looks at the painting, at himself revealed, a man with a beast's face, his face, his features so beautiful and so hurt, beckoning, the torturous hiding curves of the maze twisting behind him in lush, verdant greenery, neatly clipped hedges surrounding this chiseled monster of unassailable strength and sorrow, all the contradictions of his character, the spirit of darkness and the light of hope combined, undone only by the ball of string slowly unspooling, disappearing into the grass beneath his feet.

Olivia watches him, frozen, helpless. Nick is looking at himself as a man, so sexual and yet so innocent, as a naked creature yearning for whatever crumbs of love are strewn at his feet. He blinks, as if disbelieving, then laughs, and I realize I have been holding my breath.

"Is that me? Is that how you see me?" he asks, finally, when his laughter fades. "Is that how I really look?"

Olivia can only nod. Her heart is thumping so loud she can barely hear him.

I see them see each other. I wonder for the briefest of seconds if it could have been me, but I push the thought away. There is no point in such speculation. Instead, I will marvel at the thoroughness of her skill, like luggage being X-rayed in the airport: The machine sees what is packed away, revealing every little thing in stark clarity, all hidden secrets, no matter how careful the wrappings binding them tight.

"You did this," Nick says, "you did this for me. It's impossible. An animal, but he has a heart." He turns to her, tears standing in his eyes that he quickly blinks away, tears in hers. "You found my heart. You made me live."

I can't remember the last time I saw tears in his eyes.

His arms are around her, crushing her, crushing her lips before she can move, or try to protest. "Please," he says, "please," kissing her so she cannot answer.

She pulls away. "I can't," she says, her voice shaky, one tear trickling down her cheek. She rubs it away. "I can't be with you that way. Don't ask me to do that."

"I won't," Nick says, looking again at his face, painted, vibrantly enigmatic, his eyes hooded, violet shadows, following the gaze of the viewer, the secret sharer, waiting, in a maze, then back at Olivia, prolonging this rare moment of unblemished happiness.

"You'll call me, when you want to, and we'll celebrate. That's the least I can do for you. Please let me. It would give me great pleasure."

He smiles at her, grateful beyond expression, unable to articulate why the painted beauty of his beastliness has brought him, in an instantaneous rush, such profound, simple satisfaction.

I know why. She has seen through him to his heart of darkness, somehow penetrating his facade to link up with his spirit in a swift rush of terrifying exhilaration. Here, before him, she has conjured Nick as he could have been, as the boy he was never allowed to be wishes he could be seen, had fate not left him to be jerked awake by nightmares populated by lurking creatures, prowling and hungry, dreams that sent me down the hill into the after-hours clubs, where even though my face was known and feared the women were willing, leaping into the backseat of the black car, tying on the blindfold, eagerly succumbing to the desperate desires of the man who awaited their submission.

She will call him, he knows, because at this moment she no longer fears his desire. She only fears her own.

CHAPTER 7

The table, the waitress, the bottle of champagne chilled just so, all the same, the glances, murmuring, hushed, expectant, room abuzz, blazing with anticipation. It is all the same, except this time Nick knows what he is waiting for.

He arrived early, irritation with his impatience masked behind the usual polite facade, smile frozen, small talk distracting, a flirting gaze, his hands through his hair. He smokes, inhaling his nicotine deep followed by a languid exhale, women watching enraptured, wishing they were his cigarette, his lips on theirs while he sits, willing Olivia through the door, his heart pounding slow, slow, he is lost in his world, alone with unpardonable thoughts, wishes swimming deep, waiting, always waiting, watching her as she stood behind her easel, fingers hovering over his painted face, watching, waiting, and wanting, certain now she will not come.

He looks up. Olivia.

A smile lights his face, surprised into gentleness, a pure

sweet smile she had not thought possible, and she smiles back, sliding into her seat, her hair pulled back, tidy, prim, its glories tamed, because she is nervous.

"I'm not late this time, am I?"

"No, I was early."

"Were you wondering if I'd come?"

"Maybe." He pours her a glass. "Cheers," he says. "Here's to . . ."

"To what? Your portrait?"

"No. To lunch."

The air between them is saturated, heavy with anticipation, the pulsing unseen, desire breathed out, breathed in, hypnotic, steady, and as relentless as his eyes upon her.

Olivia's anxious fingers, slim and paint-flecked, sliding up and down the stem of her wineglass, unconscious mimics of unwanted thoughts. "It's funny that M's not here," she says. "I almost expected him to be."

"What do you mean?"

"You're always together," she explains. "He's like your shadow, isn't he. Behind you, and you don't even think about it, because you know he's there. He makes you feel safe, right? Well, at least he made me feel safe, when I was painting."

Nick frowns. This is dangerous territory. Who we are and what we do together, so much a part of us, so long taken for granted, is not meant to be talked about.

"M doesn't usually make people feel safe," he admits, trying to find the right thing to say, to steer her away.

"Of course he doesn't. He's damaged goods in a world that expects perfection, isn't he, like a fat person in an ice cream shop, so who can be bothered to find the man behind the scars? He must have been really handsome, once," she muses.

"He was. Much better-looking than me."

"Why, Nick," she says, trying to tease away her nervousness. "I do believe you're jealous."

"Me? Jealous of M?" Nick smiles at the impossibility of that thought, and shakes his head. "No, but what I'm jealous of right this minute is the implication that *I* don't make you feel safe."

"Nick," she says, laughing, "how dumb do you think I am? Of course you don't. Nor do you want to. That's why I shouldn't have come," she says. "I know I shouldn't."

"Then why did you?"

"I think you know why. The portrait's finished, and you like it, so what else is there to talk about?"

He has to bite the inside of his lip to refrain from grabbing her tight and pushing her down, flinging her on the table as he'd wanted to do in her studio, plates and silver crashing at their feet, wine spilled, soaking through white linen a bloody stain, kissing her, devouring, while everyone sits, transfixed with lust, envious, equally desirous yet never daring, sitting and watching him ravish her with complete, relentless impunity.

"How much longer are you in London? Shooting, I mean," she asks, if only to say something.

"A few months. So far we're a few days behind schedule, but it's difficult with period pieces, you know, and—"

There is a shadow falling over the table.

"My dear girl," says a mocking French accent, "and you said to me that you so dearly hate to go out to lunch."

"Jean-Michel," she says, her voice curt, turning her cheek for him to kiss. "So nice to see you. What brings the world-famous pianist to London?"

His eyes alive with mischief, eager yearning for some small humiliation to send winging along the grapevine of gossip. "Recording, what else, abusing my ghastly producer with long lunches and many martinis. The usual." He shrugs. "And where is the charming Olivier?"

"You know very well he's in Japan," she says, a small flush

rising into her cheeks. "But before he left he suggested that I paint Nick's portrait. You do know Nick Muncie, don't you?"

They nod to each other, coldly appraising, instantly wary, the knowing gaze of the professional seducer catching a fleeting glimpse of his own hard face in the mirror.

"I don't know," she goes on, "should I paint him? I'm getting the feeling he might be difficult. What do you think?"

The wicked smirk fades imperceptibly in Jean-Michel's fervent haze of delirious conjecture. So Olivier knew, did he, or perhaps he didn't, no, she was bluffing, the cool lying bitch, trying to trap him, sitting for all the world to see in a public place, or is it a blind, the perfect cover for duplicity, but no, she is too straight and this is Nick Muncie, superstar, what could he see in her anyway, what did Olivier see in her anyway but devotion, she's no great beauty, she is too quiet to be charming and she's just a painter and besides she slapped me when I pinched her ass.

The cool lying bitch.

"Hmmm," he says, regarding Nick's famous profile. "I see him as Cardinal Mazarin, or perhaps Richelieu. No. More legendary. A Borgia. Napoleon. No. Too European. He needs to be an American legend."

"But he already is a legend," Olivia says slyly. "At least in his own mind."

Nick laughs. Heads turn. He is deeply impressed with Olivia's collected performance, that instantaneous, seamless whiff of mendacity far more alluring to his senses and sensibility than anything else she could have done. "I've only heard that about a thousand times," he says.

Jean-Michel smiles, stiff, outfoxed. He lifts Olivia's hand in a farewell kiss, scrutinizing her face for even a vague hint of deception, and, finding none, says goodbye and returns to his friends.

"Serves me right. Now I know I shouldn't've come," says

Olivia, a tinge of bitterness in her voice that Nick finds intoxicating in its ferocity. "Jean-Michel is a second-rate—no, failed—pianist who's insanely jealous of Olivier's success, and he loves nothing more than to see his name nearly as large as Nigel Dempster's, and I don't want Olivier bothered with this nonsense."

"This isn't nonsense."

"Isn't it?"

She is agitated, her eyes shiny with stress. That damn French prick.

"Olivia."

"Don't. Please, please don't."

"Okay," he says, leaning back and stretching his legs. "Relax. I can wait. We've got all day. Have a drink. Let's order."

"I'm not hungry." She tries to smile. "Besides, I don't think you can wait."

"That's where you're wrong, my darling Olivia, because I can. I'm going to wait as long as I have to for you to revise your opinion of me."

"But why should I?" she says soberly. "I admit that you're a lot more surprising—or substantial, I guess—than I thought you were, but I expect you're still a rake, a cad, and an abomination to women."

His eyes spark with some unnamable hurt, a flash no longer than a blink, but Olivia catches it, sees that window opening only an instant to the bitter secrets locked inside his heart, buried, forgotten, willed by his ambition to lie dormant and sleeping, far away where they cannot touch him. She sees it and as so she sees him now, outside the sealed calm space of her studio, sees him as she'd painted him, sees the shadow of a raw terror she knows must be real, for no actor could possess a skill so rare as to break his own heart.

Her defenses melt, she is sorry, ashamed of her harshness, because she is kind, and pain is no stranger to her thoughts.

She brushes her fingers across the rim of his glass, a feather, a spontaneous gesture so unbearably erotic that Nick quickly picks up the glass and drinks, his lips touching the spot she'd so briefly caressed.

"Well," she says, her voice lightening, apologetic, "maybe not an abomination."

"I've had my moments," he says. "Believe me, I've had way too many."

"Why am I not surprised?"

He pours more champagne. "You shouldn't be. Bad boys in Hollywood usually deserve their reputations. When I told my agent I wanted to do *Faust* even he thought I should be playing Mephisto."

"I don't pay any attention to gossip."

"I know that. I just really have no idea what you think about me. You studied my face, who I am. It's all there; I can see how you *saw* me, but not what you think."

"Why is that so important?"

He does not know how to start what he wants to say, although we have rehearsed it so much I never want to write another word for him again, hours spent pacing in our suite in the Savoy, curtains drawn against the cold and dull throb of dreariness outside our window, hours spent on Olivia that should have been given to *Faust*.

Or perhaps in his mind's eye the quest to conquer both has been inextricably melded.

"What do you think?" he'd asked me, and I'd hidden my amazement. Nick did not ask my opinion, not about anything important, unless it was work-related. He just told me what to do.

"She's not Belinda."

He laughed. "God, no. No, she's definitely not Belinda."

"She's a woman."

"I get the point."

"But why her, you mean. Why now."

Nick looked at me, silent, waiting. We know each other too well. We sat there for a long time.

"She's so much smarter than I am," he said, finally.

Nick has been with other clever women before, in whatever context of his choosing, but their purported intelligence has never mattered, not when he'd never cared enough to remember their names or what they did or anything they might have said. There was no need to listen.

"You're smarter than you think you are," I told him. "I've always believed it. It's just that no one expects you to be. Intelligence is a burden to actors like you."

He ignored my comment, because there's no point arguing with that Hollywood truism. "So tell me what to say to her."

I got up and pushed back the draperies to stare out at the blackness, punctuated by bright round suns of the headlights wavering below us. "How do you mean?"

"You were there, watching. How did it make you feel?"

I was not going to tell him how it made me feel. I can't even tell myself.

"You mean how it made *you* feel," I said.

"Whatever." He shrugged. "Just do it."

I did it, of course, and he repeated what I'd given him so often that it became his own.

Sometimes even I underestimated the determination behind his talent.

And so he sits, staring at the tablecloth. Nick, unaccustomed to the truth, wherever it came from, to telling it or feeling it, finds himself wanting to be honest with Olivia, wanting to confide in her, divulge and reveal. Why should this woman, this odd, truthful, strangely protective woman whose heart belongs to another, have fixed her peculiar eyes upon him and cracked through to his heart? How can he hope to understand why she makes him feel, so fiercely, that he wants whatever stolen moments he is to have with her to be real?

That with her, far from home, he can be real.

"I would watch you, you know, when you were painting, there and not there, so remote from me," he says finally. "I'm not used to that. To being seen, but not acknowledged. To having a woman look at me and not want to take something."

"But I wanted you, to paint."

"That's different. Now it's yours. You made it. You made me immortal on a canvas. But I would watch you, I'd be talking, or maybe I wasn't but it didn't matter because I knew you weren't really listening. You'd nod or say umm-hmm but you were lost in the work, and I'd stand there watching you with such envy, such *envy* at the easy rhythm you'd fallen into. You'd paint, glance at me but not seeing me, and I am standing there, useless, a captive audience that can only watch in silence, my actor's ego dented, watching yours at work, giving me nothing, needing nothing more than my face, or my body, no role to play, no lines, no being, no director giving me cues, no camera in my face, no one there but you, and you didn't even see me."

Olivia is astonished by his words. My words.

"Sometimes you'd push your hair impatiently off your forehead or chew on a knuckle or even talk to yourself, so lost in thought, concentrating, remote from me, from the world, it had disappeared, I no longer existed because you didn't need me, you were turning me into another, and I was standing there silent in a maze, lost, with only my eyes upon you in your painter's dance, and there was nothing, *nothing* I wanted more in the world than to hear you say, 'Come with me now and we will dance together.' "

She doesn't know Nick, or me, well enough to have heard that subtle shift in his voice, she has not seen him act before, act truly, and she would never have guessed that all these words are not the spontaneous outpourings of his soul, that I thought them up, wrote them down on the Savoy's smooth stationery for Nick to repeat to her, caring only that she would hear them.

She doesn't know.

Nick has leaned closer to her as he spoke, that famous voice made magical with the rawness of truth unexpected, and she cannot help herself from leaning in to hear him, knowing without knowledge that he is speaking full from the heart, nakedly yearning, auditioning for a role he never thought he'd want to play.

Their heads are so close he could have kissed her, his loins full of heat, burning, they are breathing hard, together, lost, until she pulls away and sighs, breaking the spell, leaning back to sip her champagne.

"But isn't acting like that?" she asks after an excruciating moment. "I mean, don't you feel that you can lose yourself completely in the character you're playing, be whoever, be Faust, lose yourself in this journey and yet still be yourself, and then when you see it on film you can't believe you said what you said or remember how you felt in that moment, because it wasn't you, Nick, talking, you had disappeared, and all you hear is the voice of your spirit?"

"Like a personalized Ouija board?"

She laughs. "Not quite."

"I know what you mean," he says slowly. "That kind of acting is what you're supposed to feel, except of course you don't when you're playing idiot parts in idiot movies."

"*Faust* isn't idiot."

"Which is one of the reasons I'm doing it. I've said I wanted to do this for years, and no one believed me. Everyone laughed. You can't imagine the fights that went on to pull this together. Muncie's Madness, they called it."

"Even M?"

"No, not M. It was his idea, originally. We were out by the pool and I picked up this book he'd been reading and saw that he'd marked a passage: 'I stagger from desire to enjoyment/ and in its throes I starve for more desire.' So I asked him what the story was about. 'Faust is insatiable,' he told me, 'seeking the unattainable. He's willing to surrender eternity in a quest for one perfect moment.' He looked at me, as only M can look at somebody. 'You're born to play him,' he said."

"Did you believe him?"

"Of course not. I laughed. But M knows me, all too well, and he kept on at me. 'You've got it in you,' he kept saying. 'You're always complaining about the movies you do—so package this for yourself. What do you care what anybody says?' "

"But you do care," Olivia says softly.

"Of course I care. My whole life as an actor is at stake. My whole life." His hands through his hair. He finds it hard to look at Olivia, surprised that he is telling her what he'd never admitted to himself. "I mean, the story struck a chord, some-where, one I usually don't let myself think about."

"Why not?" Her voice is gentle.

Nick clasps his hands in front of him. This conversation is harder than he thought, even with all our rehearsals. "What's the point? In the business I'm Nick Muncie, valuable commod-ity, nothing more. And then at home I'm reading these lines, at first without really understanding them, but still knowing that this is me."

"What lines?"

"Oh, it doesn't matter," Nick says, smiling, as anxious to veer away from the pangs of confession as he is to dazzle Olivia with every utterance. "It sounds pretentious."

"Tell me."

" 'I awake with horror in the morning/and bitter tears well

up in me/when I must face each day that in its course/cannot fulfill a single wish, not *one*!' " he recites, his eyes far away. " 'The very intimations of delight/are shattered by the carpings of the day/which foil the inventions of my eager soul/with a thousand leering grimaces of life.' "

There is a long silence. "Nick," she says, finally. "Is that how you really feel?"

His heart in his eyes as he looks at her. "Sometimes."

"So you fought for this movie."

"That's an understatement." He leans back and relaxes. "Jamie helped. He can be a fool sometimes, but a worthy one, and he battled for me and believed I could pull it off, even though McAllister and the studios were ready to croak." He grins saucily. "For that reason alone it was worth the aggravation. But the knives are out, sharper than ever. It's so pathetically predictable. I should let you see what people—my estimable colleagues and so-called friends who hate my guts and want nothing more than to see me flop big-time because I pull in so much more than they do and am such a bastard about it—are saying about my pathetic attempt at 'acting.' "

"Well," she says, "I think you can do it." She cannot meet his gaze, she does not know what to do now with Nick, earnest and truthful, Nick so unbelievably charming, so sweetly candid and articulate with words of poetry falling from his lips, so suddenly unlike the image she'd formed of him, the image she made herself believe because being alone with him is dangerous and wrong. There is something palpably shimmering before her eyes, she sees it, mocking, taunting her that she has already succumbed to the magic of his seductiveness, whispering to her that his sweetness may be true right here, right now, but what lies hidden under that honeyed candy coating is equally true and vividly blazing, out of control as it has been, unchecked, for years, twisted and implacable.

"If I can it's because of you," he says.

"Me?"

"Yes, you. Having watched you lose yourself in your paint-ing is making me try harder to lose myself in my acting." His voice is harsher, sad. "I need to do it."

She looks down at her fingers, stubborn stains spreckled across her nails, clasped tightly around the stem of her glass.

"Not just to prove something," he says.

"Yes."

"You know why."

"Yes." She looks up at him with tears standing in her eyes. "But I don't want this to happen. I don't even really like you. I don't know what to do."

"Come with me."

She sits unsmiling, still as if etched in granite, barely breath-ing, her eyes luminous, wavering.

Don't do it, I would have willed her silently, telepathic, if I had been there instead of here, in my little room at Porchester Square, waiting for the inevitable. Don't do it. Don't believe him. You don't know what he can do.

Don't, I would have said, stunned at myself in this unaccus-tomed role of protector, not procurer. Don't, please, this time it's for real, I can't help you, I can't help myself. But even as the words would have died on my lips I'd have seen her as she is now, unheeding, her ears roaring, she doesn't hear me because she does not want to know.

At least not yet.

She rises so suddenly that even Nick is surprised, she tucks her purse under her arm, blows a kiss to Jean-Michel, whose eyes she knew were upon her, makes a minute adjustment to her jacket, and strides out.

Nick leisurely pulls out two fifty-pound notes and leaves them on the table, gets up and slowly follows, nonchalant, relaxed and smiling as he acknowledges his fans while every muscle in his body is screaming to run, run fast, run after her and catch her before she slips away forever.

This time she is waiting for him at the top of the stairs.

He is careful not to touch her, fearful, worrying that any brush of his fingers will make her bolt, a frightened filly, fearful that if a taxi doesn't come as one does as if summoned by some benevolent goddess she'll disappear into the rain, fearful that traffic will move so slowly that she will push down the door handle and leap out, dodging other cars, elusive, no more real to him than a shadow obscured by fog.

That is all he can think, that she will leave him as they sit, not touching, mute, staring out the windows until at last the taxi stops at the fat white pillars of Porchester Square.

The keys are in his fingers. She is behind him, please, be there, they are in, inside his secret house, the carpet thickly cushioning, the walls creamy smooth, prints of flowers found in the market on Portobello Road hanging in ascending rows, sedate in their frames, the balustrades polished, gleaming, a faint whiff of lemon oil, her footsteps soft behind him, Eurydice, if he could paint her she would be his Eurydice, and if he turns back to look she will disappear forever.

He unlocks the door and pushes it open.

Oh, she says as she sees it when he switches on the light and turns down the dimmer, activating the cameras, the muted glory of the hours I have spent, the sumptuous luxury of a room made solely for pleasure, hothouse peonies in a blown-glass vase, iridescent. She looks at Nick with eyes full of bewildered doubt and delight, fingering the velvet petals that have dropped on the table. It is too much to believe.

"Nobody has been here but me," he says, leaning back against the door that closes with barely a click, instantly locked. "And M, of course. He found this for me. It's the only place where I can hide from the world. Everyone always knows where I am—on the set, at the Savoy, walking down the street, eating lunch. If I didn't have this place to disappear in I think I'd go mad."

She cannot move. They are alone, for the first time, truly alone. The room is tranquil, the light softly glowing, the heavy drapes pulled against the dull gray of thickening clouds, traffic a dim hum, the ormolu clock on the mantel calmly ticking as loud as her heart. No one else knows where they can be found, alone together in a golden room.

Time stills, and stops, until Nick takes two large strides to Olivia and touches her, finally, his hands on her, her warm flesh, perfumed with bergamot, unleashing the furious passion that has been gnawing his bones, kissing her breathless and easing her over to the bed, his hands, finally, free to touch her as he wishes, the petals falling from her hands, scattered randomly in her hair.

"I don't want to," she tries to say, tears streaming down her cheeks, unaware. "I don't want to."

He kisses their salt sweetness. "I know I know I know." He runs his fingers over her lips, brushing across them till she bites him to stop. "Don't say anything," he says, "just kiss me. Kiss me."

"I don't want to," she says again, it is all she can say, trying, vainly, to twist her head away from Nick. "Let me go let me go let me go."

"It doesn't matter," he says, his lips in her hair, "it doesn't matter because I have never wanted anyone as much as I want you, never ever ever, and I'm not going to let you go. Ever."

Tears still falling, rolling into her ears. She closes her eyes.

"There is nothing here but me and you," he says.

And the camcorders, silently whirring, preserving the most tender outpourings of his heart for the endless pleasure of the perpetual rewind.

DURING

Lunchtime, and only then, Olivia says. Her voice has tightened again, she is fighting him with rules, regretful, guilty. Not every day, and never on weekends. An hour stolen, maybe two, when she can dash across the park and into the flat, and then leave, fleeing back to safety. If she can. In the secrecy of this hideaway, never at her studio. Never call her at the studio, the machine is on all the time, of course he knows that already, she never answers the phone when she is working, and will not pick it up now even if she hears his voice. She will leave a message on the machine he'd installed in his suite at the Savoy. That's all. Take it or leave it.

Nick takes it, accepting with such alacrity that I must bite my inner cheek to prevent a spasm of surprise from flitting across my face. Oh yes, how lucky he is scheduled for night shoots, how convenient his call for makeup at three, the weekends are for sleeping off exhaustion, this is a sign, don't tell me it's not. Oh yes, I can see the wheels of mischief already rolling in devious pleasure, let her pretend the control of her time is the control of his mind. Let her pretend that the parameters of what has been her life will not be breached. Let her pretend that this tempestuous hunger is satiable with snatched moments and bites of lunch.

Once a week will become twice, twice thrice, he is thinking. The clock smashed, an hour stretched. Languorous lingering. The afternoon shadows deepening when Nick finally pulls himself away to dash into the awaiting fury, later than he's ever been, me feeding him lines unrehearsed as we speed through traffic into the life of fantasy that is the only reality he has ever truly understood.

The game is on, he thinks, a crown of laurel already encircling the fervid imaginings of the victor, king of pleasure.

He does not reckon with Olivia.

Perhaps if she had called him sooner Nick would have taken longer to lapse into this rage of frustration. Eighteen, Nick says, eighteen days and she hasn't called. His fever of impatience infects the set. He can't slip into character. He is overacting. He sulks, locking himself in his trailer between scenes. He calls in to the machine every hour. Silence. He screams at Toledo. Toledo screams back. Producers appear, publicists. Cajoling, pleading lectures. Even the great Nick Muncie is replaceable, they are muttering, even if this project is his brainchild. I hope they are not bluffing. Nick needs to think he can be fired.

Only one time together, and it is already spinning out of control.

We are all waiting for Nick to come out, a molten lump of self-pity, and I knock on his trailer door yet again. "Fuck off," he shouts. I kick in the door, fed up.

"I think I'll bring her on the set," I say. "She'd like this a lot. Very impressive."

"Fuck you."

"You know, you might find a more creative outlet for this temporary setback, one that Olivia might even respect."

"What the hell are you talking about?"

"Your work, you fool. What you do. What she does, is doing this very moment. *Using* your frustration. Creating something more important than your own deluded image. And then when she sees this film, when she sees *you*, she'll *know*."

He slumps down, runs his hands through his hair, a flicker of hope. He has never looked better in his life. "Do you believe that?"

"Yes."

"If you're wrong, I'll kill you."

"You'll kill yourself first."

He apologizes to Toledo, effusive, he apologizes to the crew, abashed. He begs forgiveness. Nerves, he explains. He wants to do his best. He's counting on them for advice and support. Where's the best pub, let's all go and have a drink. My treat.

No one begs better than Nick. Dark mutinous mutterings dissolve into mindless, pleased nattering. Film brothers bound by a humbled oath of fealty.

How could these worthy working souls possibly understand that this pledge was the first heartfelt, selfless plea that Nick had uttered on a set in more years than I could count.

It is Olivia's doing.

When we arrive, weary beyond talking, to the Savoy, the usual messages are neatly stacked on the table, square white notes. Nick ignores them, heading for the machine's blinking yellow light. Tomorrow, he hears her say. Noon.

Nick looks at me, quietly jubilant, and shaky. Nick does not get shaky.

"She must be a witch," he says.

"She isn't a witch," I say, "she's a woman. Treat her like one. There is time enough."

Time enough.

"There is all the time in the world," he says.

Nick sits in one of the Regency chairs, staring at the peonies,
lush and blowsy. A fat round petal drifts down to lie like a
swan's feather on the polished surface. He fingers it, velvet.
Like Olivia's cheeks.

He is hours early.

He appears calm, sitting so still and trying not to smoke
because he knows she hates it, his legs crossed, his feet bare.
The boots kicked off into the corner the only sign of impatience. An impediment.

The buzzer sounds. Nick nearly jumps out of his skin to let
her in. He opens the door and returns to the chair, the petal
still in his fingers.

She walks in, closes the door, leans against it, drops her bag.

The cameras are whirring.

Nick smiles. "Do you like my flowers?" He pulls one out
and offers it to her.

Its beauty is quite irresistible. Or perhaps it is that Nick is
holding it. When she takes it, Nick stands up. She backs away,
skittish, as he knew she would. He circles around to her,
pulling another bloom into his hand, careful to keep his distance as she stands deliberating, glancing at the door and gaug-
ing how long it would take to fling it open and run, panting,
run far away to the safety of the life she thought she knew.
She does not realize her back is now up against the wall, hitting
her mark exactly, right where Nick wants it.

He always knows the best angles for the camera.

"I shouldn't have come," she says.

"You said that last time."

"But it's what I feel."

"You're still here, though, aren't you?"

"I don't know what to do."

"You don't have to do anything. Let me do it for you."

"I can't."

"Why not?"

"Because I shouldn't be here."

"Then why are you?"

"I don't know."

"But you are, so let me."

"Let you what?"

"Touch you."

He is closer. She begins to tremble.

"Let me."

"I don't want you to."

"You do."

"No."

She is whispering now. I can barely hear her.

"Let me," Nick says.

"It won't work."

"It will."

"It will end in tears."

"I won't let it."

The pulse in her throat is throbbing wildly. The very relentlessness of his longing has eased his features into a deceptive, reassuring calm. She is puzzled, wary, unaware of the desperate eagerness hidden behind a facade etched by years of experienced seductions.

He has never waited so long for any woman in his life.

The peony brushes gently across her throat, a feather caress. The shock thrills through her veins. She is pushing back into the wall as her knees buckle. Stand up, she tells herself, go. You let yourself do it once already, that's enough, you don't need any more, you don't want this, not from Nick, not what he wants to take. Go now, while there's still a chance.

"Don't move," he says, reading her mind.

"I can't," she says. The flower swaying back and forth against her flesh, back and forth.

"I won't touch you if you don't want me to," Nick says. He is so close.

"Nick," she says. Pleading.

"Are you afraid?"

"Yes." Her eyes wide, her voice a faint whisper.

"Afraid of me?"

"Yes."

"Afraid of what I might do to you?"

"Yes."

"Afraid that you might like it?"

"Yes."

"Like it too much?"

"Yes." Yes yes yes.

"Do you want me?" he asks. A curl of her hair wrapped around his finger.

"No."

"Do you want me?"

"No, no. I can't."

"Yes, yes, you can. Say yes." His lips on her pulse, she is burning. "Yes. Say yes."

"No."

"Say yes." His lips on her chin.

"No."

"Say yes." His lips on her cheeks.

She twists her head. He pulls it close. His eyes, unblinking. "Do you want me?"

She cannot speak.

" 'I want you.' Say it."

She cannot speak.

His lips in her hair. "You came because you want me. Say it. Say it."

Her head is swimming. He is too close. Her body is alive, every pore magnified. Time stills. She sees nothing but his face, she feels his breath in her hair. His hand buried in her hair, caressing. His lips on her throat. She is dying. There is no breath left in her body. She is drowning. She cannot move.

"Say you want me. Say it."

She says it.

He sees her, a tremor flits across her face, her parted lips, her cheeks flushed with fear and desire. One hand in her hair, his finger tracing a line from her ear toward her eyes, around them, down her nose, the curve of her lips, her chin tilted up.

"You are mine," he says. "Mine."

Now she is more afraid, trembling, alight. She dares not touch him. She will explode.

He takes her hand, kisses it, licking the palm whose scratch had healed many weeks before. He places this palm on his cheek.

Mine.

"Touch me," he says.

She leans harder into the wall without realizing it. He is so close. She puts up her hand, an unconscious gesture, fending him off, but he touches it, so gentle, tracing a path across his face with her finger as he had just done to hers.

"Say it," he says. "Say 'I want you.' "

She closes her eyes.

"Say it say it say it."

"I want you," she says, barely a whisper.

"Again."

She can't. Her heart has swelled so much she can no longer inhale, the breath has left her body.

Nick has not moved, but there is a shift in the very air because he has grown with the inexorable power he has over her, that has brought her here despite her frantic efforts to push him out of her thoughts. He stands now, giantlike, loom-

ing over her, his prey, helpless, he is huge, she tries to blink
him away, back to where she can see him, but there is a film
dancing in front of her eyes, and her legs can no longer hold
her up because she cannot breathe, she is drowning against
the wall, all she hears is the roaring of the sea she is drowning
in. He is so close, immense, his palm cupping her cheek. He
has not moved.

Her eyes are glued to his. "Please," she says.

"Please what?"

"What do you want?"

"You."

She closes her eyes and shivers.

"I want you," he says. "All of you. You are mine. You need
me, you need to be mine. You need me to touch you." His
fingers caressing her cheek. "I will touch you. See?" His fingers. "It's so easy. So easy. You want me. You want me to."

"Yes." Another whisper.

"Close your eyes."

"No."

"Close them."

"Why?"

"So I can touch you."

"I want to see you."

"You will. Do as I say. Keep them closed."

She closes them. With one hand he covers them, he feels
them flutter, helpless, blinded. With the other he unbuttons
his famous black jeans, they drop to the floor, freeing him,
rocklike already in anticipation, ready, so desperately ready.
Her eyes are shut, and she is trembling violently, knowing.

He pushes up her dress, gently pulls down her tights and
panties, the air is cool between her legs but the fire there is
unquenchable.

"Open your eyes. Look at me."

She opens them. He is still a giant, immense, the room is spinning, the roar has engulfed her, she is afraid.

"Say yes," he says. "Say it."

"Yes," she says. "Nick."

He is in her so quickly, so roughly, slamming his weight hard into her pressed up against the wall, so hard, that she cries out in shocked surprise even as he is lifting her legs around his hips and thrusting into her like a madman.

"Say it," he says now, his voice thick. "Say it now."

"Stop—"

"Say you want me."

She could not say it even if she wanted to, his lips are on hers, forcing open her mouth, bruising her lips, biting them. She has no weight, no strength to fight, the waves are crashing in her ears, pounding in rhythm to what Nick is making her do. This rhythm is inescapable, and she feels herself submitting, because she cannot breathe, because she knew he would do it so, because she has no choice.

The slightest gesture of capitulation. He feels it. He carries her to the bed, a few steps only, he is outstretched, on top of her, she is melting, drowning into the bed, disappearing. She hears, dimly through the roar, a voice moaning stop stop stop—

His first frenzy stilled, he withdraws, a fraction.

No, she hears a voice say, but it can't be her own, no, it is saying, come back—

He is laughing softly, kissing her. "You want me."

"Yes."

"Where?"

"Here." She tries to touch him, but he won't let her, pinning her arms over her head with one hand, he is still a giant, with giant fingers on his other hand, how can they be so tender when they are so large, make it stop, it's too sweet, too sweet to bear.

He smothers her moans with kisses. He is torturing her, slowly, pulling back, probing her again, relentless.

"You want me," he says. "Say it."

"I want you I want you let me go."

"No."

"Let me go." She is struggling, gasping for breath, he has been waiting for this, for her to struggle back to life, to fight him, her body squirming under him in indescribable pleasure.

He is still laughing, biting her breasts. He is too strong, he has both her arms pinioned hard, too hard, with one hand like a band of steel, the other caressing her as her legs flail helplessly till he pins them with his own in a scissors grip. She is helpless, totally helpless, that delirious helplessness that is opium to his fevered senses, swirling into his brain, intoxicatingly uncontrollable. It is what he lives for, this oblivion, this craving, what he wants for himself and for her to feel, this power, to take, keep taking, she will cry out, she will beg and plead and moan, she is his, his prisoner in bed, absolutely defenseless.

Olivia will not capitulate quite so easily, he knows, he teases and torments, he wants her to fight him, because every time she does, he will shudder with the pleasure of forcing her to submit.

"Mine," he says, "mine."

Her legs are pushed up around his neck, he is insatiable, it is too much, it is unbearable.

She knows he wants to hear her scream.

It is easier to drown. Her eyes close, and she gives in, utterly.

She hears ticking, her arm still above her head, no longer pinioned. Her watch. It is not yet one. Less than an hour. It cannot be.

Nick is propped on one elbow, watching her, smiling tenderly at her. Olivia.

A tear trickles down her cheek, she can't help it. He kisses her gently.

She lies there, deep in the down comforter and Porthault sheets, watching as Nick disappears into the loo, she hears water running. She closes her eyes, too dazed to move, and does not hear him till she feels a cool wet cloth, perfumed with lavender, between her legs, around her breasts, at her nape, his hands gently turning her over to trail down her back. A brush slowly pulled through her tangled curls. She still cannot speak, it is too new.

It is too terrifying.

Without a word Nick gathers her jumbled clothes and dresses her as if she were his child, she cannot move herself, she sits, numb, as Nick throws on his clothes and runs his fingers through his hair.

"Come," he says. "M will take you home. I came on my bike."

That is my cue to turn off the equipment, shut off the lights, and hurry down to the car.

"Olivia," Nick says, tilting up her chin. "I can't wait three weeks to see you again. I won't."

She shakes her head, still dumb.

"Promise me." His lips on hers, sweet, his lips, harder, insistent, pushing her back down into the comforter, sinking, if she stays down there she will drown. "Promise me. I won't let you go till you tell me when."

She cannot think. Where is she what has she done what day is it why is she here, dizzy and drowning. What has he done to her. His lips, bruising, biting hers.

"Tomorrow," he says.

She shakes her head, no, it is too soon, it is unthinkable, she cannot breathe.

"Thursday."

No. Today must be Tuesday, this is London, she is in a flat near Porchester Square, she is sinking, down, deep down into a place where she should not be. Nick is kissing her. She is kissing him back, she can't help it, she can't help herself, there is no one to save her except herself.

"Friday," he says.

"Friday." A whisper.

"Same time. Here."

She nods.

"You promise."

She nods again.

"Your solemn word."

"Yes."

He scoops her in his arms, carried softly like a baby down the stairs into the car where I am waiting. He does not say goodbye. The door slams. She cannot think. Cars flash by, trees, the sun in her eyes, no, wait, it is raining, there is a storm, there must be, because she hears a roaring in her ears.

"Olivia." I am shaking her gently. Her eyes blink, focus on me in confusion. "You're home."

She looks out the window, and awakens. She bursts out laughing, to my surprise.

"What happened?" she asks, not expecting an answer.

"Friday," I say. "Do you want me to pick you up?"

She shakes her head. She will be there.

She promised.

She disappears into the house. She will run a bath, I imagine, she will lounge back in steaming warm bubbles, soothing her aching limbs, tracing with much disbelief the vivid bruises blooming like hothouse peonies on her pale skin, wondering why she cannot remember the very instant that Nick's fingers kneaded her breasts so roughly to leave such violent fingerprints like squares on a crossword, or when her wrists became ringed with cuffs of blue and ocher. Cerulean blue and Indian yellow, she decides, colors, that is all she can think about, colors, as the burning heat between her legs slowly diminishes to a slow steady ache.

How could she have done what she did?

It doesn't matter. She drowned, and he brought her back to life in an enchanted room, his Frankenstein creating another creature, a siren calling, luring him to his doom, her voice sweetly enticing, he will hear it, and come, and they will both drown together.

Three days till Friday.

C H A P T E R   9

"Tell me about your boyfriends," he says, sweat-glued to her, his fingertips doodling up and down her back, suffused with lazy passion. The intense ease of their coupling makes him want to be nice. He is trying harder than he's ever tried to be nice, to restrain the urges that have been permitted him for so long. This is Olivia. She doesn't want to talk about herself but he wants to know, and this is how she'll tell him.

The cameras are rolling, noiseless. I am watching.

"What do you want to know?"

"Everything. Everyone."

Olivia swats him, playful. "How many do you think there've been?"

"A lucky dozen or two."

"Is that all?" She laughs. "Of course, in comparison to you, I must seem positively virginal."

Nick rolls away and lights up a cigarette. His eyes narrow

as he exhales, and she frowns. He stubs it out. How much
can I tell her now? he wonders. He looks in the mirror.

"No one else matters."

"Not even Belinda?"

He lies back, smiling. "How do you know about Belinda?"

She shrugs. Annette told her, suppressing a smile at the
curiosity Olivia did not want to acknowledge. Nick is staring
at her, intently. He doesn't want her to know. To know anything of the life that exists outside this room.

"Tell me about your boyfriends," he says again.

"You really want to know?"

"Yes," he says. "Everything."

"When I lived in New York, before I went to Chicago, I
used to go running in the park," she tells him, her voice dreamy
with memory, Belinda forgotten, "running in the summer,
around the reservoir, when the stinky-sweet smell of the leaves
and the undergrowth made me dizzy. There were weeds, and
prying eyes hidden in them, and their rotting smell even in
the heat of summer made me lose my pace, and so sometimes
I'd mix colors on a palette in my head as I ran, the water
Payne's Gray and the sky Stephenson's Blue and Rose Madder
for the windows on Fifth Avenue, or Cadmium Red Light,
and then all the colors blurred together and became the same
shade as the stones crunching beneath my feet. I crushed them
all, those colors."

Nick is fascinated, her voice singsongy, faraway.

"Or I'd write letters in my head, as I ran, letters to old
boyfriends, and I could never remember if I put them to paper
and mailed them or not, but fragments stayed in my head,"
she says, "and sometimes I'd dream them, and if the dreams
were vivid enough they gave me ideas to paint."

"Like what?" he says.

"Like the man in black. *The Birthday Present*, I called it. I
painted him as a centaur."

"Who was he?"

"I met him at a party. An Italian, Robertino, his name was. It was a going-away party, and I was frosting the cake, for some reason," she says. "He was watching me, dressed all in black. He had this lazy look around his mouth like those spoiled by unearned wealth. I know that look, it really bugs me." She sighs, and sits up, hugging her knees. "He stood there, staring at me, and when I asked him what he wanted he said: 'Come home with me—tomorrow is my birthday.' "

"And did you?"

"No. Not then, at least. He was a photographer, and he was always off somewhere on assignment. He sent me scarabs from Egypt, and paprika from Prague, loose in the envelope, so it stained my fingers when I opened it, and once, a funny lumpy package, and when I opened it dozens of rose petals came fluttering out. He was very strange."

"What happened to him?"

"I don't know. He only needed me when he was on the other side of the world."

"How could he leave you?" Nick says, pulling her back down. "Tell me another."

"Once," she says, trailing her hand lightly up and down the arm he's wrapped around her, "once I was in a club downtown, oh, this was many years ago. As you walked in there was a horseshoe-shaped bar and a crowd of people waiting for a drink and the deejay at the far end, wearing headphones like a tiara, and the dance floor was behind her. She liked old-fashioneds. Everyone else was shooting up or snorting or smoking in the bathrooms."

"But not you."

"No, not me. I was Miss Pure and Proper."

He laughs. "I bet."

"No, honestly. I didn't need anything. I'd never've been

able to work if I'd done them. Drugs interfered with my pleasure, believe it or not. I wanted to remember."

"You mean you wanted to be in control."

She shrugs.

"I was standing at the bar," she goes on, "waiting for a glass of water. There was a feather in my pocket and I was waving it idly under my nose, listening to my friend Charlie talking the usual nonsense, I don't remember. I looked straight across the bar and saw this man staring at me. His left arm was in plaster, and there was something about his cast that turned me on. It glowed as if it were a living thing, phosphorescent, and I felt this overwhelming, perverse desire to pick it up, feel its heft in my fingers, to touch *it*, not his warm, real flesh underneath.

"We stared at each other for a while, and then he smiled and pointed to his glass. I left Charlie and maneuvered around to him. 'What happened to your arm?' I asked. 'Oh,' he said, 'I fell on some concrete and broke my thumb and part of my wrist.'

"I said I had to touch it. I did. It wasn't smooth, it was rough and chunky and white, radiant white. I lifted it gingerly, his whole arm. It weighed much more than I thought. 'Does it hurt?' I asked.

" 'Yes,' he said. 'The weight of it.'

" 'You're so little,' I told him. He was. Wiry. Intense.

" 'I lost weight. It hurt too much to eat.' He laughed. 'I can't believe we're discussing my waistline at the bar.'

" 'I'm sure that's what you come here for.'

" 'No,' he said. 'I like to watch. Watch the faces here.' "

Nick is laughing.

The laugh is intended for me. I can smell his arousal. "No wonder he turned you on," he tells her.

"No, it was the cast," Olivia says. "And then he said: 'You

know, you're not so strange up close as you are from a distance.' That's why I still remember this, not because he was a boyfriend or anything, but because he said that. Then I asked him what he did.

" 'I'm a gravedigger,' he tells me, and sees the look on my face. 'But only for the money. I'm really a filmmaker.'

" 'Are you? Do you shoot them in cemeteries?'

" 'Nah,' he said. 'Too morbid.'

"We stood there for a moment. The music faded away. I wanted him, I wanted the feel of that cast on top of me.

" 'You have scary eyes,' he said, 'but they're not as scary now that you're by me as they were when I first saw you.' He smiled. 'I think I want your phone number.'

"I stared at his cheekbones, as alabaster as the plaster. I wanted to pick up his cast and smash it on the counter."

"Did you?" Nick asks, delighted.

"No. No, I didn't."

"Did he call you?"

Olivia is staring at the ceiling. "No. No, he didn't."

"He was a fool," Nick says, pulling her close. "Who wouldn't want you?"

I wonder. Olivia does not fit. She is an outcast from the fields of beauty plucked and harvested by Nick with such blasé regularity. He, whose implacable requirement of ravishing statuesque proportions untethered by character made the procuring too easy and too boring, would never have looked twice at this woman in other circumstances.

But in this room as it is now, the drapes drawn against the day and illuminated only by the light of candles flickering across her face, her hair seeming to me, through the lens, not dissimilar to a writhing mass of Medusa's coils, she resembles a strange goddess, a ripe figure, curved and rounded, sound of stature, sound of spirit, and made for love.

"Him, obviously," she is saying. "He didn't want me. But sometimes when I shut my eyes I can still see that cast."

"Maybe you should paint it, now. Again."

"Maybe. But what I have to paint is sitting in my studio right now, so let me go."

"Stay. Just one more minute."

"All right." She snuggles close to him. "Now you tell me a story."

He sighs, and waits a moment before starting to speak.

"I was with some kids I knew, and we went to a farm. We were drunk." He entangles his hands in her hair, caressing her head.

"When was this?" she asks.

"I don't know. A long time ago. It doesn't matter." He stiffens, imperceptibly. "I saw a huge rock, with a rope tied around it, near the edge of a well, and those guys said I couldn't lift it." His hands whirling, harder, hair bunched in his fingers, flowing through, helplessly.

She shivers.

"So I picked it up and I carried it over to the well and I threw it in." He starts to laugh. "And then all of a sudden this goat comes tearing around the corner, screaming, bleating, and there's a rope tied around his neck and I think oh no and before I can do anything the poor little mother is down the well."

"You mean you couldn't get it out?"

"How was I supposed to know? Stupid goat."

"So it died."

He buries his face in her hair.

"You let it die, just like that. It's the most revolting thing I've ever heard."

"No, it isn't."

She ignores him. "Then what did you do?"

"We ran. We ran like hell." He reaches down to the wetness between her legs. "So this is what turns you on?"

"No," she says, trying to push his fingers away. "That is a horrible story. You are a monster."

He won't let her go, kissing her, gently, till she stills.

"Would you like a rope around your neck, and a little bell for the shepherdess to find you?" she says, placated, ready to tease him once more. "Would you like me to chase you across that field with my staff and throw you down the well? It's what you deserve."

"Go ahead. I dare you."

"Would you like me to tie you to the post in the barn and run a comb through your coat because it's all tangled from running through the fields?" He has let go of her arms and she is stroking his legs, her nails leaving white traces as she caresses him slowly. "Would you like that, you horrid nasty little beast?"

"Do it," he says.

"Monster," she says.

"Yes," he says, "yes."

"You are thoughtless, and cruel, and that poor little goat is dead because you had to prove how strong you are."

"Do you know how strong I am?"

"Show me."

He shows her.

He shows me, too, what he can do, and though I've seen the motions countless times already, I've never before watched with such a gnawing compulsion of my own, unable to tear my eyes away, not from Nick's smooth and sensual performance, but from the conflicting emotions racing across Olivia's face like clouds blown swiftly across a sky, she oblivious to her own bewilderment, fear, and the thrilling shock of sexual enthrallment even in the very instant she feels it.

This must be akin to what she sees when she is painting. For her, then, time slows, and its effects are prolonged, lingering, cumulative, and controllable.

For me, here, watching in a tiny room, time is traveling with such speed that I cannot stop to wonder why it hurts so much to breathe.

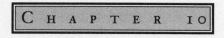

CHAPTER 10

He is already late for the set when he hits the buzzer, leaning on it a moment too long.

"Who is it?" Her voice floating down, annoyed.

"Acme Messenger." Perfect Cockney accent.

"I'm not expecting anything."

"Are you Miss O. Morgan? Delivery."

"From whom?"

"Medusa Records, miss. From a Mr. Chabrol." He pronounces it Chab-roll.

"Can't you leave it there by the door?"

"No, miss. It says urgent. I need your signature."

"Okay," she sighs over the intercom. "I'll be right down."

She opens the door, a whiff of cerulean, a brush in one hand, her painting smock askew, tendrils of hair curling around her face as she pushes them back impatiently in an instantly familiar gesture. She looks at the package. "Where do I sign?"

"Here." He holds out a clipboard. "Line eleven."

She scribbles her name and takes the package. "Thank you." Turns to leave.

"I also have a message for you."

She looks at him, curious, but cannot see his features hidden behind the opaque black faceguard. She can barely hear him.

"Yes."

He unmasks himself.

She blanches, then steps back, enraged, startled away from work by a face she is unprepared to see.

"You son of a bitch," she says. "How dare you? I can't see you now." She tries to push the door shut. Nick is too quick. He wedges in his boot. Steel-tipped. No fear. "You can't come in."

"I don't want to come in. I only wanted to see your face."

"Well, you've seen it. Now go away."

He pulls back, and bows.

"Tuesday," he says. "Tuesday lunch."

Olivia leans against the door she has slammed and slides down to the floor, trembling, her hands shaking as she tears open the package, not from Medusa, no, that was such a nasty trick, but a small blue box tied with a white ribbon, a small heart glistening on a bed of cotton, a small ruby heart, deeply red and circled with gold.

There is no card, no note, no apology, just a dazzling gem, gleaming in the light on a thin gold chain, blood-red to flicker between her breasts.

CHAPTER II

He senses her mood the instant she closes the door, but does not indulge her by asking what's wrong and rubbing her shoulders to ease the tension away, murmuring soothingly that he understands. He does not help because he likes seeing her human and real and frustrated, he is expert with weakness. The silliness of his charade on the bike was deliberately provocative, the dopey prank of an infuriating juvenile, growing up into an infuriating man who knows how to find her when she does not wish to be found.

He only wanted to see her face.

Now he is sitting on the bed, waiting, pages of his script littering the floor where he has tossed them, memorized and discarded, he is waiting for her to explode, and when she does he knows exactly what he's going to do to her.

Anger is easy, for Nick.

He senses her mood and will not give in to it, teasing her when she finally comes to him, she pushes him away in annoyance but he is too strong, and too wily, and he knows what she likes, and he always makes her come.

"Tell me about your boyfriends," he says as they lie, sated, finally.

"Not now," she says. "I have a meeting. I've got to go."

"In a minute."

She sighs, restless.

"Then tell me about your husband," Nick says, his fingers stroking her hair.

Olivia pulls away, her eyes narrowed. "How do you know about him?"

He shrugs. "I don't know anything. Just that you were married."

"Don't ever ask me about him."

"That awful?"

"Not awful. Just over, a long time ago. I was very young, and naive. It ended badly."

"In tears, you mean."

She stands up, looking for her clothes.

"Sorry," he says. "No. I'm not sorry."

"What do you mean?"

"If you hadn't married him, you wouldn't have come to London, and we wouldn't be here right now."

"Thanks for reminding me. I've got to go."

"No."

"Yes. Leave me alone."

"I won't." He sits up and grabs her wrists.

"Let go, you bastard." She tries to pull away, not in play or fear but real anger, the anger of pain and betrayal, and then she lashes out, kicking him, wanting to hurt him, to sink her teeth into him and watch him bleed, not knowing how much he enjoys this display of temper, how he thrills to the fierce fury in her determination, her muscles taut, her mouth set, her breathing hard as he frees her wrists, suddenly, so she topples, off-balance, into the soft comforter, and is instantly up on all fours, trying to crawl as far as she can, still lashing out and catching him full on the shins. He grabs her around the middle and whacks her bottom, hard, as if he were spanking a wayward child, two handprints appearing, ghostly pink images, Nick loosening his grip for a second to admire his handiwork, and Olivia twisting onto her side, trying to get away.

I have been waiting, with dread, for this all along. I knew it was coming. The dreadfulness is not merely the anticipation of Nick doing it, but that I have been wanting so badly to see Olivia try to fight him off, push him away till she can fight no longer, and then succumb.

I disgust myself.

This is the scenario Nick had been dreaming of, wondering how to entrap her into the games and props as delightful to him as the sight and feel of her body, and as necessary. And here she is, the familiar joy of a soon-to-be vanquished woman clawing at him, scratches running across his chest, venting her rage on the kind of man who, early in his career, had taken a small part as a sailor in a film that he knew would be awful, simply because he wanted to learn the intricacies of the Blackwall hitch and the fisherman's bend from a real professional.

Nick tells himself she is begging him to subdue her.

It takes no more than a second to yank free the silken cords holding back the brocade drapes, looping one first around her right wrist and then the bedpost, and as quickly repeating it with the other despite her shocked, frantic thrashing.

He kneels over her, smiling, savoring the moment, content now to watch her as she struggles helplessly against the cords, smiling when she tries to heave away as he reaches out to caress her breasts.

"Don't you touch me," she screams at him.

"Why shouldn't I?" He is maddeningly calm.

"Because I hate you."

"If you don't stop screaming I'll have to put a gag on you."

She is too angry to be frightened, too angry to realize how her wrath arouses him. "You wouldn't dare."

"Wouldn't I?"

She is still trying to kick him.

"Are you going to calm down, or should I tie your legs, too?"

That provokes the reaction he knew it would, and he rolls over on top of her, propping his weight on his elbows, pinioning her body beneath his, delighting in her thrashing response.

"You can't get away, you know. You are totally helpless, and I can do anything to you that I want."

"No, you can't, you bastard," she says. "Let me go."

"I will, but only if you apologize."

She looks at him, aghast. "Me? For what?"

"For screaming at me because someone else made you mad, and otherwise insulting my character."

"*Your* character? You're a monster. Now let me go."

"Am I?" His fingers have found their mark, incessant, swirling. "Would a monster do this to you?"

"Get away," she says, more feebly.

"You like it," he says. "Say that you like it."

She turns her head away, and he turns it back, biting her lips, kissing her, devouring.

"Say it."

"I hate you."

He pulls away, instantly, leaving her there on the bed, he wants to hear her plead, craving satisfaction, as he saunters into the kitchen to open a bottle of champagne, coming back to sit on the edge of the bed, bemused, smiling at her childish tantrum.

"Care for a drink?"

"You fuck," she says. "You're never going to see me again."

"That's what you think." He drains his glass, and stands,

looking at her, his hands on his hips, his body taut, virile, his eyes darkening, and she stares back at him, a slick knot of fear tightening in her gut, but still she will not back down.

"What are you looking at, you sadistic pervert?"

"You, my darling Olivia," he says, as he lies down atop her once more, this time his arms pinning her legs, his head in her belly, his tongue incessant, demanding, unyielding, till she moans.

"You want me," he says, sitting up. "Say it."

"I want you," she says, because she can't stop, "but I want you to go away."

He laughs, plunging into her with long sure strokes, maddening, rhythmic, stronger and stronger, endless waves of stroking pleasure from the weight of his body, and the sureness of his fingers, and how he feels inside her. "I am not going to go away," he says, "not now, not ever."

"Yes you are, you bastard," she says, his smugness infuriating her yet again. "Get off me."

"I've had just about enough of your lip," he says, pulling out of her suddenly and turning her on her side, her arms smarting against the cords, and spanking her again, hard, harder, till she is kicking and screaming at him to stop, but he won't stop now, no, he is not close to stopping, the thrill of her sweet body beneath his, bound into compliance against her wishes, he is not going to stop, not now, not when he can have his fill of her however he wants it. "Take it," he says, "you know you can take it," and he makes her, screaming, tears soaking the pillows as she tries to squirm, fighting, twisting away to fight, but she cannot because he has turned her back and is kissing her, kissing her deep, his fingers deliriously maddening yet again, and she hates him more than ever for her helpless submission to his will, her effortless initiation into his twisted, expert manipulation of pain and pleasure, and her certain knowledge that this was only the beginning.

Strange how stories begin. Usually you're in them before you think they could possibly be worth remembering. All those endless, mindless encounters that fueled our days, those overheated sagas of instant gratification so vivid to the players, so boringly habitual to us that the actual recollection lasted no longer than a sneeze.

This story is different. It started at lunch, yes, but it doesn't end there; stories like this, born of innocence in the full light of day, never do. No, they end in the black of night, when the moon is obscured and a bleak winter wind rustles the leaves, and those well-fed eaters of pasta in trendy restaurants are tucked safely in bed, dreaming of deals and dates and buffalo mozzarella with a hint of basil and extra-virgin oil, their sorry simple minds never daring to unleash the dark webs of dangerous impulses spun like quicksilver in their synapses, lurking, desperate, just beneath the veneer of their respectability, waiting to be released.

This story begins not with a chance encounter on a day full of rain, nor with the light-diffused sessions in a white studio scented of hyacinths and oils, nor with the inevitability of his willful seduction.

No, it begins when Nick is lying in bed, he is lying in the flat, the pillows grasped to his chest, inhaling the lingering scent of Olivia, the essence of Olivia mingled with vetiver and sex, the essence of desire. Nick is lying there, his fists wrapped around the sheets, and Olivia will not come that day, I know it, she is afraid, and Nick is lying, dreaming, waiting, waiting in vain for the soft rush of footsteps up the staircase, the metal clink of a key in the lock, the knob turning, the door opening, the woman blowing in, breathless, raindrops on her face, raindrops in her hair, she is warm and laughing and full of life, kicking off her shoes that are sodden with wet. These were suede once, she says, and smiles. Nick pulls her down, kissing her, drinking in a whiff of her, this essence of desire, he cannot hold her long enough before she is gone, she will not stay.

He cannot keep her.

This is when the story truly begins, with a pain Nick had not allowed himself for more years than he can remember. It is the pain of refusal. Olivia does not submit, she will not come, and even if she did, she would not stay.

Nick has no tolerance for pain, spoiled as he is by the facile leap into the kind of fame that is incomprehensible to those who'll never live it, his senses dulled by the endless procession of shapely bodies yielding to his will.

The rage starts small. He ignores it, as long as he can, obscured briefly by the essence of desire.

The rage starts only as a tiny match sparked into life, but it grows, yes, it grows, it is a small steady flame, it is a warming campfire in the middle of the forest, it is fed, fed too much, it is burning the trees, they are glowing, crackling with fire, burned, then gutted, incinerated in the maelstrom of heat so intense it consumes the very air that feeds it, and dies.

The pain is palpable, growing like a tumor in his gut. It is palpable, and it is out of control, inextricably, hopelessly entrenched, living, breathing, an all-consuming obsession.

Olivia is not like the others.

She is unhavable.

This story truly begins when it is already beginning to be over.

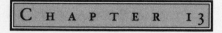

CHAPTER 13

They do not speak of their lives outside the flat. they meet at lunchtime on weekdays, and then leave, quietly, on separate paths.

She tries to keep their meetings short despite Nick's calm requests for other times, burdened, she says, by her schedule, and Nick must get to work, mustn't he, put on his face, learn his lines, be who he's meant to be, become another. She tries, she tells herself, a flurry of self-righteous justification, she is trying, she is still in control of this thing, she will put an end to it, he's leaving anyway in a few months, it's only because Olivier is away, it must stop, he wants too much, he wants her.

He wants.

Each time he pushes the wanting, the games of their lovemaking, just a little bit farther.

Each time she lets him.

Even a woman like Olivia has found herself ensnared by the

force of Nick's sexual charisma, and on such a completely fundamental level, going beyond all rational thought or deeds. Thoroughly unaware is she of precisely what she's doing till it's done, and still she can't believe she is capable of such abandon, of what under other circumstances would have automatically been judged as depraved or unthinkable. Nothing else, no drug, no potion, no money in the bank, has that power, and quite that devastating a result.

It is easier to pretend it isn't there.

She does not speak of her friends, the steady rhythm of her days, the familiar patterns of her life and the faces of those she loves, or of the commissions, her flurry of impassioned energy, the newest portraits painted with such sure quickness, the seeing of them so much easier, with a dazzling clarity. Nick has changed her work, though she does not want to admit it, the force of him enlivening the subtle shifts of color and form she paints on faces more vivid and free, full of hidden depths of character.

Will that be lost when she ends it, she wonders, is that what pulls her feet across the park to this flat? She does not speak of the jumbled confusion such thoughts bring during her long walks in the cold, longer each time, and back again.

She never mentions Olivier.

Nick does not speak of the astonished delight glistening in Toledo's eyes during dailies, watching Nick's scenes shot the day before, or of the cast, pouncing on this unexpected vigor, grabbing it quickly and feeding it back, rallying around their superstar's surprising willingness to share, to shoot and reshoot, endlessly patient during difficult technical scenes on dank cobbled streets, questioning, willing and open, to work, and then work harder even as his breath traces an aurora of steam in the chilly damp air. The work is there, all-enfolding, all-sustaining, says Faust, it is harder than Nick had ever imagined to actually be present in it, and it is satisfaction unexpected to revel in the seriousness of creation for its own sake. To Nick's surprise he is capable, if only because he can close his eyes and see Olivia's impassioned dance behind the canvas, the wrinkle of concentration between her eyebrows, her mental absence as she painted his face more potent than her presence.

His Gretchen is madly in love with him, melting at his touch, offering him every opportunity for a seduction he once would have welcomed but now spurns, gently, joking, flirtatiously friendly and respectful. Everyone is respectful.

If it weren't for Olivia, I might almost be pleased, but if it weren't for Olivia, this filming would most likely have crossed the line into the fiasco I'd feared, even though I'd always believed Nick capable of such a role, and encouraged him to play it.

If it weren't for Olivia.

Nick does not speak of the elated late-night phone calls to the Coast by gloating executives already deep in the quicksand complications of strategic marketing for a film they'd thought would last for a week and then be yanked straight to video. We never thought he had it in him, they say, when only weeks before they'd been calling Nick's indulgent fantasy *Faust's Folly*, and yet here it is, shimmering to life before their very eyes, a real story, thrillingly told.

Nick does not speak of it.

There is a new and shifting mood in him, one that so perfectly suits the character he is playing that even Toledo does not credit himself for its gradual deepening. He sees only a gravity in Nick's eyes that had never been there before, a somber worry, a questioning passion, elusive, ineluctible, and, were he aware of its effect, devastatingly sexy.

If I didn't know Nick as well as I did, I might even have called it something like love.

* * *

She hears a bell ringing, disturbing her reverie. It has been
ringing for quite some time, her machine is not on, she wonders why not in that brief second before she picks up the
phone, she must have turned it off, yes, because Olivier is
meant to be calling, and she wants to pick it up on the first
ring and tell him Darling, please, please, come home, come
home to me, I can't bear it anymore, don't leave me alone, I
am going mad.

The phone has been ringing and ringing.

"Olivia," he says.

"Is it really you?"

"Of course it is," Olivier says, a faint echo in her ear. "Who
else would call you this time of night?"

"You," she says, "only you. But it's your night. My day,
and I should be working."

"Is that why you let it ring so many times?" He is teasing,
but she panics.

"Oh, I couldn't paint, so I was running a bath."

The briefest hesitation. "What is it, *ma petite*?"

"I just miss you too much."

"Is there something else? Something that's bothering you? I
hear it, in your voice."

She is sitting on the floor, gripping the receiver with both
hands. Hear it. Hear it in her voice. Not possible. "Yes," she
says.

"Tell me."

"I can't wait for you to get back, so I'm going to get on a
plane tomorrow. Well, I can't tomorrow, I have a sitting. The
day after, then. Soon," she says, although she has only just
decided. "It was going to be a surprise."

He is amused, and pleased.

"Let's get married, now," she says abruptly.

"Why now?"

"I don't know, let's just, please. Please."

"You are very adorable," he says, chuckling softly at her impassioned plea, "but you know that's not possible. Your American paperwork takes days, anyway, and I haven't got a spare moment to myself."

"Except at night."

"Except at night. But I won't allow myself to believe you're really coming until I see you. It is too much to hope for."

"Good. Then I'm really coming."

"Darling, what is it?" he says. "Something else. Tell me. Tell me now."

"I just want to see your face, that's all, and it's cold and dreary here, and raining all the time, and I'm sick of it."

"Are there problems with the portrait, that actor?"

"No, of course not. I finished it weeks ago, and he was really pleased with it. At least he said so."

"How did you do him?" His voice drowsy, sweet. "I've forgotten."

"A minotaur," she says, "standing in a maze."

"Oh yes. A beast. Lost."

"I'll call you as soon as I have the flight number."

"It's such a long flight."

"I don't care. I'll take a sketchbook."

"Silly girl."

"Mmm."

"I'll fetch you at the airport. I don't care what I have to cancel."

"Will you?"

"In a big black car."

"Naughty." She shivers. "What did you play tonight? I'll put it on."

"The Mozart program, but I missed the cadenza in the D minor Fantasia."

"Because you were thinking of me."

"*Sans doute.*"

"How many encores?"

"Four."

"Only four?"

"I must be slipping."

"Go to sleep now."

"I will. *Je t'embrasse.*"

"Me too. Soon."

"Soon," he says, "but not soon enough."

Her heels on the cobblestones of the mews, walking past the car dealer, the pub where normal people are having a pint and a sandwich, gossiping during their lunch break, her heels dragging as she walks up Queens Gate to the park, past the Albert Memorial, up the paths by the neatly tended shrubs and flower beds, past the Watts statue, brushing her gloved hand along the horse's hoof for luck, and knowing she would not find it as the wind whips her hair, past the American students trying to throw a Frisbee, past the obelisk, past the fat man walking his corgi, "Come along, you little nipper," he says, nodding to her in greeting, past the pond, looking across it to the Henry Moore sculpture, a gleaming white beacon.

Where are you going, she imagines she hears it whisper, and why are you going there?

It is not me, not my true self going there, she tells herself, letting him touch me this way, wanting him to, the fear and pleasure jumbled so helplessly and intoxicatingly together, craving that recklessness dragging me down to places I don't want to go.

She can acknowledge it in her painting, she realizes as she walks out of the Lancaster Gate and past the tube station, her pace slowing as she heads up Queensway, past the kebab stands and pinched faces of hurrying shoppers. She wants it there, in her work, there where she can control it.

Still her feet keep moving, taking her past the baths where she should be lying, sweating the shameful duplicity out of her body, seeping in fat drops from her pores, trickling down her body and away, far away, there she should be lying, instead of in the arms of her lover, waiting impatiently for her in his gilded flat just around the corner.

Each time she is a little later, she who so hated to be kept waiting. The relentless sweep of the hands on her watch, blithely ticking, another minute gone, her wishing it by, wanting and not wanting, loathing the knowledge that her footsteps might slow at the familiar sight of Porchester Square, yet they will always take her up the stairs, and through the door.

"I shouldn't be here," she says as soon as she walks in.

Nick is lying on the bed, reading a script, smoking, and he looks at her, his instinctive response to her petulance making his expression go vacantly wary.

"Then why are you?" he says, careful to keep his voice low and perfectly conversational. "You could've called, to cancel. It wouldn't be the first time."

"I know. But there's something I want to say."

"Then say it."

"I can't when you look at me like that."

"Like what?"

"Like you're so maddeningly fucking calm."

"What do you want me to do, when you come bursting in like this?" His eyes begin to sparkle with the pleasure of a fight as he stubs out his cigarette and stretches languorously before sitting up.

She still does not know him well enough, or perhaps chooses to delude herself, I cannot decide which, to realize how one tiny chink is all he needs, a hole in the dike, one tiny crack, to sidle in wherever he wants to go, his strength taking sustenance from weakness, the slightest hint of it swelling him, empowered, a snake swallowing a rabbit, engorged with gluttony.

"Last time you came here—when was it, oh, just a scant few days ago—you were in a bad mood too, weren't you? It's becoming a regular habit. You're almost always late, and you're usually in a snit about it. It's not like you to be so cranky."

"So now you know what I'm like?" she mutters, her eyes straying to the bed, the covers rumpled from Nick's lounging. The silken drapery cords are linked around the bedposts, where he'd left them, where he always leaves them, taunting reminders. He sees her eyes upon them, and smiles, wickedly.

"Have a drink," he says, motioning to the champagne. "It'll calm your nerves."

"There's only one thing that'll calm my nerves." She turns to the door, but he is too quick, blocking her path. She cringes, waiting for him to pounce, but he stands there, his face a cipher, watching her, assessing all the possibilities.

"At least take off your coat, and then you can tell me what you came to say," he says, his voice mild, blandly reassuring. He eases her coat and scarf off, draping them over one of the chairs, careful not to touch her. "Are you hungry? Thirsty? Want some tea?"

She shakes her head and sits down on the other chair. He sits on the edge of the bed, nonchalant. The role of the sympathetic, docile suitor fits him as sleekly as his jeans. It is a part he has played many times before.

"Tell me what's wrong."

She takes a deep breath.

"It's guilt, isn't it?" he says, not wanting to hear anything he can't say first. "You shouldn't make yourself feel so guilty."

"How do you know what I feel, or don't?"

"Okay, maybe I don't know. I'm *imagining*," he says. "Even

someone of my limited education can recognize a guilty conscience when he sees one. It's written all over your face."

She flushes. "I don't believe you," she says, unconvinced.

"Then don't. We believe only what we want to believe,
anyway, you and me, Olivia." This is not like Nick, to speak
of such things, but he is clever, far more clever than she
thinks at snapping up her confusion. He has encouraged this
anger in her, preferring it to the calmer disposition that
exists outside this flat, for it is the perfect counterpoint to
his temperament. He baits it, eagerly awaiting it only to
subdue it, conquering her and her desperate moans. Just
when this anger is about to overcome her saner instincts he
transforms himself into a sympathetic ear, a loving brother,
a trusted friend.

I shift the camera as he gets up and goes around to the back
of her chair and starts massaging her shoulders. I have to
move, stretch my legs, do something. Nick is enjoying his
performance far too much.

Olivia shivers when he touches her, but does not pull away.
"You're one solid lump," he says, probing her clenched muscles. "Relax. Close your eyes. Calm down."

"Nick," she says.

"Yes."

"I can't—"

"I know." His fingers sure and strong, soothing away her
tension. "Just relax."

The room is silent, the sounds of the street muffled into
indistinct mumblings of noise, a child shouting, a siren, the
heavy rumble of a truck. It is warmer outside than usual, the
sun shining, and I forgot to light the fire.

"Lie down," he says, his voice barely louder than a whisper.
"I want to rub your back."

"No—"

"Lie down," he says, sweetly insistent, pulling her up and

propelling her to the bed, pushing the comforter out of the way. "It will make you feel better."

She thought she had the energy to fight him today, to say this is the last time, and mean it, but she hasn't, she can't when he is being nice. I have long thought that men who know when to be nice, these skillful practitioners of seduction and elicitors of orgasms who transfer their niceness into the bedroom, these men who are so skilled at sex are in truth those creatures who cannot love. It is all put into the act itself, so that their niceness is never selfless, but a shiny mirror meant only to reflect their performance. Only then can they bask in its glory, distill it into all their other, equally meaningless acts, their smooth hellos and busy days and vapid, useless nights.

Nice, from them, is easy.

Nice, from Nick, is irresistible.

He pulls off Olivia's boots, and her socks, eases her sweater over her head, unhooks her bra, not touching her jeans, and covers her bare back with the comforter. "Don't move," he says, and unlocks the trunk, rummaging for the bottle of scented oil I'd put in there weeks before. Then he quickly unbuttons his shirt, takes it off, and throws it in the corner.

He rubs the oil between his palms, to warm it, then bends over to the ripe warmth of Olivia's skin, glowing white, delicious. He wants to sink his teeth into the divine taste of it, but instead he is calmly massaging her neck.

"Yummy," she says, "this oil. Where'd you get it?"

"M got it. Elixir of Life, it's called."

He feels her chuckle softly, relaxing further, gentled, his hands steady, pushing the comforter away, concentrating, up and down her spine, her arms, back to her neck, stealing down again.

She turns her head to the side. "Who lives here?" she asks him.

"What do you mean?"

"Alderson, Andrews, Fairley, and Scott. The names, on the buzzers."

"Sounds like a law firm."

"Mmm, it does. But I never hear anybody. The building seems so empty."

"I guess it does," he says, his voice so steady and even you'd never presume that he was lying through his teeth, "but I never much thought about it. It's not like I spend so much time here, or you." Her muscles tense reflexively, and he rubs it away. "It's one of the reasons I like this flat so much, the quiet, I mean. The privacy. Nobody knows who I am here, and nobody wants to know. I haven't been chased down the street once. Must be slipping."

"Do you get chased so much?" She turns her head to the other side. "That's a stupid thing to say. Of course you do."

He looks up at the mirror, and me, and smiles.

"Flip over," he says even as he eases her over, then stretches across the bed to turn down the light. "Give me your hand." He takes it, sitting at her side, not touching any other part of her body. "Hands are the nicest." He is thorough, his motions firm, assured, lingering over the paint specks freckling her fingers.

She opens her eyes to watch him, absorbed in his task, concentrating, his features almost boyish, and he is pretending that the heat of her gaze is not burning a dull throb deep in him. He shifts to her other hand, then, slowly, his fingers move up her arm, over her shoulders, down to her breasts, swirling, dulcet fingers, her nipples are hard and he won't touch them, he ignores her desire, moving down to her ribs, her belly, unbuckling her jeans, easing them off, leaving her panties on, rubbing more oil between his palms, rubbing it, lavender and rosemary and geranium, smoothly into her heels, the soles of her feet, her ankles, her calves, her knees, up her thighs, soothing her into lazy tranquillity.

Her anger, the long despair of her walk across the park, has disappeared, dissipated into the silence of the room, absorbed into the brocade and gilt, sunk into the luxurious comforter, tranquilized by his knowing fingers. The familiar ache replaces it, not leaving her, the aching burden of pleasure and the aching burden of guilt.

I see it all so clearly on her face.

She's not ready to say what she came to say. That's why she's here, why she didn't call, why her feet dragged her across the park. She still wants it, I see the desire shining in her eyes like molten silver, a sword's edge, flashing in sunlight. I see it transformed by a blink into remorse and a biting sense of shame for her greedy grasp of the pleasure Nick gives her. She knows it's not just what he's given to her painting, she still wants him, here, in the flat, her body wants him, awoken from a long slumber, his body taking her relentlessly, she will let him devour her whole as long as he doesn't stop, not here, not now, not yet.

Every relationship needs a touch of madness. I see it so clearly every time I look in the mirror, my own desire reflected back to me, coolly mocking.

"Feeling better?" Nick says.

"Yes."

"Do you want me to stop?"

"No."

"Do you want to go home?"

Her eyes fly open. "That's a trick question."

"Sorry," he says, caressing her thighs, "forgive me." His hands straying closer. "Is this okay?" She nods, helpless now, and closes her eyes. "Tell me when to stop." His fingers on her, stroking the crazy, infuriating ache, pulling down her panties, calm, deliberate, in ever-narrowing circles, her arms on his, gripping him, pushing him in closer.

"No," he says, "let me do it. Don't move." He takes her

arms and binds them with the cords on the bed, but she doesn't protest, not this time, no, she wants him to, wants him to do anything as long as he hurries back to her and makes that maddening ache go away.

His fingers, his mouth, his tongue on her, her back arching, involuntarily, her arms straining against the bed, her skin alive, screaming to be touched, her head lolling from side to side, her breathing hoarse.

He has never been so gentle with her before, so patient, so generous. It is so easy, to succumb.

"Don't go," she says, "don't leave me."

"I won't," he says, even as he pulls away, only slightly, teasing.

"Come back," she says, gasping, "I want you to come back."

"I'm here," he says. "Tell me, tell me what you want. I'll do anything you want."

"Kiss me," she says, "just kiss me."

"Like this?" he asks, pecking her on the cheek.

"No. More."

"Like this?"

"More."

He will kiss her, again, over and over, he will leave her breathless, delirious, he will stop only to do it again, until the desire is quenched in her, and the frenzy stills.

It is worth everything, to hear her beg.

Olivia quietly gets dressed, yanks up her boots, runs a brush through her hair, puts on her lipstick. Her sure, sweet, capable artist's hands are trembling.

"When?" he says. "I've got to shoot all day tomorrow. The day after."

"I can't." She buttons her coat. "I'm going away for a few days."

There is a long pause. "Going where?"

"Cairo."

"Why?" He sees her face. "Oh." He is still playing nice, he
will be nice, he will let her go, flushed and satiated, glowing
with sex, her lips swollen from his kisses, what a perfect mood
for parting, if indeed she must go. Let her, he has work to do.
Revenge will come later, it can wait. For now he is thankful
in an odd selfish way that he has not bruised her, perhaps
that's what she was afraid of, unwittingly, when she came in,
her steadfast self-loathing such divine aphrodisiac. He still
smells it on her, lingering, she will sit soaking in the bath,
scrubbing her skin, washing it away, desperately grateful there
are no divulging, telltale signs imprinted on her body, the
stigmata of duplicity, to compound her contrition.

Calmly, Nick lights a cigarette. "Is that what you wanted to
tell me when you came in?" She wants him to react, he feels
it and he ignores her, she wants him furious, because anger
she can try to understand, although no one can quite divine
the deeply hidden depths of Nick's wrath. Except me.

"Partly."

"I see." He exhales, small, flawless circles. She waves them
away. "When are you coming back?"

"I don't know yet."

"Well, have fun. I'll miss you."

"I know."

"Kiss me goodbye."

She shakes her head no.

He smiles at her, and shrugs. "Then you owe me a kiss."

"Bye," she says, frustrated yet grateful for the reprieve, and
is flying down the stairs.

Nick is staring at the ceiling, still blowing smoke rings, when
I come in.

"I'm fucked, M," he says. He starts laughing, the unimaginable pleasure of her pleading demands lingering in his mind,

his body languid, lying on the bed, naked, her scent on the sheets, a whiff of the scented oil escaping as he turns to me, the essence of Olivia, the Elixir of Life. His eyes are glowing more fiercely than his cigarette. "Can you believe the little bitch is leaving? Not after this."

"Probably because of this."

"Do you know," he says, needing to talk, the postcoital conversation almost as vital to him in this exultant state of physical awareness as the cigarette, "when I'm touching her, when I'm inside her, I'm so—I don't know how to say it— *aware* of her, so intensely *alive*, feeling the texture of her skin, her flesh underneath me, every bit of her body, goose bumps, a bruise, purple, or fading to green, that I put there—I must have, I don't remember—and all I want to do is give to her, give something back that I know I'm taking, making her feel exactly what I'm feeling."

"Which might be hard to do when she's strapped to the bed."

He doesn't even hear me, lost in his soliloquy.

Audiences are supposed to be quiet, and listen. Especially me. I can watch Olivia, he wants me there to watch her most intimate moments laid bare to Nick's inexorability, but I am forbidden to intrude. Look, but do not touch. Those are the rules. Until now, they were unassailable.

"It's like I am moving outside of my own body, moving within it, it is me, mine, yet I'm removed, so I can watch myself," he is saying. "I can't get enough of that feeling. I'll never get enough of it."

"You mean she won't let you."

"No, not like that. I can remember, literally, controlling the motion, Olivia was on top of me so I could see her face above, her eyes were closed, and I was saying to myself, not imagining it, but knowing it to be true, that I will never again feel this close to death." His voice is rapturous. "I was feeling her, Olivia, on top of me, inching up and down, inch by fraction of an inch, with so little margin of error, a membrane away from death."

Disbelief that Nick has himself found the words to articulate these shared secrets so precisely is etched on my face, but he doesn't see me, lying on his back, lounging into the pillows, his eyes narrowed by memory and smoke, small, flawless circles floating up to the ceiling. He doesn't see me, because I don't matter.

It hits me with a tiny jolt, realizing how little he cares. I push the thought away. I don't want to think, watching them is too exhausting. I only want to disappear, I only want to sleep.

"And you know," Nick is saying, "I didn't want it to be so intense. Not at first. But now, between her and this damn movie, it's better than any drug."

"The Elixir of Life."

"Yes," he says, laughing again. "The fucking Elixir of Life. It was perfect. Where the hell did you find it?"

I shrug. I don't remember.

"What am I going to do?" he says, stubbing out his cigarette and throwing on his clothes. "We've got to think of something. A nice welcoming party at the airport, perhaps."

"What do you really want to do?"

"Make her come home, of course. When I can't have her I only want to hurt her for leaving me, and when I do have her I only want to make her beg me to stop. So it's simple. She tells the Frog bastard she's really sorry it won't work out and comes with me."

"Simple."

"Fuck off."

"What if it's the other way around?"

"It won't be."

How convenient to have a memory so selective, erasable like chalk after a few blissful hours of lunch. The truth is too

painful to confront, too painful to deny. It isn't love, I want
to say to him, not what you want, not what she knows to be
love.

He who has loved nothing, who, I thought, had like myself
no heart to give, only the Pinocchio heart beating mercilessly
in the same entrenched rhythms, wooden and yearning, beating unaware, blinded by the dazzling light of pain beaten into
us so early, with such brutality, that he would never see the
possibility of surrender.

This time he is on his own. I can no longer help him.

His world has been reduced to a room perfumed with the
essence of Olivia.

I am standing guard.

The wardrobe mistress was glad to oblige, anything for Nick, so happy to be of service for the costume party he says he's going to, thank you very much indeed for thinking we could help, thank you even more for the payoff I swiftly palmed to her. Money does buy freedom, don't believe anyone who says it doesn't. Enough of it also buys silence.

So does my face.

The chauffeur uniform suits me, much better than Nick's dishwater-blah janitor's jumpsuit. The large peaked hat and the Ray-Bans cast a deliberate shadow over my face, and I am not stared at quite as much as usual. Twin rows of gold buttons run down my chest. Olivia Morgan is written in smooth black block letters on my sign.

Her face when she sees me, coming out of customs, a stunned, tenuous grin of nervous bewilderment. She looks ravishing, like a woman who's just been endlessly fucking the man she loves, relaxed, calm, lost in thought, until she recognizes me. I realize that except for those two lunches and the one time I took her home, I've never seen her outside her studio or the flat, moving purposeful, apart from Nick, apart from us, herself, her needs not ours in her own daily world.

"What are you doing here?" she says, confused, coming up to me. "How on earth did you know I'd be on this plane?"

An explanation is not really necessary. A few quick phone calls, the usual payola. Simple.

"Never mind," she mutters. "Let me guess."

She sees Nick, then, leaning against the wall near the restroom, mop in hand, and stifles a laugh at the fake beard glued to his cheeks and the cap pulled low to hide his famous face from curious eyes, a mock ID tag dangling from the breast pocket of his uniform.

So much for security in airports.

She sees him, then, leaning against the wall in the same pose as when she'd painted him a lifetime ago, leaning still and watching, waiting, and she stares back in perplexed astonishment, torn between indecision and desire, too stunned by the shock of his presence to be furious that he's dared find her here, so soon after, when she's defenseless.

Run, I want to say, run back onto the plane, fly away, fly to Cairo or wherever he is this week, run quick, find a taxi, lock your door, don't look back.

"Go on," is what I hear myself saying. I wonder if she will forgive me for saying it, but I tell myself she won't even remember that we spoke. "The coast is clear."

Indeed it was, but even if the restroom had been filled with drunken soccer hooligans Nick would have stood there, lounging, patient, mop in hand, because he is waiting for Olivia to come back to him, his eyes liquid with lust, moving only to stroke her cheek, tender, gentle as she draws close, telling her softly, oh so softly, that he was going mad without her.

Olivia places a palm over the fingers caressing her cheek, and without her noticing I take her bags. In a flash the light in Nick's eyes deepens and he grabs her tight, twists her off-balance as he hauls her inside and quickly into the stall we'd prepared, the handicapped one because it is larger, an out-of-order sign taped to it, and slides the lock behind him. So quick she couldn't have articulated a word of protest, for he'd performed this variation on a theme so many times the motions were seamless to him, practiced and easy, and that was half the joy of it. He is kissing her so deep she can barely breathe, forcing her to kiss him back, his mouth delirious on hers, murmuring her name, over and over, one hand in her hair, pushing her back up against the back wall, one hand moving down between her legs, parting them, her head spinning, her legs melting, liquid, but it is too much, he is too strong. This is what she feared from him the last time, the last perfect lunchtime when he made her swoon, this is the fury she knew he was hiding under glib goodbyes and flawless circled smoke rings.

She does not want him here, he has no right to trap her like this, catching her unaware, the feel of Olivier still lingering on her skin, she does not want Nick to touch it so, not now, not like this.

She is beginning to struggle against him, to try to pull her mouth away, and that is all he needs, the intoxication of extorted surrender, and he leans all his weight against her, into the cold tiles of the stall, forcing her mouth to stay open to his longing.

"You owe me a kiss," he says, "you owe me," pushing her hands rudely into the handcuffs that she hadn't seen already dangling from the pipe, put there hours before, when we arrived and changed into our uniforms. Pushing down her panties like a flutter of silken toilet paper. Pushing down his black jeans and into her with such force that her smothered scream nearly tears his hand away.

I have brought Nick's mop and her bags inside, and am busy washing my hands, trying to drown out the muffled sounds no listless tourist can hear but me.

"How could you," he says in a vicious whisper, "how could you leave me?" How she fights him, squirming, her eyes shiny with tears of rage, trying to bite the hand that imprisons her, shocked and furious at his instant transformation from sweetly tender to tyrannical, waiting for her, off-guard, waiting to pounce on her travel-weary confusion, waiting for her when she hasn't the strength to push him away, even if she truly wanted to.

And then he is kissing her again, biting her lips, biting the tears away, pushing her harder up against the wall, her legs around his waist. He knows her limits, and she hates him for it. He knows what she likes, he knows just how far to go and when to withdraw, he knows how to melt her anger so she can no longer fight him off, and she succumbs.

I timed it. Seven minutes. Enough time to sit in a trendy restaurant, eat the olive from a martini, scan the menu, and order *osso buco*.

Enough time to suck out the marrow.

Enough time to say a few prayers, and light a candle for your soul.

Later, we watched the video. We had experimented on the angle of the mini-camcorder packed gently in foam in Nick's mop bucket and started from a remote I held, following them into the men's room, watchful and wary, just in case. We had concentrated on angles and focus for endless hours, busying our hands with preparation, anything to keep Nick's mind from straying to thoughts of the hotel room in Cairo where Olivia was sleeping in Olivier's arms.

Despite our careful planning the focus was off, grainy, jerky. The video is no more real than an abstract painting, a shifting landscape of cloth, of knee, of parted thighs, of hisses and muffled moans, of enraged yearning less.potent than a whisper.

An unwitting viewer would see it and shrug, not realizing that this tape had captured the most authentic image of the fury of Nick's passion, unleashed.

Unseen. Uncaught. Seven minutes.

It was all the time he needed.

She is running in a maze, lost, the hedges growing higher against her, their branches intertwining, darkening, she is running in a tunnel, her breath hard and harsh, raggedy sobs in her ears, running away, she hears footsteps behind her, echoing, she is afraid to stop for even a second because he is following, relentless and implacable, she is running in the maze she has painted, greenly rich and lush, high hiding hedges, a forest prison of her own creation.

She awakens with a jolt, her heart thumping, her fingers clenched around the comforter, and realizes with a shuddering sigh of relief that it was a nightmare, and it's over. She gets up and pulls back the drapes. The stars are fading, a last gasp of dark before the sun, but she has no wish to return to bed and the horrible dreaming.

Foolish girl, she tells herself, thinking you can ignore him, imagining you can extract a payment, so well and richly deserved, after what he did to you in the airport, how he dared touch you when your body was still glowing with Olivier, how he dared, and how much you liked it.

She runs a bath and makes coffee, watching the sky lighten. She has not talked to him in over a week, he called her answering machine once, leaving a sober entreaty she erased immediately. There are floral tributes at her doorstep every day at lunchtime, small carefully swaddled baskets of scented blooms, lilac and night-blooming jasmine, tiny, exquisitely wrapped golden boxes tucked among the blossoms, the first with a heavy golden link bracelet, each ensuing with a different golden charm, marvelously carved, a paintbrush, an easel, a miniature hyacinth in a pot, a pillow, an ormolu clock, a tiny mirror in a gilded frame.

The last one was my idea.

She has always accused him of playing games, and now she is no different, she realizes as she nibbles a muffin, abashed, punishing herself to spite him. How easy it is to be like Nick, a petulant spoiled child lashing back at the wanting. She knows how much he wants her, but whether the wanting is simply habit when his wishes are denied him or the genuine craving is something she cannot answer.

Today she will resolve it, and she calls his machine to tell him she'll be there, for lunch.

It is still very early, and she is restless, tidying the studio, flicking through her sketchbooks until she finds one blank, smoothly expectant, and knows what she will do, throwing on her coat and bundling up against the cold.

Her feet, this time hurrying across the park, past the dog walkers still yawning and the intrepid joggers padding past, striding up Queensway, past the glassy blank stares of people lining up for buses, the dull boredom of their days only beginning, up the street and around the corner, keys in hand, up the silent padded staircase, and into the flat.

She has never been here so early in the morning, so hushed

and dark, muted by the thick carpeting and the drawn drapes, she has never been here alone, without Nick waiting, sprawled on the bed, his eagerness tampered by the idle speculation of how late she will be, because she always is, only her feet acknowledging what her mind will not, knowing he is there, the guilty awareness that this must soon end seeping out of her pores and growing on her like a weight, a silent, scolding accomplice warning her to stop, warning her that he feeds delirious on her wavering fears, wearing her down, each time inching a little deeper till she can fight him off no longer, and that is when he knows he has her.

She shakes the worries out of her head, opens the drapes to the dull gray outside, yanks off her boots, pulls one of the chairs aside, and begins to sketch. She is drawing the room, this gilded dungeon, the peonies fresh in their vase, the curved legs of the table, the heaps of pillows, the trunk at her feet, the empty expectancy an unseen creature she can feel, pressing in on her, glancing over her shoulder, curious.

She works hard in the silent room, her fingers fluttering furious, fast and sure, until the room grows, alive, on the paper as she intended. She looks at the clock with some surprise that hours have flown by, and puts down her pad, and pencils, and stretches luxuriously. It is so warm in here, and cozy, her jeans are too tight, she will take them off, lying down on the bed to take a break, so cozy, closing her eyes, just for a minute, and quickly falls into sleep.

Nick stops dead at the astonishing spectacle of Olivia asleep atop the bed, a sketchpad at her side. One pencil has fallen to the carpet and he stoops to pick it up, turning back with a signal for me to check the tapes that must have been running since she came in and turned on the light.

For a brief moment he stands deliberating, pleasure flooding his senses, the unexpected joy of her body clad only in a saggy fisherman's sweater and her panties, there, so long denied him like this, pliant and supple, helpless in the innocence of sleep, waiting for him. He hurriedly draws the drapes, moves back to the door, and quickly strips in silence before placing her sketchpad on the table and gingerly lowering himself to her side.

He will awaken her with a kiss.

Many kisses.

She stirs beside him, his fingers stroking her into a calm haze, half asleep, wondering where she is, disoriented, those delicious fingers already inside her, sweet, she arches back into him, more, she wants more, she is dreaming, if she keeps her eyes closed it doesn't matter where she is, the aching dream will never end.

"Don't stop," she says, totally unaware that she has spoken. "More, do it again."

The docility of her desire inflames him, but he forces himself to stay as he is, steady and even, calm strokes gradually deepening, slowly wakening her body into rapture. He has no intention of stopping, not now, not this gentle tormenting bliss of her moans beside him, mingling soon with his own.

I cannot say what moves me more, sunk so deep in the watching, remembering the last time he touched her, crude and violent and furious, in a reeking stall in a public lavatory, or seeing their need for each other now, expressed truly, the only way they know how. Theirs is a language of touch, of sighs and gestures and moans, punctuated by rhythmic breathing and the occasional jarring slap of flesh upon flesh.

But it is Nick's language, and only he knows all the words.

Only with Olivia have I ever known him to make love without props or nasty games. Without a struggle. Without anything but a gentle heart.

It cannot last.

* * *

"I fell asleep," she says, snuggling into him, too contentedly lazy to move, lulled by his tenderness, or think.

"I noticed," he says. "What were you drawing?"

"The flat."

"Can I see?"

"Mmm."

He pulls away, kissing her shoulders, then reaches over to the table, bringing the pad into the bed, between them like a nestling baby.

"I'm afraid to look," he says, joking.

"Why? It's just a sketch."

"You know why," he says, and then turns back the cover. He sees the room I have furnished, the rumpled bed he is lying on, the peonies, petals drifting, he sees the lush folds of the drapes, the curved fat feet of the clock and the table. It's only a drawing, but it feels alive. There are prickles at his nape.

It is alive, watching him.

And then he sees a smudged blur that must be his face, a faint dim ghost, staring at him from the mirror, he sees M's face, as if underwater, in the other, and he shivers.

She can't know, she can't possibly know.

"You don't like it," she says.

"No," he says, careful to keep his voice calm, "I love it. It just startled me, that's all, my face in the mirror like that."

"Always watching, the pair of you."

He whips around to meet her gaze, but sees nothing but innocent pleasure in her handiwork.

"What?" she says, puzzled.

"Nothing," he says, kissing her. "Just you."

"You can have it, the sketch, I mean. A souvenir."

His face darkens. What is a souvenir but a token of memory, embodied in an object? A souvenir is not what he wants.

She pulls away, shrinking back into the pillows, watching him. "Don't, Nick, please. Don't spoil it."

There is a blankness seeping into the pores of his face, and he turns his head away. She sighs, relieved. Perhaps it was only a shadow.

I am watching him closely, curious. The fury building in him is always so predictable any director worth a tithe of his salary would have yelled cut, but for the moment Nick is acquiescent, retreating into that hiding place he rarely lets me see, because it is unbearable. I marvel, actually, at his skillful and near-instantaneous rearrangement of his features into calm, reassuring solicitude.

"Does this mean you've forgiven me?" he asks, his voice soft, pleading, as he turns back to her with a tenuous grin.

Her arms pull him down, his head in her lap. "Nick," she says, in between kisses, still intoxicated by the limpid unreality of her arousal, "will you do something for me?"

"What?" he says. "Anything."

"Let me."

"Let you what?"

"Let me." Reaching over to him.

His delight a beacon stabbing the darkness, shining in his eyes. "Why, Miss Olivia," he drawls, completely bemused, "I do believe you are a slut."

"Thanks," she says, blushing even as she fastens his arms to the silken restraints. "Coming from you that's a real compliment."

Nick is not about to tell her he knows how to slip out of these knotted cords whenever he wants to. This is far too much fun, pretending.

He watches, his eyes heavy-lidded, as her hands slide over him, stroking him, her own cat, the scented panther, her mouth, taking him, deep and engulfing, how he wishes he could touch her, and take this cool stranger as he pleases, how he strains against the cords binding his hands as she torments him.

I am engrossed, watching Olivia take charge of him, surprised that his arrogant dominance has acquiesced so meekly.

If only she knew what lies hidden in the trunk at her feet, but how can Nick dare tell her? How could I?

He shudders as she pulls away abruptly and hops out of bed.

"Come back, you bitch," he screams as she pads down the hall to the kitchen, bringing back a cold bottle of champagne and sitting down on the edge of the bed, where he cannot reach her, to tantalize him with her prolonged fussing with its opening.

She takes a long drink directly from the bottle, wiping her chin with the back of her hand and making Nick laugh. Her head spins, she wants it so, she cannot understand why this crazy mood has come over her, so outrageously unlikely, why all her determined anger has dissipated into nothingness, droplets of fog evaporating in morning sunshine, and all she wants now is to remain shut out against the world, suspended in the shadowy half-world of dreams and delight, the mindless delight in her body and his, and the airy denial of all the thoughts and aspirations that woke her in the middle of the night, drenched in sweat and too terrified to breathe.

"Shut up," she says, lightly slapping his cheeks, although she is secretly aghast that she can do so, lay a hand on someone, with such gleeful impunity.

She places the base of the bottle on his cock, stroking it up and down, cruelly slow, and he jerks stiffly against its cold wetness, telling her to stop. She smiles and ignores him, then pours a thin stream of champagne on his torso and begins to lick it off, languidly tantalizing, only her tongue touching him, lapping it up as it trickles off his chest to stain the embroidered sheets, circling his nipples, his lips, light as a spider's legs.

She drinks again, deeply. I have never seen her so brazen, so fearless, mounting him, teasingly, riding him as she pleases till she throws her head back, heedless of Nick, he is no more than a body beneath her to serve her needs, heedless of anything save the excruciating torment of the implacable, yearning passion she means to satisfy however she can.

She arches back into his knees, his legs bent up to support her weight, and cries out, then slowly slides down, stretching out languorously along his body, suffused with pleasure, before reaching over to stroke him into willingness, cajoling without uttering a word, making him do it again.

She is drunk, she knows, insatiably drunk with this shocking, unrelievable craving for libidinous oblivion.

When she is mine, Nick says to himself, straining against her, moaning softly, mesmerized, the stroking of her hands almost unbearably erotic, intoxicated by her transformation into this liquid creature he is sure he has molded, when she is mine this is how our days will pass, like this, boundless bliss binding them together, castaways from the demands of the world, demanding only this from each other, lost in themselves, awash in lust, the essence of desire.

Were his hands not bound, were he able to touch her and pull her close, I can almost imagine that this is how it is for other people, when they make love. The pure banality of straightforward coupling, so normal for other lovers, is as aberrant to Nick as his twisted games and choreographed ravishings would be to them.

What I saw between them today I have not seen in countless years of watching Nick, who cannot bear to be vulnerable in bed, or out. I had almost forgotten there are lovers who love.

This is the tape he will watch more than any other, I know, rewinding and watching, alone, over and over again.

I will make my own copy, editing out as much of Nick's body as I can, wanting only Olivia, engrossed in her sketching, or lying there dreaming, or telling Nick to shut up, brazen and selfish, her head thrown back in ecstasy as if she knew I was there, aching to see it. I will keep this tape hidden, safe from Nick's prying eyes, so I can watch it too, alone, in the dark.

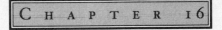

C H A P T E R   16

I have a headache, watching.

It is a dismal day, dank, a sky like seed pearls, milky layers
of gray, more opaque than Olivia's eyes, dense with damp,
the cold seeping into your bones like moisture trickling slowly
downward on an overwatered plant, raising goose bumps on
the flesh above them. All the color sucked dry. The room
needs colors, yes, that's it. Olivia's head is buried under a
white linen pillow, hand-embroidered by indentured servants
in Manila, no doubt, muffling the swelling roll of her moans,
endless and even as breakers dwarfing foolhardy souls, the
bobbing ants I used to watch from the cliffs over Malibu who'd
dared surf those constant rolling waves. I can't see Olivia's
hair, the bright mass of it hidden as Nick smothers her, moving
languorously up and down, he is taking his time, it is his
rhythm, pushing in deeper. Even the healthy ruddiness of his
skin, usually made even more rosy by the soft lighting and the
sheen of sweat from his exertions, seems a pale wash by the

creeping grayness of the lunchtime air. Too tedious, the dull
metallic glint of the camcorders. I am so weary of gloom and
wet and the oppressive walls of this room that I, for only half
a second, imagine what a scintillating diversion it would be if
Nick tore himself away and flipped open the lid of the trunk,
quickly rummaged through until he found the cat-o'-nine-tails,
and brought it down to leave thin precise slashes of crimson,
sudden dark welts breaking this monotony driving me mad,
scattering drops of blood on the crisp sheets like so many rose
petals.

Roses. Flowers. Yes, flowers. Fronds and palms. Green
grow the rushes-so. Peonies, poppies, baskets of pinks. I will
go to the market at Nine Elms tomorrow. Rise in the black
night and load my arms with blooming live things. I will smile
at a flirty flower girl grateful for attention from a man whose
face she cannot read. Neglected by a droopy husband who
still lies, snoring, beneath clammy sheets and dismal dreams,
she will not be hard to find. She will be breathless when I say
I want them all. All of them. Every last bloom.

She is puzzled. No one can want that many.

I do, I say, quietly unfolding a chunk of pound notes, I do,
but only if you help me load them in the car. Her eyes will
widen in disbelieving pleasure, two round patches pink as
anemone flushing her cheeks. I will follow her guileless and
giddy as we load cartfuls carefully in the car, her day's wages
earned so easily, oh how grateful those eyes will shine in the
dark as we coast to a secluded edge of the parking lot and I
push back the seat and her back with it. Yes, how grateful,
how eager when I sweep her cheeks with petals plucked from
a rose, how willing to submit when I kiss her tenderly, how
she will open herself to me, the fragrance flooding the car as
the blooms lie crushed under our weight. Oh yes, her eyes
will widen, large now with surprise when I push her arms
roughly above her head. No, she will say, a soft moss of fear

rising damply from her skin, pushing to get away, rolling her head spasmodically from side to side—

—as Olivia is doing now—

—no stop it, what are you doing let me go. No, *don't*—

Shhh, I will tell her, sweet, it's so sweet, you are my darling little flower, shhh. I will muffle her protests with kisses and her eyes will glisten like dew because she is helpless, crushed, she can only kiss me back, gasping, straining away from me as I push into her, hard, harder—

—as Nick is doing now—

—deeper into the blooms, she is buried in a rainbow. She will disappear, yes, her flesh now even pinker than anemone where my fingers trace delicate lines leaving a riot of color in their wake. She will moan now, no longer quite so fearful when my hands cup her breasts, when I kiss her cheeks downy with tears, shhh, I murmur when I push her down, filling her mouth until she gags.

You are my darling little flower.

Her eyes will close because she is mine. It is too easy, her surrender. I need her struggling, I will slap her anemone cheeks, pink, pinker. I will kiss the tears once more, anointed, perfumed by lust. Only now will I make her bloom, surrendering, flushed. She has no choice. Lift her face to the sun, breathe in the warmth, widen in delight or die, drooping. She does not want to die. Oh yes, she will breathe in her surrender, intoxicated with the fragrance of crushed beauty, oh *please* she will breathe.

Please.

Later, I will stand outside the car, smoking. She will pull on her tattered frock, dazed, running her fingers over bruised flesh as if it belonged to a stranger. She will not see, as I do, the faint polka of dots, tiny pricks of thorn, dancing like constellations across her backside. She will not feel them. She will not feel.

My darling little flower.

I will get in the car and drive in silence. The sky has barely lightened, the usual neon flash of Piccadilly dimmed by morning gloom, the statue of Eros appears to sleep, drooping. I will pull up in front of the shuttered Boots, and place the banknotes in her hand. She will not look at them, or me, but will hold them tight when she pushes the door handle and slides out, stumbling. I will close the door and drive away.

There are rose petals at her feet.

There is no color in this room.

Nick and Olivia lie still, sated.

I no longer have a headache.

I am still watching.

CHAPTER 17

There are days meant for languishing in bed, although few of us have the freedom to do so. There are times when the weight of the world presses so heavily on your shoulders that you think there is no reason why your lungs fill with air and you are not poisoned by the thoughts flashing through your mind more evanescent than fireflies. And there are times when the vast yawning abyss of anticipation so jangles your nerves, so awakens your senses, that even the smell of newsprint smudged on your fingers as you read your paper over a hurried cup of coffee is cause for celebration, the faint whiff of yesterday's perfume lingering as you sit next to a yawning young clerk in the subway, her shoes scuffed down at the heels because she is too poor or too dull to notice, so alive are you to the very cells in your body, aching to be awakened.

I stare at shoes a lot, they fascinate me. The true worth of character. Not only what is worn but how, and why, and what could that person possibly have been thinking when the laces were tied in clumsy drooping knots.

It was one of those days.

Nick does not look at shoes or smell stale perfume. He prefers a more pragmatic approach, even in his fantasies, even as he lies, waiting, his nerves jangling, for the sound of Olivia.

"I've been imagining what I'd do to you when you came in," Nick says as she is shrugging off her coat, her eyes stormy. "It's very passive-aggressive, you know, always being late."

"As if you'd know." She laughs, despite herself. "God, I haven't heard shrink-speak since I stopped seeing my therapist after my divorce."

"Actually, I do know," he says smugly. "I played a character like that once. Very handy, the psychological profiles, you know, all the free advice I get from overpaid so-called experts."

"I bet they just love you."

"They do."

"They believe what you tell them, don't they?"

"Of course."

"Do they have any idea what you don't tell them?"

Nick says nothing, stubbing out his cigarette, and she is sorry, biting her lip. His stillness scares her.

I sit up, a dark knot of foreboding looping through my gut.

"So, tell me," she says, if only to break the dreadful silence, clambering onto the bed next to him.

"Tell you what?"

"What you were imagining."

His face clears instantly. "What I was imagining," he muses. "What I've done to you before and what I'll do to you again."

"Don't you have anything better to think about?"

"No. There is nothing better to think about."

"Nothing at all."

"Of course not."

"Not your career."

"Fuck my career. It has nothing to do with me. I'm just the Nick in Nick Muncie Enterprises. McAllister and all the other assholes in suits take care of my 'career' for me. And what a *career* it is, all those blockbusters, all those front-end grosses and back-end grosses and slices of the pie, all those tidy little sequels for me, the trained monkey." His voice is harsh. "All that money, and all the shit that comes with it. And, oh yes, let's not forget *Faust* while we're on the topic of shit, shall we, what a great idea for our action superstar, a real movie, a real man, just the thing for our hero to play. Don't make me laugh. As if they thought I didn't hear *them* laughing, and snickering, and spreading rumors behind my back. Even the number-one box-office draw in the world is not immune to all that fucking Hollywood shit."

He lights up a cigarette, he doesn't care if she hates it, and runs his fingers through his hair. "Have you ever thought about the unconscionable amount of money I actually earn?" he asks. "Me, Nick Muncie, superstar, the most undeserving fuck who ever lived and breathed."

I'd had that bad feeling about today from the minute Olivia walked in the door, and it tightens more deeply when I hear Nick's unprovoked candor, and see the startled expression on Olivia's face. They are talking too much of the hell on earth where he lives, too much reality is beginning to seep through the leaded windowpanes, intruding on the fantasy of their gilded wonderland when Olivia should be lying underneath him, writhing in ecstasy, pleading.

"You're not undeserving," Olivia says, her arms around him. "I imagine you're paid what producers think you're worth, and that's why you earn it. Besides, I can think of a million things I'd do with all that money."

"Like what?"

"Oh, set up a foundation for young artists, for starters. Another one for art therapy for battered children, and—"

"That's the difference between us, isn't it?" he interrupts, he can't bear to hear any more. "You have a heart and soul and I have McAllister."

"Don't say that," she says, her eyes filling with tears. "Don't say that. Don't say anything else. Just kiss me."

He buries his head in her lap, and they stay like that, locked in a frozen embrace, until Nick comes back to himself with a start and kisses her so deeply she thinks she will never be able to draw another breath again.

"You're in a strange mood today," he says to her afterward, twirling a stray curl in his fingers. "I guess we both are. What is it?"

"I'm not sure," she says, but he feels her tighten. "I just woke up on the wrong side of the bed, I guess."

"What a delectable thought."

"Very funny," she says, pretending to swat him, then nestling down to him. He pulls her tight, caressing the round curves of her belly.

"I owe you an apology," she says eventually.

"What for?"

"For being a jerk. For being, as you so succinctly put it, passive-aggressive. Because I'm always late, and cranky when I come in. Acting like a spoiled little brat. I don't mean to, you know. I've always hated being late, actually. But when I'm walking across the park my feet just start slowing down, and . . . well, if you're going to do something, you should— I mean—" She buries her head in a pillow. "I don't know what I'm doing. I don't know who I am anymore."

He is still holding her tight. She can feel his tense breathing, and the absolute rigidity of his muscles.

They both know what she is trying to say.

The bad feeling is getting stronger, and my stomach is churning.

"What's the worst thing you ever did?" she asks, turning around to face him. It is a surprising question, even for Olivia.

I do not move from my perch, rooted with anxiety yet intrigued by their conversation, watching them, watching Nick, nerves on edge, to see if he snaps.

"I can't tell you that," he says.

"Why not? Is it that bad?"

"Does it matter?"

"Of course it matters," she says, sitting up, her eyes wide. "Everything matters. Everything that's happened has made you who you are."

"And who am I?" He sits up and snakes closer to her, pulling her back into his lap, scooting back with her until he is propped securely against the bedframe, holding her tight, one arm an iron vise across her chest, the other running down her body, bending her with him, caressing her breasts, his thumb and forefinger playing with her nipples till they harden, her belly, her thighs, his fingers swirling in that familiar teasing waltz of urgent hunger. She feels him growing harder against her back, it takes so little time for him to stiffen, and then take what he wants, over and over again.

His hands, swirling, harder, and faster. She is arching away from him, and he pulls her back, sliding up and into her.

"Who am I?" he asks again.

"Nick."

"Nick who?"

"Nick Muncie."

He claps one hand over her mouth. "Who am I?" he says, his voice raspy. "Say my name. Say it like this. I want to feel you say it."

She tries to bite his fingers, and he pinches her, cruelly, just to hear her scream beneath his hand.

"Who am I?"

"Nick." He feels her say it. "You fucking bastard, Nick." He laughs and takes his hand away.

"Why do you always have to ruin it?" she says, gasping, his abrupt changes of mood so unpredictable and terrifying, so inflaming, always leaving her defenseless against him. "You can never be nice, and just stay nice, never."

"You don't want me to just be nice and *stay* nice, so shut up and take it," he says, knowing her body too well, knowing that as long as he is moving like this inside her her protests are feeble shams and his fears are groundless. "You know you have to take it, whether you like it or not."

"Fuck you," she says, twisting away so suddenly that she falls free from him, and tries to crawl off the bed.

"So you want to play, do you," he says, grabbing her ankles and dragging her back as she claws helplessly for a handhold. "We'll play 'Who Am I?' and it's your turn to guess." He spanks her. "So," he says, punctuating each word with a re-sounding smack as she writhes frantically, trying to get away, "who am I?"

"Stop," she screams.

"Stop? No, I'm not 'Stop.' " Spanking her harder. "Try again."

"Nick," she says, sobbing with rage and pain. "You're Nick."

"Now we're getting somewhere," he says, lifting her up and telling her to blow her nose on the large handkerchief he keeps tucked inside one of the pillows, there, like a good girl, before turning her around to sit back on his lap, facing him this time, one hand gripping her wrists tight behind her back, kissing the tears away, smiling triumphant as she twists her head away from his lips, smiling still as he impales her and she shudders, despite herself. "Where were we? Ah, yes," he says, "we're playing 'Who Am I?' So, who am I?"

"Nick," she says, her eyes shut, her ass on fire, riding him, heedless. "Nick Muncie."

"Nick Muncie, who?"

"Nick Muncie, superstar." He lets go of her hands and she leans forward into him, pressing down, hard, feeling him deeper, her breathing ragged. "The most famous actor in the world."

"Am I?"

"Yes."

"I am?"

"Yes." Oh, why so many questions, she can't think. "More famous than anyone. More, more, more."

He is laughing softly, watching her, so close to the brink. "More than anyone else in the world?"

"Yes, more," she says, delirious, until she can bear it no longer, how can he hurt her and then make her feel like this, it's not possible, no, don't stop, she is falling in the sea, drenched, wave after wave of unbearable satisfaction flooding over her.

When she can think again she opens her eyes, surprised to see Nick's face so close, still with that awful smug grin, and she is suddenly aware of a sharp stinging pain on her rear.

"You prick," she says, pouting. "You spanked me."

"You deserve it, and worse. Much, much worse."

"Let me go."

"Not a chance." He is still hard, inside her, rocking her back and forth, imperceptibly, and she bites her lip to keep from crying out. "We're still playing."

"I don't like this game."

"Ah, but I do. And I think you do, too." His hands on her breasts, pulling her down. "So tell me, who am I?"

"I told you already," she says, stretching out her full length on him, as he wants her to, she has no choice but to obey the overwhelming mastery of her will when she is lying in his arms, she isn't strong enough to fight him, no woman is. Not like this. "Nick. Muncie. Superstar. The most famous actor in the world. More famous than anyone."

"Anyone?"

"Yes."

"Acting is my job."

"Yes."

"My life."

"Yes. I don't know. How should I know?"

"It is." His grip tightens, squeezing her till she cries out. "Acting all the time. You have no fucking idea."

He pulls away from her suddenly, pushing her off, and sits up, lighting another cigarette, and she is so startled by his abrupt standoffishness that she sits up behind him.

"Acting at what, Nick?"

"Acting at *living*," he says savagely.

There is a look on his face she's never seen before, worse than the silence she'd glimpsed there already and wished she could block out of her dreams. Not pain, not anguish, just emptiness, a gaping black void, his features still so starkly handsome and so terrifyingly empty, a face wiped clean of any human emotion as if a squeegee had passed over it like the one Nick used to use at the Sunoco station in Beverly Hills, retreating inward, far away, dropping deep into a fathomless cavern.

It is like looking at the face of annihilation itself.

I haven't seen that face for a long time. No one should ever have to see that face.

She doesn't know him at all, Olivia realizes with a shiver so sudden it is like footsteps tap-dancing on her grave, all she knows is how much he wants her. It is their unspoken rule not to talk of who they are, who he is or his life outside this flat. She only knows what he means to other people, what his body means to her—and hers, she guesses, to him—but not where he came from, what incomprehensible brutality molded him, what sparked that indefinable longing driving him on into life, plaguing him always to take more than is offered, even when he has her nakedness, exposed and vulnerable, dissolving into his, bending to his will, and begging him to stop.

For the first time, she is truly afraid.

He wants more. He will always want more.

"You want to know what I was like?" Nick says, the dreadful blankness fading into the simplicity of anger. "Okay, I'll tell you what I was like. I'll tell you a nice little story about what I was like, since you asked. I was just a kid. I needed money."

She doesn't ask why a kid would need money, she thinks she can imagine.

"I knew this boy, and he told me he had a secret place to get some quick change."

He sits staring out the window for a few silent minutes, dragging on his cigarette. A terrible dread is growing inside Olivia, akin to mine, and she says nothing.

"You mean M?" she asks finally, because the silence is worse than the knowing.

"Not M. Before M." He turns to look right at me. A warning. As if I could do anything now, my nerves jangling.

"We'd go the night after the funerals," Nick says. "No one ever found out, because we were strong, and quick. We'd get jewelry and watches and fence them for a fraction of their value because we didn't know where else to sell them. Once we got a guy with hundred-dollar bills in all his pockets. That lasted awhile." He leans back on the pillows, blowing smoke rings. "They were dead, and I was hungry. They didn't know."

"Go on," Olivia says, trying to keep the revulsion out of her face. "There must be more."

He stubs out the cigarette and pulls her close and she lies

cuddled in his arms, sinking into him. His fingers find their way inside her, a feather duster, idly stroking, because he can always do that, detached and mechanical, even though the rest of him is miles away. She shudders, not in the pleasure he assumes, but from nervous apprehension.

"I'm not sorry," he says. "It doesn't matter."

"I don't believe you."

"Don't be stupid," he says, his fingers pressing, insistent, harder, and she tries to pull away but he won't let her go, not now. "What do the dead know?" he asks, his voice blunt. "I can just see you, you know, you and your precious little Frog bastard up there at the gates of heaven so smug and secure, expecting Saint Peter to let you in. Do you think you'll end up there or wherever it is people like you go, looking down on all the mourners at your funeral? Or will you be some screaming ghost standing by your grave, scaring off the nasty little boys like me who come to steal the rings on your fingers and bells on your toes?"

She is struggling wildly against him, what he expects from her, what he covets, what she always does, without thinking, because, with him, it has always been that way. He wrenches one of her hands back to feel his hardness. "Does this feel better," he says savagely, forcing her to stroke him, "better than the cold wet ground? Are you as wet as the cold wet ground? Of course you are, because you know what you like, and you can lie to yourself all you want, and always show up late because you're scared, and guilty, and tell yourself that you don't really care about me or the dead, but the bitter truth is that right now you don't care about anything else except how I'm going to fuck you."

He shifts his weight away for just a second and she kicks back, wildly. "Liar," she screams.

He laughs and twists down to the side of the bed, knifing his legs around her so she can't escape, feeling for his favorite whip stashed underneath, just in case, the one he'd had made after I found the Murano vase. The artisan had sculpted a glass handle to fit exactly in Nick's hand, hand-blowing with intense precision the looping swirls of red and orange, delicate and delicious together, yet far less fragile than they seem. It is an object of exquisite beauty, perversely attached to a sleek implement of pain.

Nick swishes it back and forth in the air, testing his wrist. When Olivia hears the horrid noise she tries to bite him, but her legs are pinioned and Nick quickly turns back up, pushing her face down into the pillows and straddling her, trailing the thin end of the whip down her back, like a snake, watching her body quaver helplessly beneath it.

"You can struggle all you want but you can't get away because you're not dead and buried in the cold wet ground, and I'm not going to steal the precious little ring your precious little Frog bastard gave you." He whacks her hard across her ass, once, twice, again, the welts so darkly pink on her white skin, rising instantly, slender strips of embossed pain, and she is screaming for him to stop but he won't stop at this, no, not when he can force his way inside her, writhing under his weight.

"It doesn't take you long to beg," he says. "I didn't think you were such a wimp."

"Let me go," she is still screaming, "I'll kill you let me go let me."

"No," he says, turning her over so she lies on her back, the pressure on her welts a burning fire, swiftly fastening her hands to the silken cords as he always does, then leaning over to pick up two fat down pillows that have fallen to the floor, propping them gently under her ass, smiling as she winces. "Better?" he asks sarcastically, tracing a finger down her face, her neck, circling her breasts, caressing, slow, so slow, kissing her belly, and slipping inside her again. "I thought you wanted to hear a story," he says, moving languidly in and out, in and out, probing until she is certain she will go quite mad, but he is not even close to letting her go quite mad enough.

He has the triumphant grin again, propped on his elbows, brushing her hair gently out of her face even as he goes on, relentless. "And then do you know what I did?" he says.

She shakes her head no, unable to speak, her chest heaving.

"We got a job working for a crook in a funeral parlor. And after the viewing, when we were supposed to be loading the body into the hearse, we'd open the casket and grab whatever we could.

"One time there was this guy and we were trying to get this big fat diamond, a really nice diamond, tons bigger than yours, off his big fat finger."

"Stop," she says. "Stop."

"He was fat, that bastard, a greedy fat pig, and he was dead dead dead, but we really wanted that ring and we only had a minute to get it off. In my pocket I had a jar of hair grease, the same gunk they'd put on the stiff's hair, but it didn't work, and we didn't have time to get anything else. So I took out my knife and cut off his finger."

Moving on her, cruelly persistent, his fingers stroking her body, teasing, his eyes on hers, not letting her go, she asked for it, and he is going to watch her when she hears it.

"Do you want to know what happened?" he asks, his voice softening, so tranquilly at odds with the revulsion of his story.

"No," she says, turning her head to the side. He turns it back.

"I sold the ring," he says, whispering, his lips so close to her ear, kissing her cheeks, her eyes, kissing her, endless kisses till she whimpers, hooking her legs around him, desperate to pull him closer, she needs him close, there, just there. "Diamonds are forever."

She laughs, she can't help it, this can't be happening, it is a dream, a perverse, surreal dream, her head is spinning, there, don't tell me anymore, don't talk, just kiss me, there.

She doesn't even realize she has spoken.

"I sold the finger, too," he is saying, sweat dripping into her eyes, salt, like tears, blinding her to all but the hypnotic drone of his voice and the feel of his body on hers, a captive audience. "It was worth more than a ring. A lot more. A lot. A lot," he says, biting her lips until he can't bear it anymore, and he grinds into her, ecstatic, for the briefest of seconds, transported away from all memory of what made him.

He loosens her arms and kisses her sore wrists, then strips off one of the satin pillowcases and dips it in the ice water of the champagne bucket he always keeps by the bed, delicately wiping the angry welts he'd inflicted only moments before.

"Is that really the worst thing you ever did?" she asks, trying not to flinch at his touch.

"What do you think?"

"I think not," she says slowly.

"Well, what about you?"

"The worst thing I've ever done?" she muses. "The worst thing you can do is deliberately hurt someone you love."

"Is it?" He pulls away, wads the pillow, faintly smeared with pink, into a ball, and throws it in the corner. "Is it?"

She turns around to face him, wincing, and sees the same terrifying emptiness robbing all character from his features.

"The worst thing is no love," he says, his gaze locked into some primal memory, blinded. "The worst thing is when you do it because no one's ever loved you."

He is talking to a ghost.

I can't watch this.

Olivia's face is troubled. Does she love him or simply pity his pain, does it matter, and if she does why can't she say it, what will happen to her if she does, what more will he demand of her? She should be flinging her arms around him with no hesitation, holding him tight, she should be smothering him with kisses, deeply reckless, she should be saying I love you I love you till there is no speech left inside her.

Instead she is lying on the bed, sore and stinging, with tears filling her eyes, wondering wildly what to do, she must say something, something real, put into words the ineffable moments of their time together. But it's not real, she tells herself, these fantastical interludes in a secret gilded hideaway, created of lust, of amusement, and no more substantial. That's why she can be here. She can shut the door behind her and it no longer exists. There is nothing to hold on to but a sketch in her studio, his portrait long gone, crated up and shipped away to the house in the hills, nothing to remember save a fading scar on her leg, the faint imprint of the lash, or the bruises, brightly colored horrible blossoms slowly fading into greens and yellows, soon to disappear as he will back across the ocean.

Does she love him, does it matter, it's not possible to only love him at lunch, that's not what love is, it isn't love.

She has to think before she speaks, and that is answer enough for me.

It's too late, anyway.

Nick does not even know that he's been waiting for her declaration, only that the emptiness is so habitual he no longer expects it to be filled.

Only Olivia came close. Not the real Olivia lying here beside him, the woman fearful of the truth he'd see if he looked upon her face as I do now. The dream Olivia, the Olivia who is coming with him when he leaves, although he has not yet asked her. The dream Olivia knows instinctively, and will oblige him, whatever he says, and wherever he goes.

Her body is throbbing as she walks quietly back across the park, her feet dragging with lassitude over the frozen grass, her breath puffs of white smoke in the dull sky, her hands clenched deep in her pockets, replaying the unbelievable scene they have just enacted, in slow motion.

He didn't say he loved her, and she is glad, grateful for the words unspoken, and the silent, immeasurable chasm that will always keep them apart.

CHAPTER 18

I would drive along the coast, just after dawn, lost alone in a world dissolved in mist, the fog obscuring the waves, the world condensed in gray droplets. Early in the morning, when the sky is that peculiar damp blue threatening never to fade into the brightness of day; early in the morning, when only the garbage trucks and the hungover and the displaced of the earth are moving, when even rats and roaches are expected to sleep; then, early in the morning, I would get in the black car and drive, just drive, up the coast, drive a little too fast, too fast for the Harley that would only be skidding on the dew-soaked asphalt, concentrating on nothing but the rhythm of my foot on the clutch and my fingers on the stick, caressing the knob, shifting, hit the clutch, shift, move forward into the murky air, mind empty of all thoughts and pain, wide and vast as the ocean crashing soundlessly to my left. It was as if I were still, stranded in place, and the world were unrolling through my window, rushing past me, I could not stop it. If

I saw the horsemen of the apocalypse galloping past into the enveloping mist it would not be surprising. Only when other cars began to creep into view would I turn back home to where Nick lay sleeping, legs entwined with a blonde still blindfolded, she too exhausted to dream, yet eager to resume whatever contortions he demanded of her.

I cannot drive in London, I cannot breathe this damp air of a landscape so contained, as if the very hills were squashed down into the earth. Nowhere here can I imagine the endless open vistas of the desert, shimmering mirages and land parched into empty salt flats and twisting alluvial canyons. I should have driven to the moors, bleak, cold, and enshrouded in gloom, seeping into your skin, the moss oozing, alive, the wet pulsing, a wild creature skulking just under the surface, wanting to eat, waiting to devour anyone who dared step over it.

I want to be hot in the desert breathing deep the dry clean scent of heat, driving, sweat gluing me to the seat, the wind a sauna in my hair. I want to leave this place, I wish we'd never come.

It will end in tears, Olivia said. It will end in tears.

It will end.

I cannot drive because Nick has forbidden me to leave for longer than a few hours, now, and then only on days when he is so preoccupied with the scenes to shoot that I am dispensable. Those days are rare, he needs me by him, he needs me.

"I close my eyes and I see her," he says to me. "I see her everywhere."

And so I give in to his needs, as I have always done, because there is nothing else to save me from it.

Toledo thinks this preoccupation clouding Nick's eyes is an even deeper concentration because the end is near, and he pushes Nick, harder, because it is so visible, and so good. What he cannot envision is that Nick's eyes are haunted all the time, seeking knowledge he knows he'll never find. All Toledo sees is Nick on the set, inhabiting the character of a man so like and yet impossibly unlike himself, living and breathing as this creature daring to take a journey in the hopes that his heart might awaken, daring himself as he wonders if he will indeed be able to embrace death, the rightful death he has challenged, with a willingness of spirit, and a swiftly murmured prayer for his soul.

What Nick started as a whim and a dare is now the only railing separating him from the plunge into the abyss where obsession calls him, echoing endlessly the sound of her name.

Sometimes I still wake at dawn, the sky the color of stale milk, and sit on the balcony at the hotel and watch the world awaken, barges down the Thames, stirring the mud, worms of cars and trucks attacking the traffic circles, clouds scuttling like the smoke rising from my cigarette, wondering what visions came wandering, unbidden in the night, fluttering gently behind Olivia's queer gray eyes, clenching tight her muscles, and disturbing her dreams.

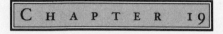

C H A P T E R 1 9

She is meandering down the mews, swinging her bag, her
limbs still languid with lingering kisses, her lips bruised, when
she sees the back of a familiar figure paying a taxi driver in
front of her studio.

Olivier. It isn't possible.

Her heart stops in an instant of stunned shock, and her knees
nearly buckle. She should be flying into his arms, so happy is
she that he has stolen time that is not his to steal, to be here,
with her as she has begged him to so many times, her voice
crackling with the effort of holding back tears she does not
want him to hear, but instead she steps quickly into the shadowy recess of a doorway, shivering with guilty, anxious dread.
She can't let him see her now, not after lunch, not as she reeks
of Nick, still feeling the imprint of his body, the soreness of
her wrists, his lips toying with her nipples, the endless caresses, the sticky wetness between her legs. Her fingers still

laden with him, he took her fingers and licked them one by one, suckling them, and she was helpless.

She runs down to the end of the Mews, and flags the very same taxi that has just dropped off Olivier.

Porchester Baths, she tells the driver, slumping down on her seat and trying to calm the frenzied beating of her heart. The baths will sweat the shame away.

I can't take it anymore, she is thinking, this is it, I can't lie anymore, I don't want to lie anymore. Olivier flying home on the few days he has for a long-overdue break, the shocking boredom of all those hours in the airplane, away from his work, jeopardizing his life, and here she is crying in the backseat of a taxi driving off in the opposite direction, hating herself as she examines her wrists to see if there are any bruises to give her away.

She sits in the steam room until she is panting, dashing from the wet heat searing her lungs to squat, breathless, for only a second, in the plunge pool, the cold of its still blue water shattering, making her nerves dance in jittery rhythm, before running back to the sauna, stretching out on the cedar bench, the only sound the ragged hiss of steam when she ladles water onto the hot stones, and the sharp intake of the deep breaths she is gulping to still the jumping thuds of her heart.

The baking heat of the ritual in the baths, purifying her pores and cleansing away the scent of her sins, soothes her shattered senses, roasting Nick's smell out of her, cooking her tortured thoughts in a steaming brew of hot burning liquid, fat drops of sweat rolling down her face past her eyes misted with tears.

In the baths no one can tell that you're crying.

After she dresses she calls the machine, telling Nick curtly that Olivier has shown up unexpectedly and she doesn't know how long he is staying, and she will call back as soon as possible.

By the time she hurries home she has no problem pretending to be surprised.

They make love in the dark, in her tiny bedroom beneath her studio that Nick will never see, lit only by candles. I want to see you flicker like a ghost, because only a ghost of you is here when you're gone, she says to him. Olivier laughs softly at her, drowsy with travel fatigue, teasing her that she has gone all melodramatic as she lights the wicks, a long matchstick shaking in her fingers.

She cannot tell him making love in the daylight might make her think of Nick. She cannot tell him she is afraid of what he might see on her body, but he is very weary and his eyes remain closed, and for the moment she is safe.

Afterward, they lie intertwined and content, all trace of Nick vanishing like the thin plume of smoke from her candles.

"Let's get married now," she says.

"Right now? In the middle of the night?" He laughs.

"Tomorrow, then. Let's go to the registry and do it. I don't want to wait any longer. I can't bear it."

"But darling," he says, "I've got to go back tomorrow morning, first thing."

She props herself up to look at him, stunned. "You mean you flew all this way only for a night?"

He shrugs. "It was worth it. I missed you."

Tears start to her eyes, and he pulls her close, tenderly, to kiss them away.

Annette is lying on the chaise next to Olivia in the steam room, patting a garishly pink clay mask onto her face, her hair sleeked back with conditioner, and her flesh glowing rose in the shimmering heat.

"You look like a big pink rabbit," Olivia says.

"And you look like a lady with a problem."

Olivia rolls on her side to look at her. "What's that supposed to mean?"

"I'm not going to ask," Annette says, pointing to the thin trail of a welt, nearly healed but still visible, on Olivia's hip. "I've always preferred discretion, as you know, so I've been waiting for you to tell me. Why, for example, you seem to be avoiding me. Why you hardly come by the gallery anymore. Why you look like you're wrestling with all the demons in hell, my darling. That sort of thing."

Annette knows. Of course she knows. Even if it weren't written all over Olivia's face, it's been written all over her body, naked and sweating in the baths, with reminders she's so accustomed to seeing that she pays no attention, not to bruises on her arms and legs that aren't the result of clumsiness, or the sideways stares of other women around her.

"Of course, I can hardly blame you," Annette adds, matter-of-factly.

"What?"

"I was there when you met, at lunch that day. I saw him looking at you like that. Nick Muncie. Your famous subject. I don't see how you could have resisted him. I wouldn't have." She puts down the jar of her mask and picks up another, rubbing a cream smelling of coconuts into her cuticles. "Quite frankly I was wishing he'd look at me like that. Adrian never does, and never will, I suppose. I don't think he has it in him, poor dear. But I should think every woman wants a man to look at her like that, at least once in her life."

"You're lucky he didn't," Olivia says, relieved to talk of it at last to a trusted friend who will not judge her more harshly than she already judges herself. "Looking is one thing. Giving in to it is another." She sighs deeply and drinks from a water bottle. "When Olivier came home the other day to surprise me I thought I was going to go mad. And you know what I did? I ran, ran from Olivier! I saw him at the door, and I ran away, because he would have looked at me and known, instantly, all I could think was I have just come from my lover, will he notice, don't let him find out, please. It was pathetic. That's the real disgustingness of betrayal."

"How very American."

"Don't tease me, Annette, please don't," she says, tears in her eyes. "It's completely out of control. I never meant for it to last so long, I never wanted . . . I'm going to crack any minute if I don't get out of it."

"Because of Olivier."

"It's more than that. You don't know what Nick's really like."

"Then tell me."

"I can't."

"Do you love him?"

"When I think of love, I don't think of Nick," Olivia says, only realizing it as she speaks. "Love belongs to Olivier, and what we have together, we just fit. Nick's about wanting, and taking what he wants, about lust, about pure animal fucking . . . he's—"

"—a beast?"

Olivia smiles, barely. "Yes, a beast. His own species, master of his kingdom. It's what I saw in him to paint. It's what I wanted him to show me."

She sighs. "He rented a flat, it's just around the corner from here," she continues, "this marvelous magical flat with the most gorgeous things in it. It's so golden and quiet, I've never heard anyone else in the building, it was as if we were sealed off from the world in it, and it was made only for us to be together. Our safe house. As soon as I'd go in, up the flight of stairs, put my key in the lock, and open the door, I felt as if I no longer existed, not me, Olivia, the person I thought I was, I'd disappeared, melted into this room where Nick was waiting for me. He'd always be there before I arrived, lying on the bed, reading a script or dozing, and as soon as he touched me the real Olivia vanished, I was suspended in some bizarre intoxicating dream, and I told myself that as long as it wasn't real then I could take it, whatever he'd concoct, whatever he'd do to me. I wouldn't wake up till I walked out the door, and I was always shocked that only an hour or two had gone by, that the air was still cold and wet on my face, and I could hear the traffic and see the people walking around, minding their own business. Only then would I wake up. I'd wake up amazed that life is going on just as it always has, me painting, you selling, Olivier at the piano, all that I had before, and all that I ever wanted."

"I understand, Olivia," Annette says, wiping off her mask. "At least I think I do."

"But how can anyone understand what he does to me when I can't understand it myself, or why I let him?"

"I don't know."

"Every time he pushed me, just a little bit further, I almost couldn't see how far I'd gone, or that he'd hurt me, till I got home. And then I'd hate myself, swear I'd never see him again, till the next time. I always let him, it's part of the game we played, it's always been a game to him, dominating me, and I welcomed it, actually, giving in to him made it easier for me to deal with the guilt, because I could tell myself it wasn't really me playing, it was some awful creature who was curious and flattered by the attention, some silly girl who was lonely and wanted one last fling, as if I were punishing Olivier because he was so far away." Her face is deeply flushed, and she wipes the tears and the sweat away, closing her eyes.

"Are you guilty because of him, and worrying about Olivier, or because you like it?"

"What are you, the shrink of sauna?"

"For the moment."

"Both, of course. Nick is . . . well, he's always been overwhelming. What got him off was to feel me helpless, and my pleading with him to stop. I never liked feeling that way, not really, it's not how—"

"—how Olivier makes love to you."

"How anybody ever did. Nick didn't make love, he fucked me as if it were the only thing he had to keep him alive. And I thought if I only saw him for a short time I'd be able to control it, but that was ridiculously naive. What a fool I am."

"How could you have known?"

"Oh, I knew, all right, that's part of what was so tantalizing, sensing that unbelievable power in him. It was so erotic, feeling the enormity of this man's sexual potency focusing on me, watching me when I was painting him. I must've encouraged it then, subconsciously, or even overtly. I know I did, because feeding off that concentration gave me the strength to capture it in his face, in the portrait."

"That's why it's the best you've ever done."

"But even when I felt that desire oozing out of him, when he made me feel so alive, painting, I couldn't understand why me, why he wanted me."

"Maybe because he sensed that you didn't want him."

"I wonder. I thought that, at first, you know, no one ever says no to a Hollywood star, blah blah, spoiled jerk, can have any woman he wants, but it's become more than that. Now I see what I can do to him, too. It's an addiction, a physical addiction. That I'd even want one bit of it after seeing Olivier like that the other day makes me sick."

"It doesn't sound to me as if you really want it anymore. I imagine you're not quite aware of it, but you've been talking about it as if it's already over, describing him in the past tense, you know, as if it's something that happened to you a long time ago."

"I wish. It's much more complicated than what I might want anymore."

"Why?"

"Because I'm afraid." She towels the sweat away. "I'm afraid he won't let me go. Last time we met he asked me to go back to L.A. with him, he told me all about his house, how he lives, and made me memorize his private number. He thinks I'm seriously considering it even though he knows I want out. He's sure he can do something to change my mind."

"Like what?"

"I don't know. Not having something he wants is making him angry. The more mad he feels, the more he feels anything, the more unable he is to suppress his anger, and it scares me."

"Do you think he's in love with you?"

Olivia frowns and rearranges her towels. "No, I don't think so. God, I hope not. I told you, Nick's not about love."

"So what are you going to do?"

"What can I do, send him a letter? I'll tell him, I have to. I'll tell him that it's over, cold turkey. The film's almost finished, and I'm going to leave." She sits up, splashing more tepid water on her face. "God, I can't breathe, thinking about it."

"You need a cold shower."

"I need a lot more than that."

"Do you want me to come with you?"

Olivia laughs, touched. "You are a darling, but it's my mess, and I have to deal with it." She doesn't tell Annette about the terrifying blankness sweeping all humanity from Nick's face, about the bonds imprisoning her to the bed, and to him. Even the heat of this room parching her skin can't stop her from shivering at the thought of it. "And afterward, I'll disappear, I can't risk seeing him. And I don't want him to know where I'm going."

"With Olivier."

"Yes."

She stands up, too quickly, and her head spins. Annette

grabs her arm, righting her. "Come on, sweetheart, time for some cold water on your face," she says.

"I'm okay," Olivia says. "It's just the heat making me dizzy."

It's more than the heat, she says to herself, it's much more than the heat.

She has carefully planned what she is going to say to him, calm and assured and unyielding, rehearsing it over and over again in her mind as if she were a young actress auditioning for a role in *Faust*, but he spoils it as soon as she walks in the door and drops her bag with a thud.

"You're late. I've been waiting to see you for a week, and you were supposed to be here nearly an hour ago," Nick says, the panic of waiting edging into his voice, barely masking the fury hiding underneath. "So do me a favor. Don't say 'I shouldn't have come.' You're here, so shut up about it."

"Okay, I won't," she says, throwing back her hair, "and I won't shut up about it either. I'll just tell you this is the last time, because I can't take it any longer."

"No you won't."

"Why not?"

"Why do you make it so difficult for yourself?" he says, exasperation seeping into his voice like mud down the slopes of Topanga Canyon during the floods the year before. "You're here, now, because you want to be, whether you mean it or not, so stop making excuses, and just . . ."

"Just what? No, go on, tell me. Just what?" She has completely forgotten her lines, and is spoiling for a fight.

Anger is becoming easier, for Olivia.

Nick has that kind of effect on people.

She still has not realized how any impatient fury in her charges him with a *frisson* of intense amusement, seeing her fueled with resentment as he so often is, masking it behind the habitual cloak of polite charm. He is already plotting with lurid anticipation exactly how he will pounce on her, in just a minute or two, as soon as she drops her guard, twisting her anger into a sharp stinging weapon, and impaling her with it.

"Time. All I want is time," he says to her, instantly relieved and confident, smoothing the vexation from his voice. As usual it is a splendid act, because I can tell from the look on her face, already thawing and less wary, that she has absolutely no idea what he's really thinking. "We're nearly finished shooting, you know that. After everything you've said—or not said—I can guess you're not exactly planning to hop on a plane with me." He is so blasé. "Therefore I assume this time left is all we've got."

"You want more than time, Nick, and I haven't got it to give to you. And I won't start my marriage by cheating, and betrayal."

"You're not married yet. You're not betraying him."

"I'm betraying *myself*," she says fiercely. She runs her hands through her hair, exasperated, and defensive. "Please, Nick, it's got to stop." Her voice softening. "Before it goes bad. Before it gets worse." Pleading, desperate. "And you're leaving . . ."

Her voice trails away when she sees him sit, rigid, with a frightening stillness on the bed, that blank look on his face again, that horrible empty expression bereft of any human emotion. She closes her eyes, she can't face it, not that look again, make it go away, she can't bear to see that horror haunting her dreams again, it is too terrifying. Before she dares open her eyes, before she can try to reach for the doorknob and run down the stairs and away from him, his arms are around her like a vise she's felt so many times before, and he throws her facedown on the bed.

"Tell me you can," he says, in an instant tugging off her coat, and pulling her sweater over her head so she is blinded, smothered by the heavy wool, "tell me you can live without this. Tell me." Slipping her arms from her sleeves and imprisoning them, viciously pulling the cords tighter than they've ever been, pushing the sweater off her face so he can see her suffer and hear her shrieking that she'll never tell him anything he wants to hear, never, he'll never see her again, ever. She is kicking at him furiously as he reaches down and pulls off her boots, throwing them to the floor, before kneeling over her legs to still them and tugging the snap of her jeans, the zipper, how he always managed it so quickly she never could quite figure, not thinking it was years of practice, twisting them off as she tries to kick him again, and fails.

"Tell me you can't take it any longer," he says. "Go on."

"You make me sick."

"Yes, I know."

He calmly backs away from her thrashing legs, and knots a leg of her jeans to the bedpost, grabs her right leg, running his fingers down her foot with a nasty tickle, his lips brushing her instep, and then ties the other leg of her jeans around her ankle. His movements are methodical and precise, as if he's performed them a thousand times, and she watches with an appalling numbed fascination, because there is nothing else she can do, as he pulls off his belt, dropping it on the comforter, and then slides down his jeans, an inch at a time, his hands on his thighs, caressing, knowing she cannot help but stare at this excruciatingly lingering striptease, taunting her in slow motion as he flaunts his virility above her, so raw and so unmerciful, just out of reach.

"Did you like what you saw?" he asks, not expecting an answer as he neatly knots his jeans next to hers, tying her other ankle to them so she is helplessly spread-eagled on the bed.

He's never done that to her, never dared render her quite so appallingly exposed, but time is running short, and so is his judgment.

She feels a stab of pure hatred as he lowers himself down and slides against her skin.

"Get off me," she says, her voice low, and he hears it catch and knows this time she truly means it, but he is already deep inside her and has no intention of listening to her, even if she is screaming that she hates him, forever and ever.

"You don't hate me," he says, "you want me."

"I don't want you. I hate you."

"Who do you hate more?" he asks sarcastically. "Me, or your own sweet self for being here?"

She opens her mouth, furious. "You, you despicable pig."

"Ah," he says. "The truth hurts, doesn't it? Because you don't hate this," he says, slowing his manic pace and swirling his fingers the way she likes it best. "You can't tell me you hate this."

"I do hate it, and you."

"Not this," he says, pulling out and leaning down to stab at her with his tongue, sliding his hands under her hips as she struggles against him, easing the ache of this familiar torment only when he hears her entreaties to let her go.

"No," he says, picking up his belt, "I'm not listening to you, because you don't know what you're saying." He whacks the sensitive insides of her thighs, once, twice, one long thin welt on each, the pain of it shocking her, then bends down to her again.

"Stop it, please stop," she is sobbing even as she arches against him in helpless satisfaction. "Let me go."

"It's only this, Olivia," he says, kneeling over her, huge and feral, "we have only this. That's all there is."

For once, I can't argue with him. He is telling the absolute truth.

"This, my darling Olivia, this is why you're here."

She closes her eyes, he's right, the bastard, she does hate herself, betrayed by her body and his wicked mastery of it, conquering her senses. But not her spirit. It is easier to capitulate than to fight him.

She cannot win. She can only escape.

"You'll always want this," he says, bringing her to the brink again, and toppling her over the edge.

"Will you do one thing for me before you go?" he asks, watching her dress, her movements jerky.

"What?" Her voice is flat, emotionless. She is still very angry, and he knows not to push her.

"Give me a weekend."

Her eyes widen, startled.

"It's always been lunch," he explains, careful to keep his voice relaxed, conversational. "We've never had any time together, not really. Not a whole day, and not a whole night."

She shakes her head no.

"Please, Olivia, please," he says, kneeling on the bed, his eyes instant pools of desperate liquid pleading. "I know you want to end this. I know you hate me. I'll never ask you anything again, I'll never see you again, I'll go back to L.A., I'll leave you alone forever, just give me a weekend." He sees her hesitating, this is how he'll trip her, persuade her to do as he says with the lovely lying promise that he understands what she wants, and he'll let her be. "Please, Olivia, I'm begging you, don't leave me this way. You said it yourself, that we should end it before it goes bad. Before it gets worse. I don't want to end it with anger between us."

Don't end it. The unthinkable.

"I'll think about it," she says.

"That's not good enough. There's no time. I have commitments, you know that. Everyone wants something from me, and I've got to let them know, soon."

They can wait. There is all the time in the world for lunch, if Nick Muncie really wants it.

She stares at him, wavering, wondering if this is an act, or some twisted trick, wanting to keep hating him and wanting to give in. After what he's just done to her, the awful specter of the blankness on his face coupled with the raw, brute force she felt shimmering, ripe and potent, coiled in his muscles, she is more afraid than ever, afraid of fighting. She hasn't got the strength for it, not when he is offering her the chance to escape.

All he wants is a weekend.

"When?" she says.

"I can pick you up Friday night, I think. We're shooting odd hours this week."

"Okay," she says. "One weekend. On one condition."

"Anything."

"That you mean it."

"Mean what?"

"That you'll leave me alone."

"Whatever you want."

"You promise."

"I promise. I'll leave you a message when I know what time I'll be free. M will pick you up."

"Fine," she mutters, not wanting him near her studio. "Why am I doing this?" She leaves without saying goodbye, slamming the door, and Nick stretches lazily, a languid cat, before he looks over at me. I turn off the tapes, wondering what kind of diabolical scheme he is already plotting in the feverish recesses of his mind, what sort of fiendish trickery can be making him smile, so spitefully exultant, as he gets dressed, humming a tuneless song, already counting the hours till Friday, when he'll have her in his arms, utterly vulnerable to the perversity of his passion, convinced that he can persuade her to do his bidding, helplessly his, for a weekend, and then forever.

CHAPTER 20

All the windows are tinted dark in the Daimler I have rented, exactly as I'd ordered, although it is already dark outside. No one can see in, nor can the passenger see through the partition separating the front and back seats. I can vaguely discern Olivia's profile when she slides in and pulls the door shut. I throw the locks with a switch at my fingertips, a click too unobtrusive for her to notice, exactly as I'd ordered, and slowly pull away.

I hit another button to roll down the glass partition. I can see Olivia clearly, she fixes her queer stare on me and then looks away, staring into darkness, conflict racing across her face, clouds scuttering as I'd seen it before, watching in the flat. Bewilderment, fear, and the thrilling shock of sexual enthrallment are all mingled with nervous apprehension and the sure, relentless knowledge that Nick will exhaust her till she is quaking with abandonment, imploring her to let her be, because she cannot endure any more.

That is what she is hoping.

I want to turn the big black car around and drive away, drive to Heathrow and put her on a plane, but my foot stays steady on the gas, and we do not speak. I turn around a curve, up a long winding driveway, stop, the car idling, and raise the partition. Olivia hears the faint thud of an automatic door, I creep up a few more feet, then stop, she hears the garage door closing behind her, and she gets out and disappears into the house.

Nick is waiting for her by the door. He beckons, and she follows him, oblivious to the furniture or the draperies or the colors of the walls of someone else's house, whose, it doesn't matter, how could it when her skin is so alive and tingling. Down a hall they go, up a wide staircase, down another corridor, up more stairs, and into a cozy warm room lit only by candles and the snapping sparks as the logs in the fireplace burn into flame.

She shrugs off her coat as she's done in the flat so many times before, and Nick hands her a glass of champagne he's just poured. She smiles and drinks, a little too eagerly. Nick smiles back, and refills her glass. It is too dark for her to see his face clearly, the lines of frustrated passion etched around his eyes.

She doesn't know it yet, but all his meticulous plans for the weekend have been thwarted by a typical production screw-up. Jamie told him only hours before that he must work tomorrow night, they all must, they have no choice, they are all so very near the end, the lab had scratched the prints or some other insanely moronic something, and an infuriated Nick had no alternative but to capitulate, sulky and brooding.

He has to tell Olivia, ask her for another day when she'd barely agreed to this, and he prefers the coward's approach. The drug he's slipped into her glass, mixed with the alcohol,

will soon render her pliant and relaxed and thoroughly benda-
ble to his will. That is all he wants from her now, not her usual
wary feistiness and stubborn refusals to change her mind, but
the lovely blissful surety of submission, numbed to reality,
hidden in this timeless cave.

"I like this room," Olivia says. "It's dark, and little. Like the
other room."

Like the flat, she means but cannot say. Like the safe house
has once done, this little room with its connecting bath eases
her fears. I recognized its suitability as soon as I'd found it,
though it will always be dark up here on the third floor of a
mansion I paid heavily for, this weekend, shadowed by the
trees in the garden overlooking the Heath, shadowed as long
as Olivia's here with Nick because I have pulled and taped
shut the shades and drawn the velvet drapes.

"I want you," Nick says.

"I know." She finishes her second glass, and nearly giggles,
falling back on the bed, relieved by her giddiness. She doesn't
have to think, she wants only to feel, and then be done with
it. "I'm getting drunk," she says. "I can't believe it. I never
get drunk."

"Never?" Nick asks, bemused.

"Well, hardly ever." She kicks off her shoes, and laughs.
"What are you doing to me?"

"Everything I can think of," he says, but she doesn't hear
his confession because her head is spinning.

"You're crazy," she says, her voice affectionate.

"Yes," he replies, sitting on the edge of the bed to enjoy the
kind of sweet silliness he's never seen in her before. "Is it
nice?"

"Mmmm," she says, "nice." It takes too much energy to say
any more.

"Does this make it nicer?" His hands, easing off her clothes.

"Mmmm."

"And this?" he asks, kissing her gently, endless tiny sweet kisses as he slips off his own clothes.

"Yes," she says. "Yes."

I have nothing to do but wait till summoned, and I sit in the hall near their door, too listless to read. There are no cameras, there was no time to hide them. Besides, Nick told me in a rare moment of introspective candor, he didn't think he could bear watching what they might catch, not this time, some part of him acknowledging that it might be the last time.

The irony does not escape us. Everything that made him what and who he is, reinvented whole, play-acting and becoming Nick Muncie, superstar, the terrors he'd endured twisted, combed, and spun into satiny threads of perversion, loomed into fine, impregnable cloth, his armor, tortoiseshell-hard, protection as he drove himself, violently, on his speeding ascent to the top, driving mindless and determined, as I am on the Harley, on the curving path up the hill, overlooking the evanescent twinkle of the fairy lights of the city below him, undeterred—all that has shaped him, dauntless.

Until one dreary day a woman he does not know is late for lunch.

This time he'd begged for, alone together, power and passion convoluted and intermingled, will live only in memory. For all the days of careful planning, the hours bereft of Olivia that he'd fill, placated with the dreaming of it, the perfection of his scheming, had been defeated by the simple limits of technology.

I have seen enough, already.

Later, I bring in dinner on a large tray, placing it on a table near the fireplace before trying to leave as unobtrusively as I've entered. When Nick motions me out into the hall while

Olivia is running a bath, I know instantly that something is wrong.

"The fuckers," he says hoarsely. "The stupid fucking pricks."

"What?"

"I've got to shoot late tonight. They fucked up." His hands through his hair. "I finally get her where I want her, and they fucked up. What if she won't come back?"

"What are you so worried about?" I ask. "It's not like she's in any shape to say no to you."

Nick slams me up against the wall, a hard thud, taking me by surprise. "Shut up," he says savagely. "Just shut the fuck up."

"She's going to hear you," I say.

Nick loosens his grip, and pulls away.

"Just ask her," I say, shrugging off his touch and trying to keep my voice low. "She promised you a weekend, and I expect Olivia keeps her promises. It'll be split up, that's all."

"It's still fucked." He turns to go back in.

"Don't let her see you like this."

It is the wrong thing to say. Nick's eyes darken and I tense, but he remembers Olivia in the bath, and instead hurries inside to her.

"What were you arguing about?" she asks, blowing fragrant bubbles to Nick that he playfully swats away.

"Nothing, really." His hand drops down, idly swirling the bubbles, crushing them. "You are very adorable, like this," he says, smiling gently as he reaches down to scoop her out of the bath. Kissing her damp neck, he wraps her in towels, and carries her to the Bessarabian in front of the fire. He pampers her as if she were a child exhausted by the day's play, rubbing her entire body with warmed oil scented with hyacinth that makes her smile, relaxed by its familiar scent.

They drink more champagne and nibble at food, without

hunger, Olivia sedated into a dream state, eagerly welcoming the intense lassitude without wondering what induced it. She only wants to exist in the moment, she is his, her body melting into a soothing, sensuous languor.

Nick feels her surrender.

It is time without end, countless dreamy hours of pleasure. He is unswervingly determined to overwhelm Olivia with a tender, solicitous passion she has never felt from him before, not an hour ago, not the other times when he'd try to be nice, not ever has she felt this sweetness of spirit and easy tenderness. He is as recklessly plagued with a need to serve only her, to do only as she wishes, to be kind. This is what she'll remember, he is thinking, this, only this, our undeniable hunger, a passion too unbearably magnificent to deny or live without, a physical addiction, this will make her change her mind and come with me, how can she not.

They doze only to wake in each other's arms, limbs entangled, she is nothing but sensation robbing her of all other thoughts. Drifting blissfully replete, she closes her eyes to sleep and is awakened moments later, or is it hours, it doesn't matter, his mouth is on hers, honeyed kisses, she wakes with him inside her, or if she turns closer to find him lost in dreams she slowly arouses him into wakefulness.

They rarely speak, no more than murmured endearments, or shared quiet laughter.

Their lust for each other's bodies is more heated than the fire crackling at their feet, their fervor insatiable as if their lovemaking could somehow slow the inexorable sweep of the hands on my Rolex, as if the world outside had died, swallowed into the cold gray rain, swept out to sea, devoured as he is devouring her, drowning, only they exist, only this, this room, this fire, his face next to hers, nothing else, because this is the end.

Olivia believes it is the end.

*   *   *

She awakens to unaccustomed brightness. Nick has gone, his face set in sullen lines of displeasure, unwilling to tear himself away, raw, exposed, leaving only because he has no choice. He is picked up by a faceless driver sent in a studio limo, and falls asleep on the way to the set, exhausted and sore, gladdened, actually, that his fatigue will force him to concentrate. Jamie notices the haggard lines on Nick's face and his snappish temper, and wisely says nothing, thankful that the unexpected reshoots are uncomplicated and short.

I have untaped the shades and pulled open the drapes, revealing a dull gray day like the one preceding it, dreamy hours that for them have already disappeared into the haze of remembrance.

When she comes out of the bath Olivia notices a pile of clothes on the bed: beautifully embroidered silk underthings, a white poet's shirt and black Levi's, a pair of black Noconas, stiff and new, scaled down to the smallness of her feet, a black leather belt with an intricate buckle of hammered silver. Last is a thick black leather motorcycle jacket identical to his.

He has pictured her, a thousand times, putting on the Nick, and now he is not there to see it. She has no choice. She looks around for her clothes, but I have folded them neatly and placed them in the Daimler. There is nothing else there for her to wear.

I drive her home in the same strained silence, Olivia lost in thought. Lost.

She is remembering their last conversation, Nick murmuring to her in the dark.

"Olivia," he'd said, his voice a caress, his lips nibbling on her ear, "you won't believe this, but I have to leave you soon. Too soon." Still kissing him, she thinks she is dreaming the implausibility of these words. "I have to work. They screwed up, and there's nothing I can do about it," he is saying, and she still does not understand. He sighs, and a sudden flood of surprised adrenaline punctures her lulled state of intoxication. She pulls away to prop herself up on her elbows to stare at Nick in amazement, at the calm distress in his features masking the angry discouragement beneath. "I'm sorry," he says. "I wanted to tell you earlier, but I couldn't. I didn't want to ruin this." His hands through his hair, his eyes imploring. "It's not fair. This is supposed to be our time together."

"Yes, it is," she says slowly. No longer dreaming, she can feel the fears she'd tried to dampen return to rise off her like the hot steam hissing whenever she'd dropped a ladleful of water onto the rocks in the sauna at the baths.

"I wanted our weekend together," Nick says. "Two days and two nights, you and me, and nothing else. As you said. As you promised."

He is trying too hard, here in her arms, and she finds it unnerving, from Nick. There's something he's not telling her, there's—

"What do you want me to say to you?" she asks.

"Say you understand, and you're sorry, and you'll see me on Sunday night." Don't be like this, Olivia, don't be your everyday self, he begs her silently, a fervent wish, I want you here for me, I want you molded, docile, into a creature I can have, and manage, and master, I could have done it if we'd had the time together as we planned, without this interruption, this horrid intrusion of my life jinxing all my schemes, but I will make you whether you want to or not—

"But I can't," she says. "I thought we would . . ."

"Would what?"

"Would be together. And then . . ."

"Then."

"Nick." Her voice, sad. "Don't."

She'd never have come with him, he can't deny it any longer. He feels a sharp jolt of hatred stab his heart, savagely. He'll make her change her mind, oh yes he will. He'll do what he hadn't dared, no one can stop him, he'll *make* her—

Even in the dark, Olivia sees that look, glimmering, that terrifying emptiness of annihilation, that gaping black void she'd hoped desperately never to see again. She will do anything, say anything, to make it go away.

"Okay," she says. "Just tell me what to do."

Nick's face clears instantly, and he smiles, grateful. "M will fetch you, don't worry." He sighs. "I'm really sorry. Forgive me. Say you forgive me," he says, kissing her with such impassioned desperation that she has no choice but to say it, and then say it again.

"What is it, M—is something else wrong?" Olivia is asking me as I stand in the mews, just outside her studio, holding a small white box. She does not know I have already placed a larger, matching box, packed and sealed by Nick, on the bed in the flat.

I am not supposed to be here. Nick would kill me if he knew I'd sneaked away on this secret errand, but I had to do it, I couldn't sit still with the foreboding, I had to move, driving badly, the bike whining the protest my voice could not.

"Here," I say, extending the box, my voice echoing loudly in my ears because I keep the visor of my helmet lowered. I don't want her to see my face.

"What's this?" she says.

"It's for you. To wear."

"To wear when?"

"Tomorrow."

All she can see is her face reflected, distorted, in my visor.

"He's got some nasty game planned, hasn't he?" she asks. "He's not going to give up without a fight."

I say nothing, frozen in habitual blankness. She pushes up the visor, before I can stop her.

"I like to see the people I talk to," she says. "You're hiding something."

"No."

Her eyes scan my face.

"Are you my friend, M?"

The question surprises me. "Yes," I say, "I hope so."

"Then you know."

"Know."

"You do, don't you?"

And so does she. Nick will deny it, but he is despairing, an unaccustomed feeling that sits badly on his heart. He asked, and asked again, for him an act of unbearable surrender, and she refused him. Soon he will be shooting the final scenes of *Faust* to applause and tears, I will dismantle the secret gilded flat, erasing all traces of what he did there, we must leave, this is not our home. There is no reason to stay.

No reason except Olivia.

The tickets are sitting in slick blue envelopes atop a pile of scripts McAllister has been couriering over with mounting impatience, and the inevitable cannot be postponed much longer.

"Yes," I say.

"Can I trust you?"

I want to get down on my knees and clasp my arms around her legs, bury my head in her enveloping warmth like a child begging his mother to save him. I want her to bend down to me, her hair falling in my face, and tell me it's all right, hush, don't worry, everything's all right, I'm here, I won't leave you, hush.

She hasn't moved. Nor have I, the little box still outstretched in my hands. I've never known a woman to manage such stillness.

"Olivier's tour is going to Australia in two weeks. I'm meeting him there."

I nod, the knotted dread in the pit of my stomach growing, monstrous, global, a horrible knot of pain.

"For how long?" I ask.

"It doesn't matter. Forever."

A neighbor walks by with her shopping, curious, sensible shoes clacking, round shapes in her string bag, apples, oranges, a leek, bright colors, round shapes, the spots of color on her cheeks, round, the buttons on her woolen coat, round, shiny.

Olivia gone, round, sweet Olivia gone, the color of her hair, the life of her, lunchtimes in the flat, watching her, all gone. Unthinkable.

"I wanted to say this to you in the car the other day, but I just . . . I couldn't," she says, her eyes boring a hole through my heart. "I have to go to him. Olivier, I mean. And if I don't go now . . ."

"I understand."

"Nick can't know. He'll try to stop me. If you—"

"I won't tell him."

"I'm asking too much," she says, her features softening. "It's not fair to you."

"I'd do anything for you." I hadn't meant to say that.

Her face changes. "Oh, M," she says, one of her fingers, paint-speckled, tracing my scars with the briefest caress. No one has ever dared touch me like that. I jerk my head back, my cheek smarting as if it had been slapped.

"I'm sorry," she says, running her fingers through her hair, and returns to herself. "I never know what to say to you. You certainly don't make it easy."

I attempt a wan grin, and she sighs. We are still facing each other, the box in my hands, outside in the cold, waiting, she is waiting for instructions, the door ajar, opening just a crack into the haven inside.

"Tomorrow," I say, "at the flat. Be ready for the Daimler to come at five." I hand her the box.

"What is it?"

"Open it and see. I don't know anything about women's things."

She laughs. "But you do know what Nick likes, don't you? Go on, then. I'll be there. And I won't be late."

She pries off the top to see an exquisite small crucifix studded with diamond-cut rubies, identical to the heart he's already given her, only larger, on a slender gold chain.

"This is beautiful," she says, her eyes somber as she lifts it out to catch the light, sparkling gems lit as if on fire, then slips it on where it will hang, coldly beautiful against her skin like gleaming drops of blood dangling between her breasts.

What will she do with it when Nick is gone, I wonder, quite wildly, will she wear it, will she hide it, will she give it to Annette?

I can't imagine her showing it to Olivier.

I can't imagine her gone.

"Is this a bribe?" she says, finally, trying to tease away her anxiety. "Is Nick afraid I'll run away and hide?"

"Just wear it tomorrow. Please."

"You don't say please very often, do you?"

I nearly smile. "No," I say, "I leave it to Nick."

"You leave too much to him," she says, and turns into her house, ready to nudge the door shut behind her.

"Olivia," I say, and she opens the door a wide crack, curious. "Listen to me. He loves you, in his way, he does love you." She cannot imagine the bitterness I am struggling to hide from my voice. "Whatever happens, he won't hurt you. I won't let him."

I watch the color drain out of her face, and curse my clumsiness. I hadn't meant to scare her. Not like this.

"I asked for this," she says, slowly. "It should've ended long ago, but I couldn't. It serves me right."

"Don't be ridiculous," I say. "It happened, that's all. No one asks for Nick."

"But we've got him, don't we?" she says. "Or rather, he's got us." With that she shuts the door.

I walk back to my bike, my hands shaking, shaking too much for me to drive.

I sit there, in the calm of the mews, on my bike, until the rain starts.

She barely sleeps, dreaming of black shapes, masks, she is lost, running in the shifting maze she has painted, there is a panting noise behind her, terrifying, and she awakens with a cry. Seconds ticking, her clock, maddeningly calm, oblivious to her distress.

She lies under the thick comforter in her bed, waiting for dawn. Finally, when she can stand it no longer, she gets up, tidies up her already spotless studio, and tries to sketch, but it is useless, the hours crawling. She tears off her smock and throws it down in a crumpled heap, goes downstairs to change into a baggy sweatshirt, jeans, and scruffy boots, masses her hair under a beret, puts on Olivier's ratty tweed overcoat that smells of oils and peat smoke from their last trip to the country, and walks out into the sharp afternoon air to hail a taxi.

She does not trust her feet to walk her across the park.

The flat is heavily silent in midafternoon. Even the peonies are drooping, petals in a heap on the table I polish diligently with lemon oil after Dulcie swipes a few cursory flicks of a dustcloth over it. Olivia's nervousness charges the sleepy air into wakefulness, expectant, puzzled, especially when she sees the large white box on the bed, her name written in Nick's slanting black script on a thick cream card taped to the top. She opens the envelope to read:

Olivia—Put everything on exactly in the order you find it.
Slowly. Think of me as you get dressed.
                                                        Nick

How could she not?

I have not forged his writing this time, and the message is abrupt, useless, explaining nothing, deliberately so. Olivia sits down next to it, unnerved. I sit watching her, my senses jangling.

After a while she cannot bear the silence, so she gets up and flicks through a pile of CDs, one after the other, all Olivier's recordings, she realizes with a jolt of panic, not the CDs she brought over because she thought Nick would like them, or that Nick chose, smirking like a schoolboy, to match her petulant moodiness. These are all Olivier's, his slim fingers poised above the keyboard, his beloved face smiling at her from the photographs on the covers.

This is not the time to think of Olivier.

She sighs with relief when she finds a recording of Ella Fitzgerald in another pile. She brought it over, when was it, she can't recall, only remembering Nick teasing her about something, a song lyric, that was it, and she brought this the next time, a delicious woman's voice, cool and contemporary, singing of lost love, to laugh at over lunch. It barely soothes Olivia's frazzled nerves as she runs a bath, soaking in the bubbles so long her fingers shrivel. She rubs cream, scented of vetiver, in her skin till it glistens, then sits, wrapped in a towel, her hair a wet snake down her back, and stares again at the box.

She is sitting exactly where Nick had hoped she would, on the edge of the bed, and she is perfectly in focus.

I cannot tear my eyes away.

She feels a twinge of dread, imagining what is inside, that awful anticipation mingled with a strange calm of wondering how Nick will try to force her out of her known, familiar self. She only knows that, because this is truly the last time, he will make her struggle, that he expects her to struggle, what he'd done to her in the airport was a mere warmup, his movements belying the practiced precision of a professional, and that he will relish this opportunity far more than any other because he has begged her to do it, and has been thwarted even by her consent.

And then she understands. She understands what the game is to him, that in the playing he means to have her and hurt her, that for him pain and fear are the purest expressions of his love, inextricably interwoven into a visible token of the qualms she has made so palpably alive.

She understands that whatever he's planned for her will happen this once, and never again, he knows she is leaving, has left him already, and so they can both risk it, their selves, he daring to sell his soul, Faust embodied, she daring to surrender to his will, to his deliberate, dark impulses he knows she despises and yet cannot control.

She understands that nothing in her life will ever again equal this sensation now, damp and shivering on this bed, the ormolu clock ticking, Ella's voice singing to her, blithely unaware that Olivia is sitting alone in the deepening shadows, so naked, so thrilled with her terror, so enslaved to a fleeting transient delight of the flesh.

She understands that she will never again face such an inescapable abyss of perversity and pain tangled so deeply with pleasure, and that she would, willingly, leap into the void if Nick asked her to today, holding firmly on to his hand, not knowing how long her body would float next to his, suspended, until it hit the ground.

The soft layers of tissue paper in the box are a delicate mauve, the color of hyacinths.

There is a lovely small jeweled handbag on top in the shape of a miniature panther, encrusted with jet crystals and rhinestones, his eyes glowing green emeralds, lined in ultramarine velvet, a small pouch inside filled with makeup: porcelain foundation, black mascara and eyeliner, deep crimson lipstick. She applies it carefully, her face an ashen mask with darkly stained lips, then dabs on perfume from the tiny vial also found in the pouch, a strange, pungent scent, invigorating and bittersweet, she has never smelled before. She replaces it and the pouch in the bag, knowing he means her to carry it with her.

Next is a bra, long enough almost to be a bustier, of the finest shimmery black silk like velvet against her skin. Its only peculiarity is the straps of the narrowest strips of silk, detachable, she notices, bound in leather. It fits her perfectly. Olivia marvels at the fine stitches, fingering the meticulous workmanship, wondering whom Nick paid to make such a beautiful, odd thing, wondering how he took her measurements quite so precisely, not just the bustier but the panties in matching black silk, no more than whispers embroidered with black roses, and the silk garter belt, edged in the same narrow leather, with leather garters.

It is such a cliché, this outfit, she tells herself as she rolls up the smooth silk stockings, trying not to snag them on her fingernails, and she finds herself laughing unexpectedly in nervous reaction. It is all so typically over the top, so much like Nick, this drama, so fragile and so tough, like the strange perfume, and as undeniably erotic as it is ridiculous.

The shirt is a simple white Egyptian cotton button-down, the kind Olivier had starched by the dozen, crisply ironed, and folded into neat piles in a cardboard box by the Chinese laundry around the corner, except that it is sleeveless. The skirt is equally simple, lined black silk, flowing fluidly down to her calves, fastening with one large button at her hip.

Down at the bottom of the box is a thin black leather belt,

coiled snakelike in its mauve tissue paper, its buckle glistening with the same black jet beads of the panther bag. The shoes are butter-soft and slender, with heels higher than any she has ever worn. They make her much taller, her calves painful slim knots, and she wishes she could kick them off, wishes she could run barefoot down the stairs and into the street, run barefoot across the frozen dull grass of the park, run down Queens Gate, around the corner, tripping over the slick cobblestones of the mews, her body shivering, her feet cut and bleeding, leading her home, into her studio, locking the door behind her as she slides down to her own floor, exhausted, panting for breath, home, alone, safe.

He won't hurt you. I won't let him.

Her body *is* shivering, here in the flat, she realizes as she looks at herself in the gilded mirror by the fireplace. A shiver of dread or a shiver of anticipation, she cannot tell the difference, dressed in the deliberate ritual of Nick's instructions, and she sees herself as an apparition in black and white with pale staring eyes. Were the shoes not tilted so high and uncomfortably, were she not clad in such lavishly created underthings, were the sleeves not cut off from the plain white cotton shirt that did not quite disguise the outline of the strange black bra swelling her breasts beneath, the ruby cross she'd brought with her and slipped on hanging there between them, were her face not so dramatically stark, she could almost look like any professional woman getting ready for work.

She moves closer to the mirror, unsteady in her heels on the thick carpeting, still mesmerized by her appearance. My eyes do not leave her as I quickly adjust the focus.

It is a stranger's gaze, she tells herself, it isn't me, this provocative creature, this costumed alien dressing up in someone else's clothes on the way to a ball where she and Nick will be the only dancers on a sprung floor, sweeping around the candlelit room, intoxicated with each other even as they spin faster and faster, out of control in a dizzying waltz, while I lurk behind the violins and the cellos, watching, mute.

She has never looked more alluring, more expectant, more vulnerable. More terrified.

She stretches out her fingers and touches the mirror. She is staring at her reflection, her soul full in her eyes, confused, brave, loving, staring straight at me, so close I can almost hear her breathing, just on the other side of the mirror. Gently, I place my fingers up next to the lens, careful not to jar it, or make a noise.

If the wall dissolved, we would be touching.

When the buzzer sounds she nearly jumps out of her skin.

When, finally, she turned away and went to sit on the bed, nervously expectant, careful not to muss her outfit, I shut off the equipment and hurried out, cautiously silent in the hall lest I make a sound she'd not heard before in the flat, down to the Daimler Nick had waiting. I nodded to him and he slipped out of the driver's seat, clad in his leather biker gear, pulled on a helmet, quickly mounted the Harley I'd already parked a few doors away, and turned the bike around to wait at the corner, out of Olivia's sight line, till she came outside.

He wants to see her get into the car, just to be sure.

I press the buzzer, open the back door of the car, and get behind the wheel. I see Olivia in the driver's side mirror, and when she slides in and pulls the door shut, I once again throw the locks and pull away.

It has started to rain, and the inside of the car is very dark. Olivia sits so still, rigid, near the door she thinks she can open, that a few moments pass before she notices a small box, identical to the one I gave her the day before, on the armrest in the middle of the seat. She holds it in her lap, afraid to open it.

No one saw me leave, she is saying to herself, this is completely crazy, what am I doing, no one in the world knows where I am and where I'm going, except Nick. Except M, if it is indeed he who is driving, I can't tell, the partition is up. *He won't hurt you. I won't let him.*

She opens this box to find a weightless object nestled in the same delicate mauve tissue, and unwraps it to find a simple oblong of black silk, many layers sewn together to make it opaque, edged with the narrowest strips of black leather. At first she thinks it is a scarf, until she sees Nick's embossed cream card pinned to its bottom.

Twice around your eyes, it says.

A nameless core of dread has begun to throb deep inside her, and her only means of containing it is to press her legs together, tensing her in place, tingling, she cannot stop the tingling, one hand on her knees, the other on the wide armrest as the car twists smoothly through unfamiliar streets. What is he going to do to me that he hasn't already done? she is wondering, trying not to panic. I don't want to not see. What can he do that he doesn't want me to see? The silk is so soft, a harmless piece of fabric, growing damp with sweat in her fingers for so long that I am getting even more nervous myself.

He is asking her to blind herself, she realizes, an irrevocable gesture of acquiescence more significant to him than any other, to offer herself as a willing accomplice, a faceless slave, deprived of her eyes, her true self.

She has seen through him with those eyes, and this is his vengeance.

After an interminable moment she finally bends forward so her hair falls down over her head, and winds the silk twice around her eyes, finishing with a large knot in the back.

Her chest is heaving when she sits up, and I drive faster to the rendezvous. He is waiting, on the bike, at the far, deserted end of a large parking lot, and when he sees the car he stands up, ready, poised, pulling off the helmet only at the last second in case anyone should recognize him.

He has planned this ending to their weekend together quite meticulously, I realized with a pang of anger, long before she consented to it, comforted by his somber journeys on the Harley on the weekends when sleep eluded him, timing it, every stage of it, imagining the turns of the car, how many traffic lights stop its progress, how many minutes tick by before it arrives.

Olivia feels the car turn, slow, and stop.

Her door opens, and she turns her head toward the noise. The other door opens. She is confused, but it is only me, following instructions, opening the door and shutting it again.

There is an arm around her neck. She hasn't the time to call out before a strip of tape covers her mouth. She can't help panicking, desperate, but the weight of the man who moves so quickly is crushing her, his legs pinioning hers so she can't move, she can't see, this can't be Nick, he smells of acrid cigar smoke and leather, she has forgotten Nick came to her once as a biker, she cannot think, or remember, she can barely breathe, he smells far more frightening, a sickening animal perfume of lust and anger. In a flash he handcuffs her wrists together, lifting up the armrest to attach them to the long, strong chain he securely fastened there the day before, then shoves her down on her back, unbuckles her belt and whips it free, pulls off her shoes, unfastens her skirt and pulls it down and off, unhooks the stockings from her garters and zips them off her legs, rips off her panties, rips off her garter belt, swiftly ties the leather belt around her ankles, yanks her rudely upright and rips the shoulder seams of her shirt so it falls neatly in two pieces, the front still buttoned, then unhooks the thin leather straps and the back fastening of her bra, leaving her sitting as she'd been, panting, unable to scream, or move,

suffocating in sheer terror, completely nude, stripped of everything but the ruby cross dangling between her breasts and the
blindfold wrapped twice around her eyes.

It has taken less than a minute.

She feels him watching, although she cannot see the smug
panther's smile of satisfaction curving his lips, before he finally
moves away. She hears the door open and shut, and the car
starts moving again.

The acknowledgment of her terror is unendurable.

I'd squeezed my eyes shut, my hands clamped so tight on
the steering wheel my arms were shaking, even though I
couldn't really see anything, Nick's back blocking her from
sight. He wouldn't divulge any details of what he'd planned,
only that I should drive exactly where he told me to, high-
lighting my route in the A to Z street guide, and not dream
of trying anything that might screw up his warped intentions.

I have to drive. I can't stop this, I don't know how. I have
to keep my eyes glued forward, through the windshield, on
the road, while Olivia is a helpless captive, pinioned in the
backseat of a Daimler, creeping through London.

She has been helpless before, but always in the haven of the
flat, their safe house, hidden from the world, not like this,
moving through nothingness, uprooted and suspended, blind
and disoriented, through a dark void into the unknown, un-
earthly and terrible, far from anyone or anything she's ever
experienced, her self debased, nothing more than an object
waiting to be taken.

That is the horror of it.

And I let him do it.

I drive only a short distance, stopping and turning, once
around the parking lot, actually, long enough to confuse her
further, as if she could possibly be more confused, and let
Nick strip off his leather gear, which he will hand to me
through my window.

The car stops, turns around. The back door opens and shuts, she feels him there, she cannot see that he is silently taking off his cashmere sweats but she smells the animal lust rolling off him in nauseating waves, and instinctively tries to pull away, unable to scream, trembling uncontrollably, dreading what must be coming, but there is nowhere to go.

This isn't Nick, this can't be Nick.

"Are you afraid?" a voice says, low and whispered into her ear as the man moves nearer. "Afraid of me? Afraid of what I am going to do to you?"

She has heard this voice before, somewhere, she cannot think in her panic.

"Afraid you might like it? Like it too much?" The voice so sweet, tender pleading, a cruel whisper in her ear, mocking her helplessness.

Nick said those words to her, once, a lifetime ago, a peony fat in his fingers, begging her, desperate, in the flat.

He is still desperate, whoever this is, it can't be Nick, this ghastly low voice, Nick has paid some other beast to paralyze her like this, it can't be Nick, he couldn't, I won't believe it, oh please, let me go let me go—

He won't hurt you, I won't let him. A faint echo of M's solemn pronouncement, a sudden glimpse in her mind's eye of M's stern scarred face comes to her clearly, cutting for the briefest instant through the jumbled fragments of thoughts racing frantic, spinning in her head, her blood frozen.

"Are you afraid?" The voice insistent, imploring. He hasn't yet touched her, his voice a puff of wind in her hair. "Nod your head if you are."

She nods, even more scared not to.

"Truly afraid?"

She nods again.

His hands are in her hair, fistfuls of it, pulling her head closer to him, she can almost hear his heart, skipping wildly.

"I want you to be afraid," he says, his voice still a whisper, hoarse, rasping. "I wanted you to live through one moment of undiluted, inexpressible terror." His hands clamped in her hair, lowering her head onto his lap. She can feel his eyes on her, and her panic cowering beneath them in abject dread, dark and bottomless, she can feel him, gigantic, she knows this is exactly what he wants her to feel, terrorized for what seems like an eternity of cruel suspense, exulting in his mastery, how hard he is, how strong, how despicably determined to take her, scornful and inexorable.

She is nothing.

"I want you to be afraid," the hideous voice is still saying, "I want you to know how it feels, because that's how Nick feels, all the time, without you."

If Nick hadn't taken so much pleasure in this unforgivable brutality, I might almost have pitied him.

"Afraid," he says. He is trembling almost as much as she is, tense, quavering, not in fear, trembling with the anticipation of the longly awaited gratification of the most genuine expression of his desire, the sublime descent into evil, the need to physically overpower so strong in him, so warped, that it drowns all rationale, obviating all he'd never dared reveal to Olivia, knowing she would rebuff it, and him, disgusted.

He no longer cares, he has nothing to lose. He will risk it, risk all for a few minutes of supremely venal indulgence, unmerciful, ruthlessly inhaling the essence of Olivia. She is nothing but a body imprisoned beneath him, cuffed and bound, obedient to the brutality of whatever he will demand from her.

Let her try to fly away. Let her try to end it. She is unhavable, and will escape no matter what he does to her now.

But he will not let her go without one last savage farewell.

In a swift cruel gesture he suddenly rips off her gag, tumbles her over, pushing her down before she can open her mouth to scream, pushing into her till she is choking and the tears are streaming down her cheeks, and just as suddenly pushing her back up, sitting her on his lap, one hand replacing the gag with a slap and the other cupping her breasts, pinching them, his hands a frenzy of motion, uncontrollable.

I am driving carefully through the traffic. I don't want to get a ticket.

He is holding her tight on his lap, impaling her, too tight, his arm across her chest, she cannot breathe, and then shoves her down so she falls, the long chain coiling beside her, with a muffled cry to the carpet, where he can take her like a dog, inhuman, the pain merciless, the sight and feel of her suffering more potent than any aphrodisiac he could ever concoct.

He won't hurt you—but he is hurting her, unbearably, she cannot breathe, she is limp beneath him, barely clinging to consciousness, but he is not through, no, he lifts her up onto the seat, laying her on her back, pulling her arms up over her head, and running his tongue over her skin, a glistening trail lapping up her shivering terror. His first delirium stilled, he becomes less frantic, his weight propped on his elbows, biting at her nipples, pinching her, moving inside her, relentless still, the car rolling forward, slowing, turning a corner, he moves with it, she is falling down a tunnel, screaming soundlessly.

One hand strays between her legs, fingering her, the sweet meandering gesture she used to love when Nick did it, perverting the tender motion into a captor's taunt, her fear feeding it, the last, lingering lunch of the depraved.

This can't be Nick.

Who else can it be?

It takes him forever to come, with a hugely violent shudder, grinding into her, suffocating, and he stays sprawled on top of her, unwilling to let it end. She feels his eyes upon her, through the blindfold, raking her sprawled, humiliating, violated helplessness as if his gaze were sharpened fingernails, a trace of blood following their piercing path over her skin. She feels him still, his persistent fingers unyielding, crawling up and down her like the savage nips of ants even as he pulls away slightly to reach into a pouch he's placed by the door, one he's kept buried in the bottom of the vintage Vuitton trunk, down where she never thought to look, then pulls out a syringe that he fills with the contents of a glass vial. Olivia feels a sharper pinch in her hip, but she barely minds it, too terrified is she by those hideous fingers.

He won't let go of her, that's all she knows, devouring her skin, he is taking her as he pleases, again, his breath hot, sucking the very life out of her.

He will never let her go.

She has no idea what she is anymore when he forces her head up, she hears a strange sound, liquid, it must be, poured into a glass and brought to her lips. He rips off the gag and she tries to turn her head away, but she can't, she's so tired and this drink is so cool, so comforting on her swollen lips, she is parched dry, she is dying.

The drugs work quickly. When Nick sees her dizzy, long rolling waves of sleep making her droop, he moves away, calmly pulling up his sweats. Finally, comes her last thought before total oblivion overtakes her. *Finally.*

Nick taps on the partition. It is my signal to drive him back to his bike, and when I pull up beside it, he clambers out.

I look at him, waiting impatiently for me to hand him back his leather gear, his hair disheveled, the madness of his frenzy still alight in his eyes, and I must say something. Even now, after I'd let him do it, I could never have envisioned such craven, unremitting brutality. I'd told her I wouldn't let him hurt her—I'd told her—she believed me—

"She'll never forgive you," I tell him, my voice low.

"She won't remember, not with those drugs. They never fail." He shrugs. The bastard. "Her mind won't let her. She'll blank it all out. She'll wake up and feel fuzzy and wonder what happened and where she is, but she won't remember."

"You can't know that."

"Don't tell me what I can't."

"But what if it does come back, suddenly, in bits and pieces? What if she dreams it? What if—"

"Shut up," he says as viciously as he can without yelling. "I don't want your goddamn opinion. Just get the fuck out of my face."

"You didn't have to do that to her," I persist. "She would've come with you today, anyway. She said she would."

He looks at me, a flash of guilty hatred more electric than lightning proving me right. He'll never admit it. He did the unspeakable. It's done with. It's over.

He'd do it again if he could.

"Get out of here," he says. "Take her back and get out of my face before I kill you."

He would kill me, I see it in his eyes, if he could find a way to do it, although I am much stronger, and wary, my senses keen, and have trained myself to fight. He has helped create the monster, protector and procurer, and now he must live with it, dependent on me, bitterly resentful that I am silent witness to his irrevocable degradation.

I wonder if it is possible to hate him as much as he hates me, but only for a second, because such a question does not bear answering.

Nick is not worth dying for.

Olivia stirs, her tongue swollen, her head spinning, and then awakens, thirsty. The small of her back is aching, her entire body is sore.

I hand her a glass of ice water, propping her up to drink it.

"What?" she says, thickly.

"You got dizzy in the car," I say, my heart wrenching.

The car. Her heart starts to pound, her head reeling, she can't seem to clear it, trying to remember being in the car, how she got here, in this bed, cozy under the covers in the flat, she realizes, but it is too exhausting to think. It is not unpleasant, this lethargy, her limbs are tingling slightly as if they'd been asleep, she feels too lazy to care. Somewhere in the back of her mind is a pleading little voice, trying to warn her, trying to make her remember that something awful has happened, but the images are too far away, dark and fuzzy, she couldn't see, that was it, a blackness in front of her, the blindfold. The blindfold in the car, and then . . . It was in a box on the seat. She put it on, or did she? She can't remember.

"Did I . . . ? What happened?" she says, noticing that she's dressed in the clothes she was wearing when she'd arrived here yesterday afternoon. "Where's Nick? Why am I so tired?" Her eyes close, involuntarily.

"Hush," I say. "Sleep."

When she next awakens I knock on the door and come in, already dressed in my biker gear, and hand her a helmet.

"I guess this means we're going on the bike," she says.

"Yes." It is better this way, I convinced Nick, don't put her in the backseat of that car, not now, not so soon, she needs the air on her face.

There is already traffic this early on a Monday morning, and I maneuver carefully but fast, it is cold, but I could drive forever with her arms around my waist.

"Better?" I ask, pushing up my visor and turning back to her at a stoplight.

She nods. Her head is still fuzzy, she can't remember, and she is not yet ready to ask me the truth.

No one could be ready for that answer.

When we arrive at her door I back the bike around and turn off the engine. She takes off her helmet and hands it to me, and I rummage in the back carrier for a small package.

"What is it?" she says, feeling it carefully.

I don't want to talk, I don't want to explain. I'd told Nick not to give this to her, to forget it, surely if she saw it she'd remember sitting in the back seat of the Daimler, and it falling off the seat when he opened the door. He would not listen, insistent and crazily certain that she must have it, that she'd want it because he gave it to her, just as she'd given him the sketch of the flat, an unforgettable souvenir.

She unwraps the mauve tissue. It is the jeweled panther, the handbag forgotten in the car. She unclasps it, looks inside, curious, the makeup is still there, and the strangely pungent perfume, the ruby lipstick matching the cross still dangling between her breasts.

Her hands are trembling.

Don't, I am imploring her, a silent pleading, don't remember this, remember instead how you were sated and delirious from an endless surfeit of pleasure in a calm dark room, an intoxication more compelling than all the snatched hours of lunch, across the park, in the other room.

"M," she says, her voice quivering, "why did I leave this in the car?"

I shake my head.

All I've ever seemed to do in her presence is nod yes, or shake my head no, hiding the truth of my complicity because that is my recompense for sitting, hunched forward, hours flying by, the rectangular plastic boxes neatly labeled in growing stacks in an airless room, watching.

She comes closer to me, pushing up my visor as she'd done only two days before, another lifetime ago, when those queer eyes had still been clouded with a haze of passion. Now they are tinged with drugs, somber pewter, and troubled, trying to read my own.

Eventually, she sighs, and I breathe again. "M, the inscrutable," she says. "I always wanted to paint you, you know, I know exactly how I'd do it, too, but I was afraid to ask. I know you won't believe it, but your face is much more interesting than Nick's." She tries to smile. "Don't tell him I said that."

I murmur a silent prayer of thanks that she is hastily changing the subject.

"How?" I ask.

"How what?"

"How painted."

She smiles this time, for real. "I'll never tell." She reaches up to touch my scars, as she has done before, and this time I try not to flinch.

"Thank you, M," she says, "for everything."

For everything.

"I won't ever see you again, will I?"

"No."

"But if I do, will you let me paint you?"

I close my eyes for only a second, conjuring up the unbelievable wonder of sitting for her, alone, in the whiteness of her studio, piano music soft in my ears, watching her brushes dance past the fierce concentration in her eyes, watching her watching me, wanting me there, wanting me.

Yes, I want to scream, yes.

"Maybe," I say, wanting to leave her lighthearted. "I'll never tell."

I push up the kickstand and ride away.

The wind freezes the tears on my cheeks.

C H A P T E R   2 1

Nick is sleeping in the flat, leaving only when Jamie insists
on short stints on the set, and then finally refusing to budge
at all, a harsh unnerving weirdness in his eyes, lying in wait,
silent and still, only the slight movement of his hand bringing
the cigarette to his mouth showing he's awake.

He is listening to the sounds all around him, his hearing
suddenly acute, his other senses deprived as he lies there in
the dark with no distractions but this despairing desire to
inhale the essence of Olivia. Cars in the street he hears, a
mother screaming to her brat, kids laughing on their way home
from school, the steady rumble of a taxi's engine, a motorcycle,
sirens in the distance, a wail like the foghorn off Mendocino,
the small groaning creaks of the building, settling, the hiss of
the radiator, the refrigerator, humming on and off, the soft
chinks of the icemaker, the noise of the wind, muffled sounds
he's never heard before.

He thinks he hears a noise upstairs, sitting up in a rush,

hardly daring to breathe, but that can't be, there is only silence.

He's never heard anything in this flat but the sound of his lust.

He tells himself over and over that she'll give in, that she will never remember what he did to her in the car, it was no worse, he mutters in a rare paroxysm of self-reproach, than anything he ever did to her here. She will arrive, breathless, with a suitcase and a sketchpad, and fly off with him into the California sunset of his delusions.

I stand watch. Rather, I sit in my little room, bored and weary. He wants me there, nearby but not with him. Only late at night am I allowed to hurry down to buy food from the Arab grocers that Nick leaves uneaten. Last week when he'd been working for an hour's stretch I snuck off the set to buy more books. They are a comfort. I am reading Stendhal, Chekhov, and Diderot, long, strange stories with twisting polysyllabic names and the kind of moral retribution which is anathema to anyone I've ever met in Hollywood. I memorize poetry, I like Rilke, especially, and Yeats. I work out, shadowboxing, then on the floor, two hundred push-ups, three hundred sit-ups. Stop and check after each fifty reps, but nothing has changed, only Nick lying on the bed, in the dark, smoking.

It is early evening and Nick is dozing, sprawled nude on the comforter, when he hears the unmistakable clink of a key in the lock, and he springs instantly awake, afraid he is only dreaming.

Olivia turns on the light and jumps back, startled. Her keys fall to the carpet, soundless. I hear the click of the tape starting and sit up to watch, instantly worried.

"Oh, you scared me. What are you doing here?" she says finally, catching her breath, one hand on her chest. "I didn't think you'd—that now—at night—"

"I could ask you the same thing," Nick says, trying to keep his voice even. "I've been waiting for you. I knew you would come."

"I was at the baths," she stammers. Her hair is wet, damp curls sticking to her neck. "And I thought to leave the keys. And find my silver earrings. I know I left them here. And—"

She doesn't have to say it. They were a gift from Olivier, weren't they, and she must find them.

"Is that all?" Nick says.

"Yes," she says, her voice starting to tremble. She is trying to avoid his gaze, but she can't help it, she can't not look at him.

"You weren't even going to say goodbye?"

His sarcasm frightens her. His eyes frighten her. She doesn't know what to do.

"You'd let me leave without saying goodbye?" he asks, insistent.

"I didn't know what to say. I was going to call, or leave you a note."

"You didn't know what to say. You were going to call, or leave me a note." Mocking her. She has never seen him like this before, and she is beginning to panic, fear shooting down into her feet, rooting her legs to the floor when she most wants to flee.

"Are you coming with me?" He is standing in front of her, his glorious body naked, his eyes so darkly angry they are no longer blue, they are black pools of dread, immeasurable. He sees the answer in her eyes, a solitary tear trickling down her cheek, and he traces its path as he'd done once before, ages ago, and she shivers violently.

Not like this, please, not like this.

He is boring into her, leaning his warm body as close to hers as if he wants to smother her, dissolving her flesh so there is nothing left of her but the shadowy impression of her body etched into the hard wood of the door. What am I going to do? she thinks wildly, but her thoughts are jumbling one atop the other in her trepidation, she cannot think, she cannot breathe, he smells of cigarettes and scotch, with a faint whiff of leather, an animal smell of lust and anger, she has smelled him like that once before, where, where was it, she knows he wants her to feel the full relentless hardness of his body solid against hers, and its suffocating strength.

M, where is M, he must be here, he said he would protect her, he said it but he didn't, where was he, where is he—

He won't hurt you. I won't let him.

I am standing, sickened, choked by my own cowardly duplicity. I don't know what to do. If I come now will she know I was there, will she, will he—

His arms around her, ribbons of steel, and he scoops her up and throws her facedown on the edge of the bed, his weight on her legs so she cannot kick out at him, his arms snatching off her jacket and her sweater, she is trying to scream but he is crushing her lungs, he's done this before, she realizes, gulping air as he turns her slightly on her side to yank off her jeans, he's—

The car.

She didn't think any terror could be worse than that moment of absolute blind panic in the car, but this is, Nick on top of her, shifting his weight slightly as he stretches over, groping for one of the whips stashed under the bed. Even now in this speeded-up frantic moment he knows what he wants, the slim sleek whip with the lovely glass handle, the same colors as her hair melded stunningly into something he can hold and weld and use to hurt, hurt her now, make her suffer, and make her scream.

For a second he loosens his grip on her as his hand relaxes around the handle, and Olivia tries to crawl away to the door, naked as she is. Nick turns swiftly to reach for her, enraged, but he loses his balance and slams against one of the golden bedposts, smashing the glass into fireworks of fiery sparkles, leaving nothing but a jagged edge near his fingertips, cutting them instantly, blood coursing down his wrist in thin rivers.

He feels no pain, he sees no blood, all he sees is Olivia escaping, and he flings himself at her ankles, imprisoning them, hauling her back underneath him, forcing her over with his weight and his left arm, the whip still clenched in his right, and savagely spreads her legs. The ragged sharp glass slices the tender skin of her inner thigh with a severe stinging pain, and the wound bleeds instantly, copiously, their blood mingling together on the sheets.

"Serves you right, you bitch," Nick says savagely as he hammers into her like an animal, but she doesn't even feel it, her body is deadened, even the nasty cut on her thigh has stopped hurting, there is nothing worse that she can feel past the voice screaming that she doesn't recognize as her own, a scream so hysterical, so penetrating in its fearfulness, that Nick's frenzy stops. He moves to place his hand over the screaming, to stop its horrid noise, when he hears the only words that could penetrate the mad cloud of his rage.

"In the car," she is screaming, "you, it was you in the car, it was you."

"Yes," he says, "yes. It was me."

His voice is so calm, so resigned, his body stilled, that she stops screaming, teetering on the edge of hysteria, yet startled by the silence.

"Are you afraid?" he says, his voice so soft, purring in her ears, the same hateful words, the hateful hands raping her in the car, his slave. "Afraid of me? Afraid of what I am going to do to you? Afraid you might like it? Like it too much?"

She never could have liked it, not this, she never—

"I want you to be afraid," he whispers. He has said the lines so many times before, rehearsing every second of this long-planned attack that he has no trouble remembering them now.

Nick was always good with his lines.

"I wanted you to live through one moment of undiluted, inexpressible terror," the voice is saying, inhumanly serene. "I want you to be afraid, I want you to know how it feels, because that's how Nick feels, all the time, without you."

"No," she is screaming again in unadulterated panic, she can't possibly live through that assault again and stay sane, "let me go, let me—"

The screaming is a violent rushing in his ears, there is nothing but the screaming, she'll never stop screaming, she'll never—that's what M said, once she knows she'll never—

He has to stop the screaming.

His hands around her neck, choking her, choking the life out of her, when I hit him from behind, knocking him away with a sharp cry of passionate pain, and I hit him again, anger stored for years uncounted unleashed in a hail of punches, wrestling him down as he tries to turn his fury, raging with adrenaline, on me, but I am stronger.

I have always been stronger.

He won't get away, I won't let him, if he does I know he will kill me, it would be so easy for him, hiding my body, all his secrets snuffed with my disappearance, remarked upon by no one save Jamie and McAllister, no one knows he is here, no one knows I am with him.

No one knows who I am. No one cares.

And then he will redouble his strangling wrath onto Olivia, gasping long shuddering breaths beside us.

She is still alive.

Nick and I have slipped over the side of the bed, I feel his hands searching frantically for something, the other whips he's hidden there, I can't let him reach them, and I slam his head into the metal frame of the bed, once hard, then again till I feel him slump, finally, dazed and bleeding, then haul him up on the bed, imprisoning his wrists with the silken cords he has used so delightedly and so often on Olivia, knowing they will only hold for a minute once he revives. I quickly grab the whips that were just out of reach and bind his ankles together, tight, then look desperately for my keys, the key to the trunk, before I realize they've fallen to the floor, near Olivia's, where I dropped them bursting into the room. When I stoop to pick them up I see a silver earring, delicate filigree studded with infinitesimal diamonds, like stars, caught deep in the carpet, and I pull it out and push it deep into my pocket, my hands shaking.

I flip up the trunk lid, throwing the soft embroidered linen and towels out in jumbled heaps, groping for the handcuffs underneath, finding them, and fasten Nick's wrists securely to the bedposts, just above the drapery cords.

Olivia has slid down to the carpet, leaning against the bed, her eyes closed, wheezing, blood oozing down her leg and seeping into the carpet. I pick her up gently and carry her into the kitchen, easing her down to the cool slate floor and placing her head between her knees. I grab the first-aid kit from under the sink, and examine her leg. It looks bad, but I don't think it needs stitches, so I clean it carefully and apply a butterfly bandage over several layers of gauze.

Olivia doesn't even flinch when I touch her.

I take out two ice packs Nick keeps in the freezer to soothe the aches and pains of weary muscles after a long day's work, wrapping each in a tea towel and placing them on her neck, picking up her hands and pressing them to the coldness, she deep in shock, obeying blindly mechanical, a jacquard print of fat sweet cherubs hiding the hideous necklace of fingerprints, rounded imprints of lurid pinks and purples emblazoned on her deathly pale skin like a brilliant sunset.

"Don't move," I say to her, although she couldn't have if

she tried, and I worry that she can't even hear me. "I'll be right back."

I pick up the first-aid kit and run back to Nick, who is just beginning to stir, disoriented, the gash on his forehead still trickling. I rummage again in the bottom of the trunk until I see the small box with the glass vials lined up neatly inside, all except one, and the syringes. I fill one neatly as Nick has shown me, a dose stronger than the one he used on Olivia, and jab it into his hip.

I gather up Olivia's scattered clothing and dress her calmly, she still dumb with shock, in the kitchen. "I'm going to take you home now," I tell her, shaking her slightly, sick with worry. "Olivia, can you hear me? You're going to be okay. I'm taking you home." Her eyes move to mine, and I sigh, relieved, placing the ice packs back on her neck with her hands over them. "I'll be right back. We're going in just one minute."

Nick's breathing is slow and steady, and I cover him with the comforter. I untie the whip from his ankles and drop it into the trunk, close the lid, then clean his wound and bandage it. He will be out for a long time, lost in the blissful sleep of oblivion.

When I hurry back to the kitchen, Olivia is calmer. She looks up at me, tears trickling down her cheeks in a silent stream, still holding the cherubs to her neck.

"It's okay. We're going now," I say, and scoop her up in my arms. She shudders at the touch, then buries her head in my neck.

She cries for a long time, sitting helpless in the dark on the smooth tiled floor of her kitchen, where we've gone so I could make her a cup of tea. She won't let me turn on the light there, she doesn't want to see her reflection in the polished metal gleam of the stove, or the hideous necklace of bruises she knows adorns her neck. I hold her tight, rocking her like a baby.

The comfort of the damned.

"Why did he do it?" she keeps asking. "Why why why?"

"Shhh," I say, trying in vain to console her. "It's not you. He can't help it." Murmuring over and over again. "It's not you, it's not you."

"How did you know I was there?" she asks, not expecting an answer. "You saved me."

I am glad there is so little light. I didn't save her at all, not when I could have, not through all the watching, not—

I wipe her eyes with a roll of paper towels until the tears stop, and she sighs deeply.

"Better?" I ask, determined to keep my voice benign even though I want to cry out to the heavens. "How's your leg?"

"Throbbing, but not too bad." She fingers the bandage through her jeans. "I deserve it."

She said that to me once before, ages ago, or was it only a day or two, when I said, Don't be ridiculous.

"How can you say that?" I tell her. "No one does. You don't mean it."

"Sure," she says ruefully. "But I still think this is what paying for your sins means."

I had not heard bitterness in her voice before, or regret.

"It wasn't sinful," I say, finally.

"Wasn't it?" Her voice is hard. "I mean, look at me! Look at what he's done to me! Just look at what I let him!" The hysteria is creeping back as she pulls away, turning around to look at me in the dim light. "How can you stand it, how can you live with him, or be with him, or be with yourself, how can you take it, how? Just tell me that, I have to know, tell me how I can look at myself and not want to *scream*."

I reach up to try and calm her, and she jerks back, then buries her head in her hands and sobs.

"Olivia, don't," I say, my heart breaking. "You can't blame yourself. You couldn't have known this would happen, not this way. He's never been with a woman like you before, he's never—"

"And what kind of woman am I?" she cries out. "What have I done?"

"You're you," I say. "Olivia."

She looks up at me, at my face, she is looking at me, the tears stop and her anguish clears, and for a terrible minute I think she sees me truly, and I want to get up and run away, but I am frozen here, I cannot move.

"Why do you stay together?" she asks, wiping the tears away.

I am staring at my shoes. There is blood spattered on them like drops of paint, alizarin crimson.

"There is nowhere else to go." My voice is a whisper. "It's all we know."

"But what do you owe him?" How can she ask me that, how can she be so understanding? "I should think he owes you."

"It doesn't matter anymore."

"Of course it does." She wipes her nose again, calming. "At least it does to me. I don't think I'll ever understand it."

"It's not you," I say again. "He can't help it."

"Is that what you were afraid of, when you said you wouldn't let him hurt me?"

"I'm sorry," I say, babbling, incoherent. "I tried, I promised you, I know I did, I didn't think he would—he never told me, what he—I couldn't—"

She puts a finger to my lips, and I hear myself starting to choke.

"Oh, M," she says, "I believe you. I know you did. Now hush."

She moves back, close to me, and we sit, locked together.

"I need to know where the pain comes from," she says, finally.

I shake my head no.

"Please, M, I have to know. You must tell me. I won't ask you anything else."

Her eyes fill with tears again. I cannot stand to see her cry anymore, not tonight, not ever.

"It comes from fear." My voice is so low I can hardly hear it. "If all you know is how to live without love, who can teach you how to live with it?"

I can't believe I said that.

"It's always been worse for you, hasn't it?" she says.

I close my eyes.

"You know too much, don't you?"

I try to pull away but her arms are wound tightly around me.

"You are so sad, M, I never met anyone so sad in all my life," she says. "Who hurt you?"

"Don't ask me," I say. "Please don't ask me."

"M," she says. "M." Her voice is calmer, detached, she is regaining control. She is looking at me once more as no one has ever looked at me, as she always has, without fear or repulsion. I don't want her to see me like this, not Olivia, not the woman I have watched so avidly in secret for all the hours she could give us.

I am unworthy of her sympathy, but I feel her fingers in my hair, gently caressing, and I haven't the strength to make her stop.

"You are full of secrets," she says, "many more secrets than anyone I've ever known." She can't say Nick's name, not yet. "I would have painted you as the Sphinx, you know, if you'd let me, sitting on your haunches in the desert. Forever impenetrable. That enigmatic expression on your face—it's almost impossible to paint. I wonder if I could have done it."

"What expression?" I ask, bewildered.

She scrambles up, pushing back her hair and blowing her nose. "Just a minute. Stay there. Don't move."

I'd just said that to her, hadn't I, not so very long ago. I sit frozen on her kitchen floor, wondering, until she comes back a moment later with a heavy drawing pad and pencils and a large square flashlight, the kind meant for camping trips and restful nights in a tent in a forest. She props the lantern on the floor beside her, shining it up toward the ceiling.

"You belong to the shadows," she says, "and I'm going to draw you in them."

"No," I say. The impossible wonder I'd dreamed of, watching her watching me, please don't, I don't want to see myself as she must see me, nakedly revealed, I can't. It will be the ultimate betrayal.

"Please, M, let me," she says, her voice pleading, and I am afraid she is going to cry again. "I need to hold on to something. I need to *do* something. Concentrate. Think about anything but . . ." Her hands hover near the bruises on her neck, but she can't bear to touch them. "Don't let me think. Please."

I could never say no to her.

The slight rasp of her pencil, the hunch of her body, the furrowed concentration, all so familiar. I can feel her relaxing, if only imperceptibly, into the work.

"If you don't like it you can do what you want with it," she says conversationally. I had forgotten how she usually liked to talk when she drew.

"Okay," I say.

"M, will you do something for me?" she asks several minutes later. She sounds almost like herself again, pacified by the ingrained habits of what she does best.

"Anything," I say.

"Tell me a story," she says. "Tell me a story of when you were little."

"I don't think you want to know."

She looks up at me, at my face. "Ah," she says, "the inscrutable one speaks. Don't move a muscle. That's just the face I
was looking for." She smiles, a little sadly. "Sorry. I didn't
mean to upset you. So tell me another one, a nice story. About
anything you like."

"There aren't any."

"I see." The scrutiny of her gaze, probing. She bites her lip,
deeply engrossed. "Never mind."

Her fingers always moving, dancing over the paper, the
grace of her body as she works, even seated here, on the
kitchen floor, the square brightness of the flashlight shining
up onto the ceiling, bouncing back down to her face, a glowing
madonna. Time slows, along with my breathing, and I almost
start to feel better.

"Done," she says, moments later, or it could have been
hours. I suddenly realize my legs are aching with cramp.
"Well, it's kind of raggedy, and rough, but it'll do for now.
Take a look."

I don't want her to be finished, I don't want her to stop, I
don't want to leave this place, I cannot look.

"Go on," she says, smiling. "If you don't like it I'll be
crushed."

She holds the pad out to me, and I take it, my hands
trembling as if it were a newborn I might not know how to
hold, and will drop, and then I look. I see the body of a sphinx,
its haunches curved and powerful, its tail a fat whip in the
sand, and I see a face, mine and yet not mine, powerful and
proud, a nearly imperceptible hint of a smile curving the edge
of my lips, guarding some mysterious knowledge. It seems to
be shimmering in the dazzling white light of the desert, but I
realize I am staring through a hazy film of tears at this image
of my features, handsome and whole as I might have been, no
scars disfiguring my face.

"Does this mean you like it?" she asks.

I nod, unable to speak, afraid that words of mine might break the mirage of this enchantment.

"I'm glad," she says, taking it back. "Let me sign it for you." Her pencil, hovering over the drawing. " 'To M.' No, wait, I don't like that. What's your real name?"

She couldn't be asking me that. Not now, not here, not after—

"Oh, M," she says, putting down the pad. "After all this, you can trust me."

"No," I say, and I feel myself starting to shake. It is too much, all too much, holding it back, me, watching, all that time, everything I've seen, everything, my whole life, Nick, kissing her, pinning her down, her squirms irresistible, tying her wrists to the bed, making her body his slave, moaning her pleasure while I watch, while the tapes whirl, oblivious. Nick, jagged glass in his hand, making her scream, his hands around her throat, wanting to squeeze the life out of her. Nick, hand-cuffed to the bed, blood trickling down his forehead, dripping onto the sheets.

"Baby," she says, her arms around me, kneeling at my side, her hands on my shoulder, gently kneading the stiffening muscles. Don't stop, I beg her, a silent imploring, don't let go of me, I'll tell you anything, any pain is worth the sweet touch of your hands, your head so close to mine, the perfume of your hair, the scent of you, the essence of Olivia, so close, your voice a whisper, "Baby," you called me, that word so strange from your lips, please don't go, don't leave me.

"His name isn't Nick," I say suddenly.

"What?" Her fingers stop, only for a second, then begin again, deeper as she moves closer, because my voice is no louder than a whisper.

"Nick. It's not his name."

"What is his name?"

"Ralph."

"Ralph?" I think I hear her laughing, but there is a sharp buzz in my ears, and I am still trembling at her touch. "Ralph?"

"Ralph Polachek. From Pittsburgh."

"He doesn't look like a Ralph."

"That's the name he was born with. It's not who he is."

"Something horrible must've happened, yes? His parents? What?" Her hands on my shoulders, massaging in calm rhythmic strokes. I can't tell her, I will never tell anybody, we swore it to ourselves, Nick and I, brothers in blood. "It has to come from some hideous place, that anger," she murmurs, almost to herself. "To be that afraid. No wonder you . . . no wonder he couldn't . . ."

I try to pull away. She won't let me.

"You were orphans, weren't you?" she says, cool and clinically detached, she has broken our code, deciphering our language of pain. "How many homes did he live in? Is that how you met him?"

The shadowy air, hanging, I could see the air, thick, murky, I will not breathe, not think, it hurts too much.

"That explains 'Who Am I?' " she says softly, remembering with a sigh. "How many people must have hurt him."

She has forgiven me, forgiven us all, I can hear it in her voice, so tranquil, soothing me, I can't bear it, there is no judgment there, only kindness and trust undeserving, and her hands, sweet, don't stop, please, if you stop I will go mad. "How many people hurt you, M?"

Don't go, don't leave me.

"Who is the real Nick Muncie?"

I will tell you, tell you this, tell you anything, anything but my name, as long as you don't leave me.

"Nobody," I whisper. "A nobody, like me."

"Go on."

"He was a boy we knew, a kid. Nick. We never knew his last name. But he said he came from Muncie, Indiana."

"What happened to him?"

"He died."

"Died how?"

"In a fight. On the street."

"How old was he when he died?"

"Eleven, I think."

"Is that where you lived, on the streets?"

I nod. Her fingers, comforting, stroking my neck, pulling my head down into her lap as if I were her child, "Baby," she called me, her voice an embrace, lulling my fears away, had her voice not been such a lullaby I could not have spoken.

I have quite forgotten that I am meant to be comforting her. It is such a relief to be able to say what has never been said, after all this time, her ears meant for my burden, listening to it calm and serene, taking it away and setting it free.

Please, take it away. Make it go away.

"How old were you when you met that Nick?" she says.

"Twelve."

"Is that when you got the scars?"

"No."

"How old were you when you got the scars?"

"Fifteen."

She is silent for a moment, thinking. "Three years. On the streets, together. No one came looking for you."

My head buried in her lap, I cannot stop my trembling.

"M," she says, bending down to hold me tight, her hair falling over my cheeks, "forgive me. I'm sorry I asked, but I needed to know. I'm so, so sorry."

I am trying to pull away, I cannot bear her holding me so close, the perfume of her so close to me, smothering, I cannot breathe, I am choking, let me be.

"Don't leave me, M," she says. "Please, please don't leave me." Her hands on me, she won't let me go.

I shake my head, dumbly, like a dog.

"Look at me."

I can't.

Her hands on my cheeks, her thumbs on my scars. "Look at me."

I meet her eyes, the gray in them dark with emotion, polished pewter, full of tears.

"Stay," she says, her voice so gentle I think I will go mad. "I want you to stay." There is no duplicity in her eyes, only an unbearable shining tenderness. "Just for a moment." My lips move silently in sheer disbelief. "Please. Don't leave me yet." Her voice more frantic, remembering. "I need you, M. You. I need you." Her arms around me, her face buried in my shoulder, and I am desperate, disbelieving, terrified she will dissolve into mist and melt away, that I will wake up from the unimaginable before my futile longing for her touch becomes the reality that is Olivia, here, now, sweet in my arms, asking me not to leave her.

I don't recall how long we stayed like that, secret sharers. I only know that in the twilight haze of half-sleep where the mind cannot distinguish between the wishful thinking of wakefulness and the transcendent reveries possible only in dreaming, I could see it, so vivid and real, I could feel, truly feel, at last, my arms around Olivia, lifting her gently to carry her downstairs, my foot nudging open the door that has always been locked to us, taking her into the bedroom I could not describe even now in my imagination, because there was only Olivia, easing down with me, so close, onto her bed, and me melting into her with a pleasure so pure and indescribable I wish I could have died then, beside her.

The essence of desire.

"Thank you," she would have whispered as we lay together, legs intertwined, smiling beatifically before drifting off to sleep. "You gave me my self back."

That is what she would have said.

That is how I will remember it.

When at last I can breathe again I sit up with a start, a chilled sharp ache in the small of my back. I look down at Olivia, dozing, her hair cascading down her back, tangled and lovely, but even its thick waves cannot cover the bruises on her neck, still livid and ugly, and I am jolted back to reality. Nick, in the flat, handcuffed to the bed.

Olivia stirs, pushes her hair out of her face, and sits up. "What time is it?" she says. "What are you doing?"

"I have to go." I get up and stretch, I must keep moving, I must, or I won't have the strength. "Are you okay?"

She nods. She is. She must be.

There is nothing else to say, I can tell. For once I am not lying to myself.

Everything has been said already.

She gets up and follows me to the door, then throws her arms around me, hugging me tight.

"Goodbye, M," she says, her eyes full of tears, then tries to laugh. "This time it's goodbye for real, isn't it?"

I try to smile, but cannot.

"Take care of yourself, M," she says, pleading. "And take care of Nick. Promise me you'll take care of him. He needs—"

Her voice is wavering, but her spirit is not. She has never been more a woman, scarred forever, yet with a heart full of forgiveness.

"He needs you," she says. "Only you know what to do. Don't let him suffer."

Only I know what to do.

I open her door, and step outside into the cold night, clear and sharp. The stars are shining.

"I promise," I say, and she closes the door.

AFTER

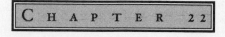

Nick sits and smokes, rocking. He has disappeared from the
world, hiding in a house I have found us high in the Jamaican
hills. This current landscape is far, far removed from everything that preceded it, the chilling, seeping, bone-rot winter
of London. Here, we are drenched with a humidity that is
warm and seething, bathwater for a baby. It is the rainy sea-
son, the downpours descending with a violent rush, drumming
on the verdant greenery at our feet, but Nick sits oblivious on
the veranda, his senses dulled by the fat spliffs of ganga
plucked and delivered each morning after toast and mangoes,
damp with morning dew, greenly moist and intoxicatingly
pungent. With the delicacy of the hand of the surgeon who so
neatly stitched and tied the sutures around the silicone saucers
stuffed inside Belinda's breasts, Nick mindlessly rolls one ci-
gar-shaped spliff after another, his gestures tidy and precise,
as unfeeling and unaware as an automaton's, lining them up
on a tray in rows as orderly as Olivia's fat crumpled silver

tubes of paint. He covers them with a silver dome to keep the raindrops and bugs away. He drinks coffee, or ice water, or Irish whiskey. He eats mechanically, without tasting the spice of jerk chicken or curried goat made in vast quantities by the housekeeper, Daisy. She clucks, she fusses over him, she clears away the plates, eyeing the shiny dome hiding Nick's pile of hand-rolled treasures and muttering darkly about that poison, and stays out of his way.

She has no idea who this man is. All she sees is the torment of his silence, enshrouded in fragrant smoke and humid mist. Of all the women in the world, the only one who has ever genuinely pitied him is a large Jamaican named Daisy, who has never strayed farther than the isolated hills where she was born, who has never seen his movies and would not care to, a sweet-tempered woman with a gold tooth and a white knit cap covering her graying hair, and an instinctive knowledge of the language of pain.

Nick sits and smokes, rocking, staring out over the valley. Sheets of tropical rain descend, thick and luscious, ricocheting off the creeping umbilical tendrils of broad plants, dripping in staccato beats on the corrugated steel roof of the veranda. That is all Nick sees, the greenness of this insidious creeping vegetation. Plumes of wood smoke rise up into the sky, thickening the mist before dissolving into the heavens, as untouchable and insubstantial as the desires captured so faithfully on videotape, flickering images, shameful and unreal. As impenetrable as they are, they cannot hide the carnal torture of his uncoupling and the burden of his memories.

I wonder what he remembers.

Nick does not speak, withdrawn into near-catatonia. He sits and smokes, rocking, unshaven, his proud muscles drooping like the wide leaves burdened with rain. It doesn't matter what he looks like because there are no mirrors, and even if there were, he couldn't bear to look in them.

It is not just withdrawal from the physical addiction of Olivia. It is the absolute abdication of his life, a thorough retreat from the possibility of love.

Belinda calls, calls again, swearing her fealty, token lying gestures, then gives up in mock defeat. She's done her bit, pretending she can't live without Nick, and now all she can do is wait. Besides, McAllister is the one assigned to all the day-to-day dirty work, that endless drivel of Hollywood business I was never equipped or expected to do, of keeping Nick up there on the scrap heap of egos even when he is hidden far away. That's what he's supposed to be paid for, Belinda screams at McAllister, her precarious position atop the pecking order *du jour* teetering with Nick's increasingly long absence from the spotlight, it's Mac's job, isn't it, to find his pretty boy, and do something, fast. Because he has disappeared, Nick is so hot he's sizzling, so hot he's practically incandescent, although that is not a word in Belinda's vocabulary, but she can repeat what she hears, and she's hearing it from everybody. Yes, we need him here, and Mac had just better find a way to bring him back home where he belongs.

McAllister calls the house once a week, sometimes more, begging, and then soon, when tired of groveling to Nick's silence and my monosyllabic explanations, the threats begin. You've got looping to do, Nick, he says, it's in the contract, you've got to get back. You're meant to be doing your next picture, you agreed to it months and months ago. Go ahead, throw your career away, everybody's talking about you, your price is up to fifteen million, go ahead, name it, everybody wants to work with you.

Everybody wants to be you.

Nick listens blankly. He says nothing, he never speaks, only the sound of the rain on the steel roof a faint echo over the phone to let McAllister know the line is still open and he is listening, and then he hands me the phone. Leave us alone, I say, Nick will call you when he has something to say, and hang up.

Sometimes, when his rocking drives me mad, I disappear into the hills on the bike I have rented, smaller than a Harley but easier to maneuver on bumpy bad roads, shifting gears, hands clenched, steam rising off my naked back as I ride through the rain as warm as the Jacuzzi by the pool, lost, the road curving up, past shacks and tethered goats, past people who stare and then smile and wave, past the verdant plots of pot, up, climbing into nothingness.

I don't want to know where I am going, because wherever I turn, the road heads back to Nick.

Nick snaps out of it weeks later, months, there are no separate days, only the same moments, the endless dreary rewind of rocking, smoke, and silence.

I have just gotten off the bike when I hear him doing push-ups on the veranda.

"Get me out of here," he says, and we leave the next day.

We have no reason to talk about anything other than the plans for the day. Nick throws himself back into his work, meets with McAllister, who is smart enough not to bring up the months lost and does not say a word about the stoniness darkening the blue of Nick's eyes. They remind Mac of a winter's twilight, a winter's evening he spent once, years ago, in New York, when a nor'easter had blown the skies clean and the air was pure, so cold the little hairs inside his nose, clipped so assiduously by Mr. Tony the barber, froze a bit more with each breath, an evening when the square, lit windows in the skyscrapers around him seemed to dance they were so alive, brightly colored and dazzlingly clean, the wind blowing the grit from their surface to reveal the jewels glowing beneath, unearthed for his eyes only as tears came to them in the wind, and the blue of the sky a deepening sapphire, hard and cold, immeasurably blue.

It frightens him, this color so brilliant and yet so bleak, so he politely hands Nick scripts to read, and as politely they discuss them. Thankfully the film Nick is scheduled to shoot has been pushed back. He isn't ready for that kind of work, so he plays the waiting game, lunching with Mac and everyone they should be lunching with, flashing his famous smile.

That is the prerogative of the superstar. He can smile, he can mope, he can laugh, he can lure women into his lair and not even know their names, he can withdraw into paranoia, but if he smiles for the camera with the babe on his arm he is there, and that's all they need for the moment, theirs to see, their beloved, Nick Muncie, superstar. Everybody wants to work with him.

Everybody wants to be him.

At first he stayed away from Belinda, and it almost worried me, realizing that he'd never gone so long without a woman. But as he ventures out into the twisted thickets of the places we know so well, the old patterns slowly reemerge by sheer force of habit. Belinda is not happy with Nick's increasingly sporadic visits, but she is not stupid, no, she will play any game Nick wants to play, easily, it suits her, she will do anything to maintain the illusion of Hollywood's hottest couple, even if it means submitting to the increasingly sadistic demands of the most adored superstar in the world.

Sex is no longer of any interest to Nick. No more the trawling ventures into nightclubs, the endless succession of choreographed pleasure taken so violently from lissome blindfolded bodies I have procured. Only pain engages him, and the idle curiosity of how far he can push Belinda before she cracks. In this they are matched, unsurpassed, because she likes what he's doing now almost too much as long as the bruises don't show, and she trusts Nick not to ruin her reputation, as well as his own. But even they are soon bored, going through the motions, tamed by their sheer banality of their excesses, linked only by an insatiable craving for physical release slowly diminishing to the odd sporadic whipping. It is tiresome, for them, and for me.

I no longer watch. Nick no longer expects me to watch. There is nothing to see.

More months fly by, a false calm, a spurious dawn when the sun's rising is a cheat, delayed by the heavens themselves, obscured by a storm. The months fly by and the whispers have started, small, a word here, bewildered, a leak, a hint, the town is soon abuzz with the unbelievable possibility that Nick Muncie has pulled it off, yes, can you believe it, how could he have found it in him, sure he's an action hero, a romantic star, but no one ever thought he could *act*.

The whispers become louder, swelling, the words husky, portentous, he has done it, this is it, it is a marvel. The marketing department continues their plotting in feverish anticipation. *"Faust: The Movie!"* they exclaim after test screenings with such predictability that even Nick laughs. *"He sold his soul to the devil! His thirst for knowledge took him on an incredible journey beyond his wildest dreams!"*

People actually believe this bullshit.

The movie theaters are booked, and the carefully orchestrated leaks are as blithely unbelievable as Nick's modest shrugs when asked about the film. Just wait, he says, just wait, and judge for yourself.

That the film is indeed a success has confounded the critics eager to deflate the hype before they'd caught a glimpse of Nick in costume. *"From heaven through all the world to hell!"* they write, claiming Goethe's words as their own, but that doesn't matter, because the author's been dead so long there's no one around who could possibly sue, much less understand what he's talking about.

Faust, a metaphor for the misery of our century, *Faust*, a metaphor for the destruction of nature, they say, *Faust*, the genuine quest that few of us dare risk, *Faust*, the fictitious man more audacious than any authentic person of our time.

Faust is fabulous, but don't bother reading the original, they say again, the movie is so much better.

Nick does not mind the daily machinations demanded of him by the studio, the numbing weariness of meetings, interviews, and the fawning public, the world's press at his feet. Why did he decide to do it, why *Faust*, why now, why him, why London?

Why London, why Queens Gate, why Queensway, why the flat in Porchester Square, why that flat, empty now, I imagine, the holes plugged and sanded, painted over with such smooth precision that no one would ever know they even existed. The furniture is gone, I gave it all away, shipping the gilt chairs to McAllister and the lovely round table to Jamie, wrapping up the pillows and *objets* and linens that were unstained with blood for the cast and crew, I gave away every last thing as presents, forging Nick's scrawled signature as I was accustomed, more perfect than his own, on his thick cream embossed note cards, thanking them for all that *Faust* was and will become, can you forgive those moments when I was a pain, I hope we can work together, soon, with love from Nick.

I wouldn't have minded seeing their faces, the bewildered gratitude for such exquisite things, such generosity, they would have been saying, this is worth a fortune, I can't believe he thought of me.

I kept the vase of Murano glass and the Mapplethorpe flower for myself, hidden away in my room, impossible for Nick to find. The sight of them would drive him mad.

The mirrors were no longer there to give away. He'd smashed them both to pieces.

An Oscar for sure, the pundits declare.

Nick smiles and looks happy, delighted, he knows he'll never win, he hasn't a hope in the world.

He isn't lying.

A tailwind, pushing the media machine, eases it gently into the slipstream, flying high, higher, soaring, giddy, when the Oscar nominations are announced and Nick's name is on the list.

Belinda, during her delirium of excitement in the weeks before the ceremony, trying to decide between the dozens of designer gowns she's been offered to wear, pays little attention to Nick's reclusiveness. He appears only at industry functions, when he has to, his habitual charm aphrodisiacal, radiant with hopefulness, and then slips away from the crowds, hurrying, out through the kitchens and the service entrances, sliding into the backseat of the black Range Rover, no more visible than a ghost.

None of it matters, not the way it should have, not the way he once would have wanted.

We drive in silence up the hill.

Nick needn't have done *Faust* to prove his dramatic skills to me, after all, for he is playing the ultimate role to a mute audience of one. He is starring as the creature he used to be. He has resurrected himself as Nick Muncie, superstar, no more alive than a zombie crawling from his grave, glassy-eyed and stiff.

His only solace, the sustenance that feeds him, is the knowledge of what awaits when he finally is allowed to go home after another day working the idiot machinery of Hollywood. He locks himself into the blue room of the pool house, locking me, and the world, out. He moves slowly, deliberate, prolonging the agony, he sits in his overstuffed leather chair and picks up the remote, he leans back, his eyes glued to the screen, his heart stopping, and he watches, watches it all, late into the night.

All that matters is locked in a blue room, waiting for the push of a button.

C H A P T E R   23

It will be better if I watch the ceremony from the television in the limo, I told Nick, and he agreed. I have never gotten used to the inquisitive stares at public gatherings, even if it is the industry and people who might know me, I don't want to feel the eyes of the well-dressed and ill-bred stars and starlets, see the wide glare of the lenses focused upon me, and hear the echoing trail of their habitual murmurings about what I look like and who I am and why Nick is with me. Not tonight.

Tonight belongs to Nick.

When he hears his name called, Nick sits stunned for a second, then as the applause begins he gives Belinda a cursory hug for the cameras. He straightens his jacket and saunters up to the podium, a dazzling roar buoyant around him, crashing in his ears, drowning out his desperate craving to call out Olivia's name to the world watching him.

"Wow," he says, his hands clasped around the golden statue. "Never, never did I think I'd ever be standing here."

A wave of delighted laughter ripples through the crowd, then more applause. He rakes his fingers through his hair, and one stray curl flops to his forehead. He is one of them, their own gorgeous darling, glowing with vitality and happiness, impossibly handsome, and unbelievably desirable.

"You know, most of us, even me, if we are honest enough to admit it, aspire to this mad dash for glory more than any other," he says slowly, adding a flash of the famous smile. "This one perfect moment."

He squares his hands around the base of the gleaming Oscar.

"This is one perfect moment for me as an actor, and for that I am profoundly grateful. All you who have helped me in my life and work—my friends, my colleagues, everyone on *Faust*, my costars, the cast and crew whose patience was tried, I know, on many occasions, and I hope you'll forgive me now— share with me in this delight. I must especially thank my agent, Edmond McAllister, who had the balls to back me up on this project, and enough good manners not to laugh in my face even though I'm sure he thought I was crazy. And I'd like to thank Jamie Toledo, my director, who had the courage to believe in me when nobody else would."

Trembling pause.

"Although I am not blessed with a family of my own, I am fortunate that my friends and colleagues, and all of my fans, have become like family to me," Nick continues, "and there are two people most dear to me, my real family, that I must also thank tonight."

Belinda preens and adjusts her dress, readying herself for the cameras, running her tongue over her teeth to make sure there's no lipstick on them.

"The first many of you know only as the Major, a friend who has been like a brother to me for many years. Wherever you are," he says with a wide grin, "I know you are watching.

"The other is someone who gave me one other perfect moment, not so long ago in my life." He stops, and steadies his breath. "And so I would like to dedicate this Oscar to her, my true beloved, the woman who gave me my heart and taught me at last the terrible power of love. Without her, the rest is meaningless. Thank you."

Who would have thought Nick capable of such public tenderness? I imagine the collective hiss of unbridled libido and wonderment sighing through the auditorium like wind in wheat. There is no woman in the audience or in the world, at that instant, not brimful of anguished desire, aching to take Nick home to hold tight in her arms, crooning sweet nothings, his head grateful on her breast, and be the one to save his soul, his true beloved.

No woman save Belinda. As she wipes the very perfect single tear of delighted pleasure from her eye in case any roving photographer should catch her reaction during Nick's moment of glory, I expect the wheels are already churning below Mr. Frederick's impeccably towering coiffure. The glint in her green eyes as hard as the emeralds in her ears, oh yes, her thoughts as transparent as the chiffon gown shielding the superb curves of her body, the jealous knowledge that Nick's true beloved has not been and never will be Miss Belinda Beverley, oh no, but whoever that bitch is, she'd better not think of setting foot in Miss B's face.

Belinda's shoulders square imperceptibly in anticipation of *le tout* Hollywood trying to divine the real identity of Miss True Beloved, but then, she realizes, why shouldn't it be her, the lucky creature, oh yes, the envious eyes of the world will be upon her. Her shoulders move back another notch, plumping forward her breasts. Yes, why not. Her dimples deepen. Why not indeed. Better call McAllister and make sure her price goes up immediately. Maybe her next film could be called *True Beloved*.

* * *

The divine delight of the obligatory grand entrances at all the right parties, Belinda giddy with joy and glowing luminous with the gloriousness of brilliance reflected, the momentary horror of his speech instantly forgotten as she propels Nick, their fingers sweat-locked together, toward the photographers calling out raucously for just one more shot. My ravaged face is not wanted to mar these pictures of perfection incarnate, so I hang back, ducking my head, little black freckles dancing before my eyes from the strobes exploding in our faces. People who do not know me stare impudently, wondering how such an incongruously rude jolt of undesirability could possibly be thrust amid their toned and scalpel-shaped flesh at such a stellar gathering, until someone whispers a few quick words of identity and I catch a sideways glance that quickly shifts away, blushing and afraid. Few dare speak, even to offer token words of congratulation, but I am not surprised. All I see around me are the yapping mouths working furiously, opening and shutting, grinning, dazzling white with perfectly polished, capped teeth.

No one will sleep tonight, buzzing on the delirious whoosh of adrenaline and drink and the spiteful delight of sharing in the underdog's gleeful victory. We have been to the Academy dinner, and two of the most prominent benefits, and McAllister's, and now we are at the most exclusive party of all at last year's winner's house up on Woodrow Wilson, a short drive from our own, the panorama of twinkling fairyland at our feet. The air is thick and humid, a storm is brewing, but it will not rain, not this night, tonight belongs to the stars on the ground light-years from those in the heavens, and it is not desired by the earthly bound to be inconvenienced by wet. It is their night, the terminally trendy, sliced and diced, poured into sharply cut tuxedos or slinky gossamer confections, teetering

on toothpick heels, necks in perpetual whiplash swiveling between Nick Muncie, superstar, and the marvelous rush of
recognition every time another guest arrives.

I catch Nick's eyes swerving to the door, as if the sheer
force of his desperate admission of love could somehow propel
Olivia over the portal and into his arms.

After a while, he stops looking.

I want to go home and lie down in the dark, alone and quiet,
isolated from the maelstrom of noise and jealous adulation
buffeting us like the Santa Ana winds, but Nick has asked me
to stay near him, to film everything this night of nights, a
splendid souvenir. The irony of the camcorder out in the open
did not elude him, and I dare not disobey, not tonight.

There we remain high in the hills, high above the world on
the pinnacle Nick has climbed.

I am standing near the bar, surveying the crowd through
the viewfinder of the camcorder at my cheek, when I catch
snatches of conversation between two men waiting for their
drinks, filtering between the noise and general merriment.

". . . never thought I'd see you and . . ." says one. I recognize him, vaguely, as a producer of art-house films. I can't
remember his name. ". . . here in Hollywood."

"My wife didn't . . . not fond of . . . but we sail at dawn,"
says the other. His accent is French. "Might as well . . . up
all night . . . Hawaii."

". . . very pleased . . . too bad she didn't keep the portrait.
It'll be worth a fortune now . . . Oscar."

Portrait. A Frenchman. There is a terrible feeling, one I
never wanted to feel again, beginning to crawl through the
knots in the pit of my stomach.

I slide closer, turning my back, until I can hear them more
clearly.

". . . quick stopover, yes, a belated honeymoon, for at least

a month or two, bobbing around the Pacific, in blissful silence," says the Frenchman. "But of course I insisted on a
small keyboard, for practice, and she is bringing her paints."

"Well, it sounds delightful, but I can't imagine anyone else
here tonight would care much for such splendid isolation,"
says the producer. "It's very refreshing to find someone who
chooses to spurn the spotlight. Almost shocking, in fact."

"Yes, but I have quite enough of it when I'm on tour," the
Frenchman says, "and I very nearly had to drag my wife out
of our hotel. She says these film people are too *dégueulasses*, but
we came with friends who insisted on this party. To them it
is very important, and you know . . ."

I step away from them and risk a quick glance, recognizing
him instantly from the photographs I have seen so many times
on the front of his CDs. He is thinner than I thought, not a
commanding presence, but a pleasant face, full of character,
deep laugh lines etched near his eyes, attractive and happy
and blessedly normal.

I keep the camcorder high, paranoid, because I don't want
Olivier to see the scars on my exposed cheek. What if, for
some strange reason, Olivia has described my face to him?

What if he knows?

What if she sees Nick? What if he sees her?

The panic is churning inside me, and I step into the throng
of people congregating around Nick, still pretending to be
shooting.

I find Nick through the lens and press the button. He is
laughing, someone shouts over to him and he turns his head
to the noise, I follow his gaze, I see the laughter die on his
lips.

Olivia.

Nick sees Olivia.

His heart stops. He is dead, but still breathing, he can hear noise, an echo of Belinda's laughter, there are bodies pressing close to his, he can still see, he sees her, the impossibility of Olivia, there, before him, almost close enough to reach.

I keep the camera on Nick, although there is nothing I want more than to drop it there at my feet and find her, to see her face, most beloved, to sink my hands into her hair wild around her, to drown my face in it and stay like that, forever.

I remain immobile, watching him, paralyzed by my own longing, and by the look of such unbearable pain clouding Nick's eyes, threatening to dissolve in tears. I was shocked by the sudden tears he willed away when he first saw the portrait, but still he has not cried for many years, and he will not cry now. A helpless wave of desperate pity for him floods me, stabbing my heart with bittersweet tenderness, replacing the bleak ache of hatred that has lived there, a dull and boring tenant, for so long it is my constant companion.

I can finally see clearly, with dazzling clarity.

There is no rage left for all that he did, the memories of the flat, or the car, or that last awful day, every memory erased by a shining beam of love. With that fleeting second, no longer than a blink, his love dazzles me, a searing flash, the pure sonar still sounding in the depths of his anguish.

"Take care of him, M," she'd said to me. *"Promise me. Only you know what to do."*

With that fleeting second the mask drops to reveal the appalling nakedness of yearning vulnerability, as if a computer suddenly realizes that it does indeed possess a soul, yet is pathetically aware of its terrible shortcomings.

But Nick is only human, and undone, wounded beyond comprehension, yet so nearly redeemed by the illusion of his one perfect moment.

A shadow moves in front of Nick, and I stop filming. I look back up to see him standing, pale under his tan, his eyes closed, forcing the emotion back to the darkness with a few deep breaths. When he opens his eyes, that look has disappeared, replaced by the habitual gaze of the emperor in his court surrounded by the sycophantic chorus of admirers. You were fantastic, you must be so thrilled, they are saying. Here, have another drink, smile for the camera, oh thank you, you deserve this, you really do, this must be the happiest night of your life.

"Take care of him, M. Promise me. Only you know what to do."

She must have disappeared, melting into the crowd, taking her own anguish with her, melting as the core of him did for one infinite second, one interminable, aching moment.

I do not turn to find her, she is already gone. She was always gone because she was never truly there, a pale shimmering ghost, a fleeting shadow dancing in delirious abandon in a gilded flat in Porchester Square, captured by the camera, frozen in unreal movements, her body intertwined with his, naked wanting made palpable on tape, a living dream of the essence of desire.

But all that remains for me is this one frozen moment.

I know what I must do. I will honor my promise, her last request.

The sun is already sneaking over the horizon when we return home, Nick, Belinda, and me. Belinda flops down on the bed, kicks off her shoes, and stretches, still reveling in her reflected glory.

Nick is drunk, drunker than I have ever seen him. There is a storm cloud growing in him, seething with electricity, his is a funnel forming, a black finger roiling, emerging just a little, so tentative, groping down, retreating, groping down again, farther, deeper, wind howling, it touches the ground, black, whirling faster, it grows, engorging, swollen and immense, it feeds upon the very air that it has sucked inside, cutting a swath of utter destruction in its wake.

Nick is standing at the end of the bed, holding the Oscar in his hand, not the genuine one waiting to be engraved, the stand-in, how fitting, I think, nothing this night can possibly be real. He is staring at Belinda, and she is too drunk to notice the glowering wrath in his eyes. She manages to sit up, and tries to grab at the statue.

"Give it to me," she says, slurring her words together. "I want to hold it." She tugs at him, then collapses in giggles.

"You want me to give it to you," he says.

"Come on, lover boy, give it to me," she pants, pulling off her dress, the perfect globes of her breasts beckoning as she lies back down. "I want to fuck the best actor in the world."

"I'll give it to you," Nick says. "I've got just what you want. An Oscar-worthy performance for Belinda Beverley, best actress in a supporting role."

He crawls onto the bed, the Oscar clenched in one hand, the other moving between her legs, her undulating hips, she is ready and willing, she is always ready. I see him pause, the turbulence of malicious loathing dimming his drunken blue eyes to black pools, darkness inescapable. "I'll give it to you," he says, "since you asked for it."

"Yes," she says, "now. I want it I want it I want it."

"Touch it," he says, the Oscar nuzzling her cheek. "It's cold, isn't it? Cold and shiny."

"Mmm, yes. Cold." Her fingers linger lovingly on it. "Sweet. Cold and sweet."

"Kiss it," Nick says. "Go on, give Oscar a kiss."

He places it gently to her lips, and she kisses it reverently.

"Kiss it again," he says.

"No." She is pouting. "I want to kiss you."

"I said, kiss it again."

Something in his voice penetrates her drunken stupor. "Oh, all right," she says and reaches for it. She kisses it deeply, her tongue caressing, licking it like a cat, then stops. "There, are you happy? Now, c'mere."

Nick looks at her again, sprawling on the bed, her eyes glistening with ready anticipation. He kicks off the Noconas he's worn even with his tuxedo, unhooks his cummerbund, unzips his trousers, and looms over her, a threatening shadow.

"Go on," he says, yanking her up by both arms till she is sitting on the edge of the bed. "Kiss it."

I cannot watch this. I open the sliding door, letting in some of the soft morning breeze to cool their heated bodies, and sit by the pool, shimmering calmly in the hazy early light, the city at my feet, the world at Nick's.

Belinda eagerly takes him in her mouth, he pushes into her roughly, she is gagging, trying to pull away, but this is how she wants it, this is Nick, and they have played this way many times before. Suddenly, he pulls away, tilts her head back farther with one hand, and brings the statue again to her lips with the other. "Kiss it," he says. He pushes it between her lips. It hurts, the metal against her teeth, his hand buried in her hair, ruthlessly entangled, keeping her head tilted back till her eyes swim, not letting her go, the metal cracking against her teeth, she is struggling, her hands reaching for his hips, it hurts, my God, make him stop.

With a vicious twist he shoves her down onto her back, she tries to get up, screaming, to scurry away from his nastiness, but he is too quick for her addled reflexes. He pulls her under him, pinning her down, forcing his way into her hard, harder than he's ever done before, so that even she is beginning to be frightened.

When I hear her scream I come running, and then I see what they are doing. They disgust me. I shove my hands deep in my pockets and walk around the pool to the garage, to the Harleys parked outside, and sit on Nick's for a long time. It would be so simple to do what I am thinking, what I have not stopped thinking about since London, or, if I stop deluding myself, for more years than I can count. So easy, a few minutes' work, and so painless for Nick. All I need is a wrench and a pair of pliers and the will to do it.

Only you know what to do.

"You want me to give it to you," Nick is shouting.

Belinda's mouth is on fire, she cannot speak, she is arching away, but Nick is glued to her, ruthlessly fucking, wanting to fuck her till she bleeds, wipe the smirk from those collagen-enhanced crimson lips, fuck her, fuck them all, fuck Hollywood, fuck the world and everyone in it.

He pulls her legs up around his waist, and she responds, she can't help it, this will always be what she wants, Nick, she is moaning softly, yes, it is so easy, she is thinking, it hurts how she likes it, the sharp aching so quickly replaced with an ecstatic rush, all other pain forgotten, she is his, he can do what he will, no other woman in the world can have him now, he is mine, Nick, mine, she is gloating enraptured, mine all mine.

"Don't stop," she says, her head lolling from side to side, her tongue thick with blood she does not feel, "don't. I want you I want you."

"You want me?" he asks, slowing down his frenzied movement.

"You. More."

"You want it?"

"Yes."

"Yes?"

"Give it to me," she is panting, dizzy with longing. "Don't stop. Don't ever stop."

"I won't," he says. "I promise. I won't ever stop." He pulls out, slowly, teasing her.

"Come back," she says, her eyes closed, her cheeks rosy,

her delectable body suffused with anticipation. Nick's fingers caress her, delicately, one finger probing deep inside her, she is so wet, she is dripping, more, do it again, when something hard and round, colder than Nick's finger, touches her, sliding up and down, lovely, cold and hard. It makes her laugh, at first. Cold and insistent, pushing, pushing Nick's finger away, pushing in, deep, deeper, it will not stop pushing.

"What—?" she says, her eyes flickering open, panicked. "Stop."

"I thought you didn't want me to stop," Nick says, pausing briefly.

"It hurts, it's too big." She pouts.

"You like it big."

"Only you—no, not this, what are you—"

He is pushing it deeper again, she cannot make it go away, please oh please. "Stop," she says. "Nick."

"Shut up," he says, slapping her face, her cracked lips, making them bleed again. "You said you wanted it, and now you can have it."

There is nothing in her but blind panic, the weight of Nick on top of her, crushing her chest, she is screaming for real with the hideous pain of it, screaming for her life, there is blood seeping through the sheets, he is tearing her apart, breaking her body in two, he will not stop, he wants her dead, her beautiful body still, her pouting lips silenced, her struggles are more feeble, there is blood soaking through the sheets, puddling on the floor, he wants to feel her die.

Somehow I manage to pull him off, the adrenaline fueling his rage lending superhuman strength to his body, but I have the advantage of surprise, disentangling him from the murderous melody thrumming through his veins.

"You're going to kill her," I yell, my arms around his neck in a choke hold. "Let go."

"Good," he yells back. "Get off me, you fuck."

I sling him down to the carpet, blood dripping down on us from the side of the bed, blood on his fingers, wrestling, he gladly fighting to the death. I keep him pinned, bang his head once, twice on the floor, but he hardly feels it.

"Get off me," he is still yelling. "Get off and get out, and don't ever show your fucking face to me again. Ever."

I say nothing but remain stretched on top of him, unyielding, until, soon, his ragged breathing slows. I do not doubt his sincerity, but finally I can tell myself that what he says to me no longer matters.

"You have no idea how much I hate you," he says, turning his head to the side just enough to spit the words at me.

I have never seen him closer, sweat dripping from my face to his, drops like tears, I have never seen such venom, sheer unadulterated malevolence shining with the true zeal of the deranged. It is not just Olivia, or Belinda, or the Oscar, or even me.

"Take care of him, M. Only you know what to do."

Only a few hours before those eyes had shone with the unimaginable bright sheen of loving despair. Now their glow is muted, the color of the sea down deep where warm-blooded creatures cannot dwell, only twisted blind crawling things.

I get up and lean over to Belinda to see if she is still alive. Barely. I wad up the sheets and place them between her legs to stanch the bleeding, wrap her in the blanket, and go to the phone.

Nick slowly stands, rearranging his tuxedo as if nothing has happened, his eyes glazed, oblivious. He wipes his bloody fingers on the trousers ogled by so many millions in the incomparable moment of his triumph.

"The ambulance is on its way," I say dully, hanging up. I don't know why I'm warning him. Habit, I suppose.

We look at each other, brothers in blood, locked together, sharing the same nightmare.

His eyes clear, for only an instant, another frozen moment.

"I didn't mean it," he says, grabbing his motorcycle jacket from the sofa and walking out, past the pool, past the blue room of stored fantasies, out to the garage. I follow him halfway, until I hear the Harley rev up, and the crunch of its tires.

I know where he is going. I know how he will get there.

There is nothing to do now but wait.

I carefully wash off the Oscar and place it on the living-room table. I fancy I can still hear the roar of the Harley, a vibrant echo.

I hear it still, roaring as if a shell were fastened to my ear, when the paramedics, their faces ashen, take Belinda away. I hear it, so loud and merciless, when the phone rings an hour later that I cannot quite understand the shaky voice of the cop on the other end, but it doesn't matter, because I already knew what he was going to say.

EPILOGUE

He died instantly, the cop told me. He was speeding, a tire blew, or maybe the engine stalled, or it could have been a coyote, maybe he swerved for a coyote, a helmet would've saved him, he should have worn a helmet, the poor cop kept saying, over and over, an early-morning mantra forged by the shocking horror of finding Nick's bloody body, limp and newly dead, the warmth receding slowly, it couldn't be him, maybe it was someone who looked just like him, yes, it was only his body double, maybe, please, it can't be true, what was Nick Muncie doing here on the dew-slicked back roads of the hills, riding his Harley, when he'd just been on the TV, everyone saw him, winning the Oscar, everyone in the world, he should have been home in bed, celebrating, he was the best actor in the world, he should have worn his helmet, it's such a tragedy, it's unbelievable, what a waste, what a waste.

What a waste.

There were so many reporters and television crews camping

outside our compound, thwarted by security, that the police had to escort me, my face hidden, inside and out, to deal with the formalities.

Only I knew the real reason Nick would never want to be buried. He left instructions for me to scatter his ashes to the wind, wherever I wanted, so I climbed up to the roof above the blue room of the pool house, the only place he'd found comfort in the last few months, and let them fly, disappearing into the hazy sunshine, little specks of gray dust dancing in the air before falling back to earth. With no grave, no crypt, no final resting place, the site of the crash became a shrine, the Père Lachaise of the back canyons, bitterly crying fans gingerly placing vivid bouquets tied with black satin ribbons near the skid marks which remained engraved on the asphalt, dark oily scars, until the rains came.

I had never seen Nick's will, which he'd clearly revised after our return to Los Angeles, and the contents of it hit me with a stinging pang of terrible sorrow. He left the bulk of his estate to fund an organization for abused children and runaways and another large sum to set up the Porchester Square Foundation for young artists, and asked me to oversee their management and the proper dispensation of the money. A sealed envelope went to a recuperated and newly subdued Belinda, whose injuries had been overlooked in the feeding frenzy after Nick's shocking death. An enormous check and dozens of compromising photographs of her with many men besides Nick were neatly arranged inside. I was certain that the look on my face when I handed it to her and the zeroes on the check would buy her silence forever. The residuals from *Faust*, his other properties, the house, and all the possessions inside it were left to me, to be disposed of as I saw fit. Nick made a pointed note of that, his intentions perfectly clear.

The portrait went to the Metropolitan Museum in New York, along with a rather large donation, and I was grateful he'd thought of that bequest. I'd handed a few king-sized sheets to one of the cops and asked him to cover the painting as soon as we got back to the house after I identified the body, and he gladly obliged me, grateful for one tidbit of gossip he could pass along to his buddies when they sat drinking later that day, shaken and disbelieving. I couldn't look at it. Nick had thought of the bequest, I suppose, for Olivia's sake, her stature as a painter. At first the trustees balked, not being altogether familiar with Olivia's work, or perhaps thinking the painted image of such a popular star too trashy for their collections, but once the record crowds of art lovers, who wouldn't know Bronzino from Batman, came thronging to see it, snapping up the poster and the postcards and the specially printed brochure in vast quantities, they quickly changed their tune.

That would have made Nick laugh.

The house needed some minor work before I could put it on the market. I plugged the hole behind the tapestry, trying not to think of the other hole I'd erased in the flat in London. I sent all the video equipment to Jamie and the cinematographer, and took Nick's assorted toys and leather goods to the dump in a nonbiodegradable plastic bag. I methodically destroyed the neatly stacked and labeled rows of black videotapes, prying off their tops, pouring acid on the tapes, then hauling the entire load to the huge crusher in the auto graveyard in Compton, watching impassively as they were pulverized into sparkling black dust.

I never looked at any of them before they were crushed into nothingness, I couldn't bear it. I saved only one. Olivia, dressing for their last and only weekend. Olivia, an apparition in black and white with ruby lips and pale staring eyes, that provocative creature, alluring and expectantly vulnerable, terrified, stretching out her hand to the gilded mirror by the fireplace, while I stood watching, trembling, just on the other side of the wall.

The house is sold and empty, the vague senseless pattern of our days, the ties that bound us all severed, all gone, snapped clean in an instant like Nick's neck, with a sound no louder than a twig breaking under a squirrel's foot scuttling through the piney underbrush, muffled by the angry whine of gears suddenly useless, upended, wheels of his Harley spinning frantically with nowhere to go.

For the benefit of the children's foundation I organized an auction of nearly all of his things. I didn't want them near me, the specter of his clothes, neatly folded and arranged, starched and hanging mementos, their silence a heavy mocking. The auction was a media circus, a delirium of passionate bidding not only for the serious collectors astonished at the quality of his art and photographs and furniture, especially the immense Gobelin tapestry and the gleaming vase of Murano glass, but for the fans who'd flown in from all over the world, desperate for a pair of black jeans he'd worn, a poet's shirt or a white cotton T-shirt, sixty-five thousand dollars for a black leather motorcycle jacket similar to the one he was wearing when he died.

I kept the belt with the intricate buckle of hammered silver and the thick gold cufflinks with the odd insignia he'd had made to match his ring, the one he called the family heirloom. A ring he stole soon after our arrival in Los Angeles, the only item he was ever able to redeem from a pawnshop, buying it back because he finally had work, a real job in the business. He never took it off his finger, a weighted reminder of what he'd rather forget. His Rolex had been smashed as completely as the Harley, but the ring remained unscathed, and when a policeman at the morgue gave it to me, his face solemn and drawn, almost reverent, I got in my car and drove up the coast, a route I had taken so many times before, parked on a lonely stretch of beach, waded in the frigid surf, and threw it in, as far as I could, a golden speck disappearing into foam and rushing waves.

I kept Olivia's sketch of the flat she'd given to Nick, and the drawing of me as the Sphinx, watching the shifting sands in ageless sorrow.

I kept the earring I had found that day. I wear it on a thin silver chain around my neck, a talisman, something to hold on to.

The house is empty, the new owners impatient to move in, eager to tell the world where they are living, but I stay on, waiting for one last thing.

I am sitting by the pool, a shimmering blue lagoon, when the phone rings.

"M," she says, "is that you?"

My heart skips a beat. Olivia.

"Yes," I say. "It's me."

"I've been meaning to call you, but . . ."

"I understand." I do, really.

"I keep telling myself that I should have known, that I should have felt something when he died, a shiver maybe, or *something*, but I didn't. We were already on the ship, and no one listened to the radio, and I didn't even know for weeks, and—"

"That's as it should be," I interrupt. "There was no connection between you anymore. It was gone. Over."

I hear her sigh. "Do you really believe that?" she asks.

"Yes."

There is a long pause.

"Are you okay, M?"

"Yes."

"Truly?"

"Truly. Are you?"

"Yes, I am," she says, and I have no reason to believe otherwise. "Time helps, and lots of work, and traveling, and a little bit of the shrink-speak." Her voice quavers, remembering the last time she'd used that word. I am burdened with the memory of that day as well, and keeping the silence of it. "Well, a lot of the shrink-speak," she adds, drawing a deep breath to steady her nerves. "But we're okay, we both are."

"I'm glad," I say, because I am.

There is a heavy silence.

"What are you going to do?" she asks me, finally.

"Travel." I'm ready to go, I have been ready for ages, but I've been waiting for this, I want to tell her, waiting to hear the sound of your voice one last time before I leave this place, go far away, and disappear from the world.

Another long pause.

"Well," she says finally, her voice shaky, "will you call me if you're ever in London?"

"Of course," I tell her. "I'll call you. We'll have lunch."